PRAISE FOR THE PEPPER MARTIN MYSTERIES

Night of the Loving Dead

"Gravestones, ghosts, and ghoulish misdemeanors delight in Casey Daniels's witty *Night of the Loving Dead*."
—Madelyn Alt, national bestselling author of
Where There's a Witch

"Sass and the supernatural cross paths in the entertaining fourth Penelope 'Pepper' Martin series mystery . . . Pepper proves once again that great style, quick wit, and a sharp eye can solve any mystery."
—*Publishers Weekly*

"[A] well-plotted paranormal mystery that . . . shares some answers that fans have had since we first met this entertaining character, and adds several surprising twists along the way."
—*Darque Reviews*

"Entertaining and amusing . . . will keep readers laughing."
—*The Romance Readers Connection*

"Pepper is brazen and beautiful and this mystery is perfectly paced, with plenty of surprise twists."
—*Romantic Times*

continued . . .

Tombs of Endearment

"A fun romp through the streets and landmarks of Cleveland . . . A tongue-in-cheek . . . look at life beyond the grave . . . well worth picking up."   —Suite101.com

"[A] PI who is Stephanie Plum-meets-*Sex and the City*'s Carrie Bradshaw . . . It's fun, it's 'chick', and appealing . . . [A] quick, effortless read with a dash of Bridget Jones–style romance. [Martin is] a hot redhead who always manages to look good . . . and suffers the emotional catastrophes that every woman can relate to."   —PopSyndicate.com

"With witty dialogue and an entertaining mystery, Ms. Daniels pens an irresistible tale of murder, greed, and a lesson in love. A well-paced storyline that's sure to have readers anticipating Pepper's next ghostly client."
—Darque Reviews

"Sassy, spicy . . . Pepper Martin, wearing her Moschino Cheap & Chic pink polka dot sling backs, will march right into your imagination."
—Shirley Damsgaard, author of *The Seventh Witch*

The Chick and the Dead

"Amusing with her breezy chick-lit style and sharp dialogue."   *—Publishers Weekly*

"Ms. Daniels has a hit series on her hands."
—The Best Reviews

"Ms. Daniels is definitely a hot new voice in paranormal mystery . . . intriguing . . . well-written . . . with a captivating storyline and tantalizing characters."
—Darque Reviews

Tomb with a View

CASEY DANIELS

BERKLEY PRIME CRIME, NEW YORK

THE BERKLEY PUBLISHING GROUP
Published by the Penguin Group
Penguin Group (USA) Inc.
375 Hudson Street, New York, New York 10014, USA
Penguin Group (Canada), 90 Eglinton Avenue East, Suite 700, Toronto, Ontario M4P 2Y3, Canada
(a division of Pearson Penguin Canada Inc.)
Penguin Books Ltd., 80 Strand, London WC2R 0RL, England
Penguin Group Ireland, 25 St. Stephen's Green, Dublin 2, Ireland (a division of Penguin Books Ltd.)
Penguin Group (Australia), 250 Camberwell Road, Camberwell, Victoria 3124, Australia
(a division of Pearson Australia Group Pty. Ltd.)
Penguin Books India Pvt. Ltd., 11 Community Centre, Panchsheel Park, New Delhi—110 017, India
Penguin Group (NZ), 67 Apollo Drive, Rosedale, North Shore 0632, New Zealand
(a division of Pearson New Zealand Ltd.)
Penguin Books (South Africa) (Pty.) Ltd., 24 Sturdee Avenue, Rosebank, Johannesburg 2196,
South Africa

Penguin Books Ltd., Registered Offices: 80 Strand, London WC2R 0RL, England

This is a work of fiction. Names, characters, places, and incidents either are the product of the author's imagination or are used fictitiously, and any resemblance to actual persons, living or dead, business establishments, events, or locales is entirely coincidental. The publisher does not have any control over and does not assume any responsibility for author or third-party websites or their content.

TOMB WITH A VIEW

A Berkley Prime Crime Book / published by arrangement with the author

PRINTING HISTORY
Berkley Prime Crime mass-market edition / July 2010

ISBN: 978-0-425-23551-5

BERKLEY® PRIME CRIME
Berkley Prime Crime Books are published by The Berkley Publishing Group,
a division of Penguin Group (USA) Inc.,
375 Hudson Street, New York, New York 10014.
BERKLEY® PRIME CRIME and the PRIME CRIME logo are trademarks of Penguin Group (USA) Inc.

PRINTED IN THE UNITED STATES OF AMERICA

10 9 8 7 6 5 4 3 2 1

For Peggy, Linda, and Stacie,
who make our Saturday night get-togethers
so much fun

Of course, there was really a James A. Garfield who was the twentieth president of the United States, and yes, he is buried in a wonderful memorial in Cleveland, Ohio. History records that he did once have an affair with a young woman named Lucia Calhoun. In an attempt to make Pepper's life more interesting and far more complicated, the ghost, the illegitimate child, the murder, and Mr. Stone's surprise are all figments of my imagination.

If I knew Marjorie Klinker was going to get murdered, I might have been nicer to her. Well . . . maybe. Unfortunately, though I have the incredibly annoying "Gift" of being able to see and talk to the dead, I am not psychic. Which means I have no way of predicting the future. That morning in late summer when it all started, I didn't know what was going to happen in just a little over twenty-four hours, and not knowing it, when my boss, Ella Silverman, informed me that I'd be working side by side with Marjorie, I reacted the way any rational human being would.

I freaked.

"But Marjorie is crazy!" I wailed. I'd walked into my office and put away my Juicy Couture bag and the salad I brought for lunch right before Ella showed up, so my hands were free. That was good, because it gave me the opportunity to add a wild gesture that I was certain said everything there was to say about Marjorie's mental state.

And Ella? She gave me that look she usually reserves

for her three teenaged daughters. The one that has patience written all over it along with the P.S. *I'm not going to put up with you acting this way much longer.*

The minute she was in my office, Ella sat down in my guest chair. Now, she popped up, the better to look imposing and boss-like. She should have known that wasn't going to work on me. I was more than a head taller than her. I was more than fifty pounds lighter than her. I had the curly red hair, the attitude, and oh yes, the style that a middle-aged woman in Earth Shoes could only dream about. Ella may have been the boss, but I had the whole imposing thing down pat.

This didn't stop her from folding her hands at her waist and lifting her slightly saggy chin. It was a gloomy Wednesday and the air outside was heavy with humidity and the promise of rain. Ella must have been watching the local weather when she got dressed that morning. Her pantsuit was as gray as the clouds that hung over Cleveland like an untucked bedsheet. Her expression was just as deadly serious. In fact, the only things that made her look a little less like one of those thunderclouds outside were the pink beads she had looped around her neck twice and the nail polish that matched them perfectly, down to the hint of sparkle. "I know you don't mean that about Marjorie," she said, and because she mistakenly thought it got to me every time, she added a motherly smile.

"It's too hot for senior citizens to come to the cemetery on tour," Ella added. "And school hasn't started yet, so there aren't any school groups requesting tours, either. That means you don't have that much to keep you busy, so you can't tell me you do. This is the best use of your time, and really, it's such a special occasion. You do agree that the commemoration is important, don't you?" She twitched away the very thought. "Well, of course you do!"

Commemoration?

Like I was actually planning on working that day, I took my time turning on my computer, the better to give my own mental data bank time to reboot. Now that Ella mentioned it, I did recall seeing something in the Garden View employee newsletter about an upcoming commemoration. *Seeing* being the operative word here, not *reading*. Since Ella was the one who proudly wrote and edited the newsletter, I couldn't admit it. At least not outright.

"The commemoration." I nodded to convince her we were thinking in perfect harmony. "And Marjorie's part in the commemoration is . . . ?"

"Well, she's offered to chair the event, of course. I mean, I really didn't expect any less of her. When it comes to President Garfield, Marjorie is something of an expert."

Ah, the pieces started falling into place and not a moment too soon. "Oh, that commemoration." I flopped into my desk chair. After four years of working at Garden View Cemetery, I should have known better, but really, a girl can hope, right? I'd fooled myself into thinking all this commemoration talk involved something exciting, or at least mildly interesting. Just like that, my hopes faded along with my smile.

Something told me Ella realized it, because her rah-rah smile faded, too. "You do remember the President Garfield commemoration, don't you?" she asked, dropping back into the guest chair. "You did read about it in the newsletter? And you were listening when we discussed it at the last staff meeting, right?"

Yes, Ella is my boss, but she's also my friend. There is only so long I can try to pull the proverbial wool over her eyes, especially when, since my dad's in prison and my mom lives down in Florida, she likes to think of herself as the calming, mature influence in my life. Ella has convinced herself—with no actual reinforcement from me, it is important to note—that I will someday follow in her footsteps and be the community relations manager of a fancy-schmancy cemetery like Garden View. This puts her in the precarious position of thinking of herself as my mentor. Every once in a while, she thinks she needs to prove it. Every once in an even greater while, I feel as if I have to live up to her expectations.

I wondered if my expression looked as pained as it felt when I admitted, "I was listening. Just not very well."

There's one thing about Ella: she never loses heart. She proved it when she explained things slow and easy: "The commemoration starts this November. That's because November nineteenth is President James A. Garfield's one hundred and seventy-ninth birthday. He's entombed here at Garden View. Of course, you know that. His monument is usually only open in the spring and summer months, but—"

"We're making an exception for that one day," I interrupted, and Ella didn't mind. It did her little cemetery-community-relations-manager soul good to know that, once in a while, I did actually listen.

She nodded. "That day will kick off the commemoration, and it will continue until next year when we celebrate his one hundred and eightieth birthday and the one hundred and thirtieth anniversary of his assassination. Oh, dear." Ella put a hand to her cheek. "I don't suppose I should say celebrate. Not when it comes to the president's death."

When Ella's in full cemetery-I'm-lovin'-it mode, there's no stopping her. Still, I was duty-bound to at least try. "I have no problem working on this whole commemoration thing with you," I told her, as perfectly honest as I didn't always have the luxury of being. "But Marjorie . . ."

I save my monumental sighs for situations that warrant them. Those usually involve guys. Or the cases I investigate for the dead. Important stuff. Things that affect my ego, my libido, or situations that involve me putting my life on the line. I wasn't sure where this one fell, but I did know that avoiding Marjorie was crucial, at least to my sanity. It was, therefore, an appropriate moment for a monumental sigh. "How about if I just do all the commemoration stuff by myself?"

"Isn't that just like you? What a trooper you are!" Ella said this like it was a good thing. "But you know I'm not going to let you do that. For one thing, it's too big a job for any one person. For another, tours will be starting up again in full swing soon, and we've got to keep your schedule open. I can't have you completely distracted by the commemoration. And besides . . ."

I knew what she was thinking, and I bet I was the only one in Garden View who had the nerve to say it out loud. "Besides, if Marjorie isn't in charge of the whole thing, she'll make all our lives a living hell."

"Well, really, Pepper . . ." It wasn't much of an argument, but since she's an honest person, it was the only one Ella could come up with. She didn't need to say another word; Ella sighed, too.

Like anyone could blame us? After all, we were talking about Marjorie.

Let me bring things up to speed here. I'll bet I've never mentioned Marjorie Klinker, right? Well, no big surprise there. That's because in the great scheme of volunteers who have ever volunteered for anything worth volunteering for (and a whole bunch of things that aren't), Marjorie is the most annoying, the most irritating, and the most astonishingly aggravating of them all.

Helping—isn't that what volunteers are supposed to do? Well, Marjorie's definition of helping doesn't exactly match anyone else's. She's been a volunteer at Garden View Cemetery since forever, which makes her a fixture in the place, and not a good one. She thinks of herself as irreplaceable, indispensable, and vital to the cemetery's operation.

Is it any wonder I avoid Marjorie like the plague? That I try not to think of her, much less talk about her? Marjorie is—

"She's really an asset to Garden View Cemetery," Ella said, finishing my thought, but not the way I would have. "There's no way our paid staff can do everything we need to do around here. We depend on our volunteers. We need to show how much we appreciate them. They give us their time and their talents, and all that is really important. And of all the volunteers we have, Marjorie is the—"

"Biggest pain in the butt?" I made sure I said this sweetly. I wouldn't want to hurt Ella's feelings. Not for the world. But I couldn't let her go on thinking these crazy thoughts, either. It was my duty as Garden View's one and only full-time tour guide to set things straight. "She's obsessed," I said.

"She's dedicated," Ella insisted.

"She's a know-it-all."

"She's well read. You know she has a burning interest in President Garfield. How many people can say that? How many people know anything at all about him? That makes Marjorie invaluable. Plus with her background as a librarian, I always know her research is impeccable. Nobody knows more about the late president than she does."

"That's because she's so loony. Come on, Ella, you've heard her carry on and on and on. She thinks she's special because she's some long-lost relative of the president."

"Which is why she's immersed herself in his life. Really, the fact that she thinks she's a descendant—"

"Is what proves she's really a nutcase, since all the real descendants say she's wrong and there's no way they're related."

As well reasoned as it was, my argument was getting me nowhere fast. I could tell because, little by little, Ella's lips pinched. Pretty soon, I couldn't see them at all. It was time to pull out the big guns. When appealing to Ella's softer side doesn't work, sometimes there's nothing left to do but tell the truth. "Marjorie horns in when I'm giving tours," I told her, and not for the first time. Four years of working at Garden View meant four years of having to deal with Marjorie's complete and total lunacy. I'd complained before, and each time, Ella had reminded me how important people like Marjorie are to the operation of the cemetery. Ella couldn't afford to step on any volunteer toes, but that didn't mean I couldn't—and wouldn't—go right on complaining. "She pushes me out of the way to be the center of attention. She corrects me in front of tour groups even when I don't need to be corrected and—"

"Marjorie does know an awful lot about Garden View and about our residents."

"So you think it's OK for her to step right in front of me and take over my tours? To grab the microphone out of my hands and tell a tour group that I'm mistaken and that if they'd just listen to her, they could find out the real story on the people buried here?"

Ella's laugh was light, but not totally convincing. "Oh, Pepper, you're exaggerating. Marjorie's just enthusiastic. She'd never do anything so rude."

"But she did. She has. She—" I was sputtering, and it wasn't pretty, and since I am more interested in pretty than I am in the workings of Garden View Cemetery, I controlled my urge to scream. There seemed no better way to end the Marjorie lovefest than by distracting Ella. And nothing distracted Ella more thoroughly than cemetery business. "You want to tell me exactly what you have in mind for me to work on?" I asked her.

She saw the question as a surrender when it was really

just a stall tactic. Thinking she had the upper hand, she scooted to the edge of her seat. "We'll set up a sort of staging area in the conference room here in the administration building. You and Marjorie can sort through all the memorabilia the cemetery owns related to the president and catalog it there. I have a feeling Marjorie will want to include some of her own collection, too, and that's fine by me. You know, she's amassed one of the most amazing collections of Garfield memorabilia in the country. Together, you'll need to decide what should go on exhibit, what special printed materials we'll need, how we should celebrate . . . er . . . commemorate. It's going to be such a wonderful experience for you, Pepper. And I know you can do it. After all, you were in charge of that cemetery restoration project earlier in the summer and—"

Ella kept talking, but I wasn't listening. The Monroe Street Cemetery restoration wasn't something I wanted to hear about. Not now. Not ever. Sure, I'd led my team in the successful revamping of one section of the old-and-moldy city-owned cemetery on the other side of town, but that doesn't mean all my memories of the project were warm and fuzzy. I'd solved a murder and finally brought closure and peace to a restless ghost, but I'd also gotten shot at, nearly been killed in a car at the top of a flag pole (long story), and lost the guy who I thought was the guy who was going to be my guy for a long time when I finally confessed to him that I kept getting into dangerous situations thanks to the ghosts who refused to leave me alone. That was when he accused me of being a liar, not to mention as nutty as a fruitcake. Not so incidentally, it was also when he walked out on me.

I shook away the thought just as Ella was finishing up whatever it was she'd been saying. ". . . good on your résumé. Not that I hope you ever need one. I mean, I hope you'll be working here for a long, long time. I'm not planning on retiring for another fifteen years or so, and by then . . ."

My brain went into full-freeze mode again. Thinking of working at Garden View for another fifteen years had a way of doing that to me. I might have sat there like that forever if not for the words that finally penetrated my slurpiness.

". . . I mean, after everything that happened with that nice policeman boyfriend of yours."

"Quinn?" Of course she was talking about Quinn. He was the only nice policeman boyfriend I'd ever had. Except that he wasn't all that nice. At least not in the ways Ella defined the word. I didn't realize I'd sat up like a shot until I already had my elbows on my desk. That's when I also realized how uncomfortable Ella looked.

"I know it's none of my business," she said. The color that raced into her cheeks matched her beaded necklace. "Though really, I suppose it is. My business, I mean, because I mean, I really do think of you as one of my girls, Pepper. And you haven't told me exactly what happened between you and Detective Harrison, but I know it's something, and not something good. He hasn't come around to see you here at work since you finished the restoration, and he usually stops in once in a while. He hasn't called and left any messages. You haven't said a word about him and . . . well . . . frankly, Pepper, you've been moping."

"I haven't. I never mope." I had no choice but to challenge her because of course I'd been moping; only I thought I was only doing it at home where nobody would notice.

"You've been depressed."

"That's silly." The denial tumbled out of my mouth at the same time I looked down at the new outfit I was wearing. Since I knew I wasn't going to be out in the cemetery that day, I'd passed on the standard-issue khakis and polo shirt with the words GARDEN VIEW and STAFF embroidered over the heart in tasteful script. I was wearing an emerald green sleeveless front-zip cotton shirtdress with a waist-clinging belt and adorable Jimmy Choo snakeskin plat-form peep-toe sandals. They were gold. And did I mention adorable?

Yes, the outfit was new.

Yes, I'd bought it as well as the three other new outfits I'd worn to work in the past week in the hopes that a little shopping therapy would make me forget everything I wasn't getting from Quinn.

No, I hadn't thought anyone noticed.

I guess I was wrong.

I pushed away from my desk and dug my shoulders into the high back of my chair. "If you're giving me this commemoration job because you think it's going to help ease some kind of broken heart—"

"I figured you'd have some extra time on your hands."

"And you think I'm crying into my pillow every night and this is somehow going to cheer me up. Number one, working with Marjorie isn't going to cheer me up. In fact, one day with her and you'll probably have to call Quinn yourself because there's bound to be a homicide. Want to guess who's going to be the victim? Number two, the whole crying into my pillow thing? Way overrated." I ought to know, I'd been crying into my pillow each and every night for the last three weeks, and it hadn't helped me feel one damned bit better.

Rather than think about it, I told Ella the same lie I'd been telling myself. "I don't miss him, if that's what you think. In fact, I'm glad he's gone. And I'm not the least bit bored. I've got plenty to keep me busy."

"Yes, of course you do. Like working on this com-memoration." Ella got up and bustled to the door. Some-thing told me she figured if she stopped listening and just kept on talking, things would work out fine in the end. She should have known by now: they never do. "That's one of the things I admire so much about you, Pepper. I know you're not fond of Marjorie. But you're still willing to work with her. That's really wonderful. It's so refreshing. And it's exactly why you're going to go over to the Garfield Memorial right now. That way you and Marjorie can talk, and you can get to know each other a little better."

"But I don't want to get to know her better." Was that me whining? Absolutely! And I didn't regret it one bit. The more Ella sounded so sure of herself, the more sure I was that I wanted nothing to do with her plan. "I just want to—"

"Be a team player! Of course you do. I knew that's what you'd say. Because that's one of the things you do best, Pepper. You help out when I need it. You step up to the plate. You pitch in and give everything you do your best shot." She emphasized this last point by poking a fist into the air.

And I knew a losing cause when I saw one. I fished my purse out of my desk drawer, flung it over my shoulder, and headed for the door.

"That's my girl." Beaming, Ella opened my office door and led the way out into the corridor. We were nearly in the reception area when we heard the most awful noise. It sounded like a cat with its tail in the spokes of a twelve-speed mountain bike.

Ella and I exchanged dumbfounded looks. Side by side, we hurried into the reception area.

We found Jennine, the woman who welcomed clients and answered the phones, standing over a tiny woman in khaki pants and one of those tastefully embroidered polo shirts I mentioned earlier, only hers said VOLUNTEER on it. The woman's head was in her hands and she was sobbing so violently, her shoulders were shaking.

Things got even stranger when the bawler had to come up for air and we saw that it was—

"Doris!" Ella beat me to the exclamation. She also beat me to Doris, but then, squatty Earth Shoes get better traction than four-and-a-half-inch heels. Even before I got over to the couch where Doris was sitting, Ella was kneeling on the floor in front of her. She took Doris's hands in hers. "What happened?" Ella asked. "Doris, are you OK?"

Doris's silvery hair was cut in a stylish bob that bounced when she nodded. She reached into her pocket, pulled out a lace-edged handkerchief, and dabbed it to her blue eyes. She sniffed. "I'm fine," Doris warbled.

"You don't look fine." Since no one else was going to say it, I figured I had to. I went to stand in front of Doris and gave her a careful once-over. No cuts, no bruises, no smudges of dirt. She hadn't fallen and nothing looked broken. I reached behind Jennine's desk, rolled her chair over, and sat down, the better to be eye to eye with Doris when I tried to get her to tell us what happened.

Why did I care?

Truth be told, in the world of cemetery volunteers, Doris Oswald is the exact opposite of Marjorie Klinker.

Marjorie is a pushy pain in the butt.

Doris is everybody's grandmother.

Marjorie likes nothing better than acting superior to everyone. About everything. All the time.

Doris is sweet and kind, and every time she shows up at Garden View to do one volunteer job or another, she brings stuff like homemade brownies or bunches of flowers from her garden or these really cheesy crocheted bookmarks she makes for everybody and I always make fun of and then keep because, really, they might come in handy if I ever decide to read a book and, besides, Doris is nice enough to make them.

Doris is about as big as a minute, and for a woman in

her seventies, she's got a sense of style, too. I admire that, and I like Doris. Honest. If I didn't, I wouldn't have cared why she was crying.

"Doris?" I tried to get through to her again because, softie that she was, Ella was crying, too, and I knew she wasn't going to be any help. "Take it slow and easy. Tell us what happened."

Doris sniffled. "The ladies from my bridge club came to see the cemetery bright and early this morning." This did not seem an especially sad incident, but Doris's voice wobbled over the words. "I showed them the chapel and then we were over in the Garfield Memorial . . ." Her bottom lip quivered like an electric toothbrush. "We'd just walked in and . . . and I was just telling the ladies about James A. Garfield . . . you know, how he was only president for six months and how . . . how he was assassinated and . . ."

"And let me guess, Marjorie showed up and told them everything you said was wrong."

Doris's watery eyes lit. "How did you know?"

I shot an I-told-you-so look at Ella, who managed to ignore me so completely, I had no choice but to shift my attention back to Doris. "Then what happened?" I asked her.

"Well, she just . . . she just took over! She acted like I wasn't there. Like I didn't exist. Like she's the only person in the whole wide world who knows anything about President Garfield, and like she's the only one allowed to tell anyone about it. I know it's no big deal . . ." Even though she said it, Doris didn't look like she believed it. To Doris, this was a very big deal; a fresh cascade of tears began to fall. "These ladies are my friends and . . . Mar . . . jor . . . ie . . . she . . . she embarrassed me in front of them. She made me look like a fool."

"Don't be silly." This comment came from Ella, of

course. She's the only one who would tell a weeping, wailing person not to be silly when silly was exactly what she was being. Me? I would have advised Doris to go back over to the memorial and kick Marjorie in the shins. Ella is a kinder, gentler person. "It's OK." Ella patted Doris's back. "I'll have a talk with Marjorie. I'll tell her that next time—"

Moving pretty fast for a woman her age, Doris bounded off the couch. "Well, that's just it, isn't it?" She sniffed, touched the hanky to her eyes, and threw back her slim shoulders. "I've made up my mind. There isn't going to be a next time. I'm . . ." Her voice wavered, but her determination never did. "I'm quitting as a Garden View volunteer. I'm never coming back here again!"

Ella's jaw dropped and her eyes got wide. No big surprise there. For one thing, part of Ella's job is making sure the volunteers are kept busy—and happy. For another, Ella just happens to be a nice person. She doesn't like conflict. She doesn't like to see other people unhappy. Every motherly instinct she possessed (and I can say with some authority that she has a lot of them) kicked in. She got to her feet, wrapped an arm around Doris's shoulder, and gave her a hug.

Over Doris's trembling shoulders, she shot me a look that said I shouldn't worry, she'd get things under control. I had no doubt of it. No way Ella was going to let Doris quit. Not like this, anyway.

"I can understand why you feel that way," Ella said at the same time she smoothly turned Doris toward her office, and away from the door that led to the parking lot. "Let's have a cup of tea and talk about it."

"I don't know." Doris wrung the hanky. "I've made up my mind. That Marjorie Klinker is the nastiest person in the universe. I'm not going to take her guff anymore."

"Of course you're not." Ella piloted Doris back toward

her office, where I knew there was a hot pot and an assort-
ment of herbal teas. "But you can't leave while you're
upset," she said, her voice as soothing as the steam off one
of those cups of tea. "So we'll just sit down and talk. And
Pepper . . ." She gave me one final glance over her shoulder. "Pepper's going over to the memorial right now.
She'll take care of everything. Right, Pepper?"

Like I could do anything but agree?

One more sigh and I headed out to where my Mustang
was parked so I could drive over to the memorial on the
other side of the three-hundred-plus-acre cemetery. If only
my mood was as purposeful as my steps. Not only did I
now have this commemoration thing to not look forward
to, I had to face the woman who had made sweet Doris
Oswald cry.

I climbed the steps to the imposing turquoise-colored front doors of the one-hundred-and-eighty-foot-tall sandstone memorial building with trepidation in my heart. Believe me, it wasn't just because I knew Marjorie was lurking inside, waiting to pounce on me and rip me to pieces like she had poor Doris. Sure, Marjorie was a royal pain, and crazy to boot, but heck, in my time as a private investigator I'd handled hit men, nasty ghosts, and all sorts of bad guys. Crazy and annoying was a piece of cake. I didn't want to deal with it, but if I had to, I could.

No, the reason a cold shiver raced up my spine and goose bumps popped up along my arms was the same reason I'd been avoiding the memorial in the weeks since I'd finished the cemetery restoration project.

Here's the scoop: While I was involved with that project, I had reason to be in the memorial, and one of the people I was working with took my picture. Little did he know (being more than a little crazy himself) that when that photo was developed, it would show exactly what he saw through his viewfinder—me next to the statue of James A. Garfield—as well as something he didn't—the ghostly shape of the president standing on the other side of me.

I suppose I should have been impressed. I mean, what with this new ghost having been president and all. But honestly, I wanted nothing to do with the old guy.

Don't get me wrong, it's not like I'm not used to ghosts by now, and I'm sure not afraid of them. After all, they've been bugging me ever since the day I hit my head on one of the mausoleums at the cemetery. And I've been a good sport about it, if I do say so myself. I solve their murders. I help clear their names and their reputations. Sure, I've considered bailing on this goofy Gift of mine plenty of times, but in the end, I've never shirked my responsibilities toward those pesky spooks. They want closure, I give them closure, even if it means risking my own life.

What do I get in return?

I get walked out on by the man I loved.

It's wrong, not to mention unfair, and after three weeks of soul searching, I had decided what I was going to do about it—I was officially out of the private investigation business for the dead.

Commander in chief or not.

My mind made up, even if my hands were trembling just a little, I inched open the door that led into the entryway of the memorial. Even I wasn't sure who I was more reluctant to see, Marjorie or the president. "Anybody here?" I called.

Nobody answered.

Relieved, I stepped forward, and the door clicked closed behind me. Aside from the fact that I knew a ghost hung out there, I had to admit that the memorial was really a pretty impressive building. It was built way back when and featured a round tower on top of a hulking, square building. Outside, there were carvings along the walls that depicted the life of James A. Garfield. Inside . . .

I looked around at all the marble and the mosaics, at the tiny office and gift shop to my right and the steep, spiral staircase to my left that led downstairs to the crypt and upstairs to a balcony, where visitors could look down on the rotunda where the president's statue was displayed. There was an observation deck up there, too, and even a ballroom, though it was closed to the public and hadn't been used since like forever. Ahead of me and up two shallow steps was the rotunda where that picture of me had been taken, the one with the ghost in it.

Fortunately, there was no sign of the presidential poltergeist—or anyone else. Relieved, I ducked into the office, saw that no one was in there, either, and thanked my lucky stars. If Marjorie was nowhere to be found, I could head back to the administration building with a clear conscience.

My hopes were dashed the moment I heard footsteps pounding on the marble staircase. I turned just in time to see Marjorie come huffing and puffing down the steps.

It is important to point out that even on the best of days, Marjorie was not an attractive woman. She was a retired librarian, after all, and while I don't think that automatically meant she had to be frumpy, she'd apparently led a life so lost in stacks of books, she'd forgotten that, once in a while, she needed to make human contact, and that when she did, it never hurt to put her best foot forward.

Marjorie was nearly as tall as I am, and as thin as a rail, but not in model-gorgeous mode, more in a yikes-is-that-woman-bony sort of way. She teased her poorly dyed maroon-colored hair into a sixties beehive and always—

summer or winter, indoors or out—topped off the do with
a filmy head scarf tied into a boa constrictor knot under
her chin.

The rest of her wardrobe was volunteer standard
issue—khaki pants and a Garden View polo shirt that was
slightly yellowed under the armpits. In fact, the only thing
that stood out about Marjorie at all—and I do not mean
in a good way—were her pointed, rhinestone-encrusted
glasses, the red lipstick she applied with more enthusiasm
than skill, and the perfume she must have put on with a
ladle. It was sweet and cloying, like gardenias, and like
gardenias, it always made my nose itch.

Marjorie's skin was usually pale, like she didn't get out
in the daylight enough. That morning, though, there were
two bright spots of color in her cheeks that matched the
red geraniums on her head scarf.

She saw me standing in the office, came to an abrupt
halt at the bottom of the steps, and fought to catch her
breath. Behind the pointy glasses, she blinked like a startled owl, and she tapped nervous fingers against one hip.
"I thought I heard someone. I thought . . ." Marjorie was
no spring chicken. If I had liked her more (or even a little),
I would have pulled out a chair and told her to sit down
and take it easy. The way it was, I counted on her figuring
that out for herself.

Instead, she pulled back her shoulders and raised her
chin before she walked into the office. I always had the
sneaking suspicion that Marjorie didn't like it that I was
taller than her.

"I wouldn't have bothered to hurry if I knew it was
just you," she said, then smiled the way people do when
they say something rude and expect you not to be of-
fended. "What I mean, of course, is that I thought you
were a visitor. Obviously, the people in charge here . . ."
She said this in a way that made it clear I was not one

of those people. "They rightly expect me to show a great deal more enthusiasm with our visitors than with employees. Employees, of course, can wait."

"Not employees with lots to do." Since Marjorie lifted her head, I did the same. I'd have her beat by a couple inches, even if I wasn't wearing sky-high shoes. "Ella says we have to work on this commemoration thing together."

"Yes." It was hard to believe anyone could make one syllable sound so sour. Marjorie's breaths were finally steadying, and all that color drained from her face and left her looking more bloodless than ever. Still, she drummed her fingers against her hip, or I should say more accurately, against the pocket of her khakis.

"I tried to talk some sense into her." Her comment pulled me out of my thoughts.

"Me, too."

"I pointed out what she obviously hadn't thought of, that we can't afford to let things get out of hand. I have experience with this sort of thing. I know. With a project this big, it can be easy to lose control, and then before you know it, things fall through the cracks. The commemoration is too important to let that happen. I told Ms. Silverman it would be best if all the planning was handled by just one person."

I wasn't sure if I liked it that Marjorie and I were on the same page. Still, I managed a smile that was far friendlier, and far less acid, than hers. "Imagine that! That's exactly what I told Ella, too."

Marjorie's smile was as stiff as her hair. "Though my argument was solid, Ms. Silverman didn't listen. I finally gave in, and I told her I wouldn't mind an assistant if it was someone who would take the project seriously, someone who has the proper respect for the president and the proper knowledge of history. Someone who's able to take direction and do what needs to be done without questioning or second-guessing me. I hate to have to be so blunt, Ms. Martin, but I think we'll get off on the wrong foot if we don't lay our cards out on the table. I told her I'd rather work with anyone but you."

"Which is exactly what I told her. Anyone but Marjorie." Because I knew in my heart Marjorie was the kind of woman who didn't approve of twinkling, I twinkled like all get-out. "Looks like we've got something in common after all."

She didn't excuse herself when she sidled past me to get to the desk. "Well, if we have to work together—"

"Apparently, we do." I rubbed a finger under my nose. Already, Marjorie's gardenias were getting to me.

"And if we have to design a celebration that will be the highlight of the cemetery's year—"

"I guess that's the plan."

"There are some ground rules." Marjorie straightened her shoulders and gave me a look that reminded me of a dead tuna. Not that I'd actually ever seen a dead tuna up close and personal, but I have a pretty good imagination. "I've watched as you give some of your tours. You play fast and loose with facts."

"Which is why you always feel obliged to shove me out of the way, step into the spotlight, and take over."

Her sigh was all about being pushed to the limit. "One does what one has to do."

"One needs to remember," I said, the emphasis on that first word, "that most of the people who come through Garden View on tours aren't all that worried about drop-dead accuracy. They're just looking to see the place. You know, to absorb a little of the atmosphere and hear some interesting stories, and maybe to see some stuff they consider art."

"Stuff?" When Marjorie's top lip finally unfurled, there

was a smudge of red lipstick under her nose. "You obviously don't take your work seriously."

"As seriously as I have to."

"You try to entertain people with cute stories. Rather, you should be working to educate them."

"Oh, that would keep them coming back." We were— what?—three minutes into this conversation, and already I was getting pretty tired of being lectured. Not to mention bored. Big points for me, though, I was doing a better-than-usual job of holding on to my temper. That is, until Marjorie started up again.

"If you're going to be working for me—"

"Hold on there!" I'd been reasonable, and more than a little accommodating. But never let it be said that Pepper Martin is anybody's doormat. It's not for nothing that my parents stopped calling me by my given name, Penelope, and started in on Pepper. It was easier to yell, for one thing, and it reflected the temper that came with my red hair. At that very moment, the spurt of anger that shot through me felt as fiery as my gorgeous tresses.

I stuck out a hand in front of Marjorie's face to demonstrate that she had to stop, and now. She swallowed whatever it was she was going to say, and sure that I had the floor, I propped my fists on my hips. "We need to get something straight, all right. Right from the start. The first thing is that I don't work *for* you. It's *with* you. Get the difference? If you don't, you might want to back off right now. I'm the one drawing the paycheck around here. It might not be much, but to my way of thinking, that means I don't answer to someone who pops in once in a while just to show off and make nice ladies like Doris Oswald cry."

"Did I? Make Doris cry?" There was a chance I might have forgiven her if Marjorie had looked surprised rather than smug. She sloughed off the whole thing with a lift of one shoulder. When she did, another wave of gardenia washed over me. I sneezed just as she said, "That just goes to show you what a flighty, silly woman that Doris is." There was a stack of weighty-looking books on a nearby chair, and before Marjorie lifted one, she scraped her hands against her khakis. She hugged the book to her heart.

"History is not an inaccurate science," she told me, her voice warming with her passion for the subject. "History is facts and it is dates and it is what happened, not what almost happened or what could have happened. You'd think anyone who took the time to volunteer at a cemetery as important as this one would know that. Yet Doris breezed in here this morning, talking about our dear president as if she knew everything there was to know about him. She got his wife's name wrong, for one thing. Called her Letitia instead of Lucretia and said Lucretia and the president were married in 1859 instead of 1858. Imagine." She snorted. Never a pretty thing for a woman to do, but Marjorie took it to new unattractive heights.

"If Doris can't stand to be corrected when she's giving the wrong information, then maybe those of you who work here . . ." She paused here, the better to put the blame on me. "No doubt you can find something else useful for her to do, like stuffing envelopes or emptying trash cans. She needs to be kept away from visitors. We owe that much to the memory of our wonderful, dear James Abram Garfield." Her voice clogged. Her eyes got all misty. "It's my duty to do everything I can to let the world know what a capable leader he was, what an asset to this country. It's the least I can do," she said and she swiveled a stony look in my direction, daring me to contradict her. "After all, I am one of his descendants."

Oh yeah, by this time I was plenty steamed. It wasn't even so much her looniness that was driving me up the wall as it was the whole superior attitude thing. Remember what I said about kicking Marjorie in the shins? This was the moment I would have done it if I wasn't worried that kicking in peep-toe sandals would ruin a perfectly good pedicure. Without the option of physical violence, I decided to get to her where it really hurt.

"I was talking to one of the other volunteers the other day," I said, as innocent as can be, and careful not to mention any names lest the unsuspecting volunteer incur Marjorie's wrath. "Your name came up."

This pleased her so much, she actually simpered. "Well, of course. The other volunteers look up to me. When I can't be here to make sure things are handled correctly, I can only hope they do their best. Someday they may know enough to take over as volunteers here at the memorial. If they pay attention and learn from me."

As if I agreed, I nodded. "This volunteer was talking about Garfield's family. You know, Letitia and the kids."

"Lucretia." Marjorie's lips puckered.

I laughed, but then again, I could afford to. I was about to get even with Marjorie for what she'd done to Doris, and I was feeling righteous. "Anyway, this volunteer told me they had a bunch of kids."

"Yes. Seven. Eliza was born in 1860, and the poor darling died when she was just three years old. Then there was Harry. He was born in 1863. Harry Augustus, that was his full name. Then James. He was born on October 17, 1865, and then—"

"Whatever!" Maybe Marjorie was right when she said I liked to ignore facts. Hers were boring me to tears. "The volunteer also told me that there are plenty of descendants of those children. I mean bona fide, legitimate descendants. You know, ones who can prove they are directly connected to the president." Wide-eyed, I traded her look for look. "You're not one of them."

She twitched as if she'd been slapped, but Marjorie never backed down. In fact, the smile she beamed at me teetered on the edge of rapturous. "That volunteer apparently hasn't been paying attention, though I can't understand how. I've told all of them the story. Dozens of times. I've told them that, in the 1860s, James Garfield had a relationship with a young woman named Lucia, Lucia Calhoun."

I thought back to everything she'd said earlier, and wondered if it was as much of a surprise to Marjorie as it was to me to realize I'd actually been paying attention. "But you said he and this Letitia chick—"

"Lucretia."

"You said they got married in 1858. Wow. You mean the old guy had an affair." I leaned forward far enough to peer into the rotunda and gave the statue there the thumbs-up. "Who would have thought an old fossil like that would have had the life in him!"

Marjorie clutched her hands at her waist. "He wasn't old. Not then. As a matter of fact, he was never old. He died before his fiftieth birthday. President Garfield was born in 1831. He was in his thirties when he met Lucia. She was a reporter for the *New York Times*, certainly an unusual job for a woman at the time, especially considering that she was only eighteen."

I made a face. "Thirty-year-old guys and teenagers should not be getting it on."

Marjorie ignored these words of wisdom. "He eventually stopped seeing Lucia," she pointed out. "But not until after his wife threatened to divorce him. That, of course, would have ruined his reputation and destroyed his political career. In the great scheme of things, I suppose it was all for the better. Otherwise, the country would have been denied one of its truly great presidents." Her chin came up another fraction of an inch. "My mother, Lucy—named after Lucia herself, of course—is the granddaughter of

Rufus Ward Henry, the son of Lucia Calhoun and the president. He, of course, was raised by relatives who took him in and made him one of their family. There really weren't other options available to women at the time. Not to women who had children out of wedlock."

Everything Marjorie said fed right into my revenge-for-Doris strategy. Did I gloat? Just a little. "Yeah. I think that volunteer said something about how you think that's true. Thing is," I pointed out, "that volunteer said there weren't any children from that affair. And that you don't have one shred of proof that says there were."

All Marjorie did was grin like she knew some big secret. It wasn't the reaction I was hoping for, and it didn't give me a whole lot of satisfaction on Doris's behalf. "Is that what that person said? Well, we'll see about that!" Humming under her breath, she did a little hop-step toward the desk and sat right down. She set the book she was holding on the desk in front of her. There was a black-and-white photo of a bearded man on the cover of the book, and I'd seen the statue in the rotunda so many times, I recognized him right away.

If I was casting a Biblical epic movie, I would have chosen James A. Garfield to play God. He was a big, burly man with a stubborn chin and eyes that looked like they could bore right through a person. Of course, the beard helped reinforce the whole Old Testament image. He had a hairline that had receded up to the top of his head, a long, broad nose, and a set to his shoulders that said he wasn't going to stand for nonsense—from anybody.

"He was born right here in Ohio, you know. Not too very far from where we are right now." Marjorie skimmed a loving hand over the picture. "He was a teacher, and an attorney, and the president of a college. He was also a staunch abolitionist, and a hero in the Civil War. He was promoted all the way to major general, and he only left the military because he was elected to serve in the House of Representatives, and Abraham Lincoln himself personally begged him to give up the Army and come to Washington, where he could be of even better service. He was elected to the presidency in 1880, took office in March, and by July . . ."

I doubted Marjorie was allergic to gardenias, but she sniffled just like I did. "He was shot by a crazed man in July and died of his wounds the following September. The assassin was put to death for his crime. He was hanged. But in spite of the fact that justice was done, our country suffered a terrible loss. The president was truly an amazing man."

And I had the truly amazing (and sounding more impossible by the moment) task of working with this Garfield-a-holic. With no other choice, I figured we'd better get down to business. It was that or tell Ella I'd lick envelopes and empty trash cans while somebody else dealt with Marjorie.

"That means we're going to want to put on some kind of amazing commemoration party for him, right?" I didn't wait for her to answer because, frankly, I didn't much care what she had to say. "What exactly does Ella want us to do?"

"Nobody said Ms. Silverman's plans were set in stone. She's thinking of a small, tasteful display here in the memorial using some of the items the cemetery owns supplemented by some of my own things."

I was almost afraid to ask. "And you're thinking . . .?"

"I've got a collection!" Marjorie's dark, beady eyes sparkled. As if just thinking about it got her all hot and bothered, she fanned a hand in front of her face. A whiff of gardenia rose into the air. Rather than start sneezing again, I went to stand near the doorway that led into the memorial's entryway. "It's a wonderful collection!

You'll see. You'll come to my house tomorrow." It wasn't a request, and since she knew it, she rattled off her address. "Seven o'clock. I'll show you some of my special things. That way I can choose what will go on display and you can—"

"Schlepp it over here for you?" I was going for ironic. She didn't get it.

Marjorie nodded. "It would be useful to have someone help me transport my collection, but only if you can be very careful."

"Oh, I can." I zoomed right past irony all the way to sarcasm, but she never noticed.

"We'll go through it all systematically. First the Garfield books, then the artworks, then Garfield memorabilia," she said, oblivious to the glazing over of my eyes. "Then we'll move on to the Garfield ephemera, you know memorial cards from the funeral service, the invitation to his inauguration. I've even got an original tintype of him taken in his Army uniform. Very rare, of course, and quite valuable."

I was supposed to be impressed. There was no chance of that, but everything Marjorie said did start to fall into place. "Aha!" I pointed a finger her way. "That explains the whole thing! You collect all this stuff because you're looking for proof that you're really related to him."

"I'm not looking for anything." She said this in the superior sort of way she said everything else so, of course, I didn't pay much attention. "What I'm doing is upholding a sacred trust. I'm helping to preserve the memory not only of one of my ancestors, but of one of the truly great American presidents. His term in office was certainly short, but it is often underrated."

"You would know."

Again, my words hit the irony wall and bounced back without making a dent. Marjorie simply smiled. "Yes," she said, "I do know. Because in case you haven't noticed,

I'm something of an expert. In fact, I would go so far as to say that I know more than anybody about the late, great president."

Oh yeah?

I wasn't so sure.

Because just as she was saying this, there was a little ripple in the air right behind Marjorie and a mist that took shape little by little until it was unmistakable, down to the beard.

If Marjorie knew everything there was to know about James A. Garfield, I wondered if she knew his ghost was standing right behind her.

3

The office phone rang, and ubervolunteer that she was, Marjorie didn't waste any time. She answered it with a snappy, "This is the Garfield Memorial. Marjorie Klinker, docent, speaking," and proceeded to ignore me completely.

Fine by me. With her busy pretending she knew all there was to know about James A. Garfield, I was free to follow him (or at least what was left of him) out of the office, through the entryway, and into the rotunda.

Only it wasn't the rotunda. Not exactly, anyway.

When last I saw it, the memorial rotunda looked like it always looked with its marble floor and columns, its thirteen stained glass windows, and that big, honkin' statue of the president on the marble dais under the dome, his head high, his chin up, his shoulders back, staring steadfastly at whatever it was he was supposed to be staring steadfastly at. Now, the whole place was filled with mist that shimmered like moonlight on water. The swirling mist curled softly around the bases of the columns and arched over my head. It blocked out the light of the stained glass windows, and made it so hard for me to see more than a few feet in front of me, I felt like I was inside a shaken snow globe.

Without a word or even a look toward me, the president marched on, and curious, I followed. By then, we should have come to the dais where his statue stood. But instead of marble, the floor at my feet suddenly turned to wood, and portions of it were covered with an Oriental rug in shades of deep blue and green.

Weird? Yes. But what happened next was even stranger. A chill breeze ruffled my hair, the mist whooshed every which way, and the rotunda was gone. We were standing on that rug in a room with a high ceiling and tall windows. Outside, sunshine dappled trees and bushes. Inside, the walls were painted white and accented with gold. They were decorated with portraits of presidents like Washington and Lincoln and a bunch of other stick-in-the-mud old guys who looked vaguely familiar from history books. There was a fireplace directly across from me, and a fire crackled in the grate. Between me and that fireplace was a long, rectangular table. Eight guys wearing old-fashioned clothes and too-serious expressions were seated around it. They were talking quietly among themselves.

"Whoa!" I stopped fast. "What's going on? Who are these guys? And what . . . ?" When I looked up and squinted through the mist, I could just make out the second-floor balcony that looked down onto the rotunda. "What's happening here? Where are we?"

"Where do you think we are?" James A. Garfield didn't talk, he boomed. His blue eyes homed in on me like radar and pinned me to the spot. "We are in the Executive Mansion, young lady. Just as we should be."

Like I was supposed to know what to say? I realized I

was gaping, snapped my mouth shut, and blubbered a little before I composed myself enough to say, "Executive Mansion? You mean like the White House? You're kidding me, right? The White House is in Washington DC and we're in—"

"Young lady, I am the president. The president conducts business in the home in which he lives, and in the unlikely incident that you have not noticed what you should, indeed, have taken note of the moment you walked in here, I am working. In fact, I am quite busy, so if you would be so kind as to excuse me—"

"Hey, I didn't come looking for you, you're the one who showed up to find me." I poked my thumb over my shoulder and back toward the way we came to remind him that while I was minding my own business, he popped up unannounced in the office. "You know who I am, right? I'm the one with the—"

"Gift. Yes. Of course I know. I am, after all, the president."

"And you sure wouldn't get far these days with those sound bites." I was hoping to maybe get a chuckle out of him, but none of the starch went out of his shoulders so I just got down to business. "Usually when ghosts come looking for me, it's because they want something," I told him though I shouldn't have had to. If he knew I had the Gift, he knew that much about me already. "Most of them want me to solve their murders, but I know that's not what you're looking for. Marjorie, she says—"

"Mr. President." Ignoring me completely, a middle-sized man carrying an armload of papers walked up to the president. He was younger than the other men in the room, but he was dressed as formally as the rest of them including the president himself, in a black suit coat and vest, gray pants, a white shirt with a stiff collar, and a narrow bow tie. The man had a long, angular nose. There was a pair of glasses with no side arms pinched onto the bridge of it. His sandy-colored hair was parted down the middle and he had a mustache. It was fat and bushy, like a caterpillar.

"We're nearly ready to begin, Mr. President," he said. His voice was polished smooth, like an actor in a cheesy Shakespeare production. He tapped the pile of papers he carried. "However, there are some small matters we should take care of before you begin your meeting. There are some papers which need to be signed, and—"

"Excuse me! Talking here." I mean, really, did he expect me to just disappear into the woodwork because he wanted face time with the president? I gave the young, pushy guy a sharp look.

He kept right on going as if I wasn't even there. ". . . and I really would like to get these taken care of today, Mr. President, if you wouldn't mind. There are a great many details and—"

"Hello!" He might be acting like I was invisible, but that didn't mean I had to put up with it. I stepped forward.

It's hard to miss a five-foot-eleven redhead in an emerald green dress. He did a pretty good job of it, and just kept talking. ". . . and there are certainly a great many things for you to discuss at your meeting today. There's no need for you to fret about these few small matters, so I will gladly take care of them for you. If you could simply sign these papers, Mr. President—"

"All right, now you're just being rude." I waved a hand in front of the man's face.

And he never once shut his mouth. ". . . I will see to it that everything is taken care of and leave you to your morning's work."

I gave the president a *huh?* look, and I guess he got the message because he dismissed the younger man with a tip of his head.

"That is Jeremiah Stone," the president said when the young man walked away. "He's an excellent aide, an eager fellow, anxious to keep the business of state moving apace. He is impatient, of course, as all young people are."

"And pretty rude, to boot." If he wasn't going to mention it, I figured the least I could do was point it out.

"No, no. It is nothing like that." President Garfield turned to face me. "Do not think unkindly of Mr. Stone. He is neither ill-mannered nor cruel. If he had even an inkling that he had slighted a young lady, he would certainly be most perplexed. He and the others . . ." He looked toward the men seated around the table. "They have all crossed over, you see. They are all firmly on the Other Side. They are not being rude in the least, they are simply oblivious to your presence."

"But they can see you?"

"That's correct." He inclined his head.

"And you can see me."

Again, he nodded.

"So I can communicate with you, but not with them. And they can communicate with you, but not with me."

"There, you have laid out the whole thing quite compendiously." I had no idea what that meant, but since the president smiled, I guess it was a good thing. "Since they are on the Other Side, they can have no communion whatsoever with the living. Now, miss . . ." Like I'd seen the characters do in boring costume dramas, he gave me a quick bow. "As you heard Mr. Stone say, there is much work to be done, and I cannot be kept from it longer than I should be. After all, I am—"

"The president. Right. But hey, I'm not the one keeping you from anything. You're the one who showed up to see me. Which means they might have crossed over . . ." I looked at the men around the table, then shifted my attention back to the president. "But you haven't. Which

explains why you're hanging around looking for me. But
you can't want your murder solved. Marjorie, she says
they found the guy who killed you. They hung him."

"Hanged." He said this in the way a teacher would to a
student who didn't get something, even though the teacher
thought it was pretty simple. "There never was any question
who shot me. It was Charles Guiteau, of course. I imagine
the history books report the facts most competently. The
villain waylaid me at a train station in Baltimore. He admitted his crime immediately after shooting me. He never denied it at all. In fact, I would say he was rather proud of
having delivered the shots which ultimately resulted in my
passing."

"Then if you know for sure it was this Guiteau guy,
you don't need me to solve your murder."

"Of course not."

Jeremiah Stone was back. He shifted from foot to foot,
expressing his impatience without having to say a word.

"One moment," the president told him before he turned
back to me. "I do not actually need anything from you,"
he said. "And yet . . ." He pulled in a breath and let it out
with a sigh. If he had been alive, it would have rippled the
mist around us, but since this was one dead president who
couldn't get any deader, those stray wisps just hung in the
air between us. "There may be something you can do for
me, Miss Martin. I am reluctant to ask, seeing as how you
are a woman and it is hardly respectable as it is not within
a woman's responsibilities to handle such matters."

No way I was going to let that pass, not even from a
president. "Things are a little different now than they were
back in your day," I told him. "Since you've heard of
me and you know I have the Gift, you must also know I've
handled a whole bunch of stuff that was—"

"Yes, yes. Such unpleasant matters. We will not speak
of them." Apparently that was that, because he got rid

of the subject with a shake of his broad shoulders and looked me up and down. "I fear that I am trying to do two things: dare to be a radical and not a fool, which is a matter of no small difficulty. It is therefore no easy thing for me to remember that, in your world, women are more free to do things for which they might not be deemed qualified for or prepared for by way of upbringing, intellect, or temperament."

Had I just been dissed? By a president?

I wasn't sure, but I wasn't taking the chance. If I'd been in my stocking feet, the president and I would have stood just about eye to eye. In my Jimmy Choos, I had the advantage and I took it. I looked down at him. "I've heard that back in your day, some women had jobs," I said, as innocent as can be. "I heard about one who was a reporter for the *New York Times*. Her name was Lucia—"

"Really, Miss Martin!" The president's beard twitched. "Though I am trying to be progressive and learn to live with the reality of women working out in the world, I have yet to reconcile myself to women—or anyone else—discussing inappropriate subjects. In order for our relationship to progress in a manner that is both appropriate and mutually beneficial, you must certainly remember that."

"In order for our relationship to progress in a manner that is . . ." No way I could remember the rest of it, and I screeched my irritation, not to mention my frustration, and cut to the chase. "How about if you just tell me what you want."

"Well, there is one small problem." He seemed almost embarrassed to mention it. "It does not, of course, make me waver in my resolve to execute the duties of my office, but it does make it devilish hard to—" He caught himself and cleared his throat. "You must excuse me, Miss Martin. I have not had the singular pleasure of communicating

with a member of the fairer sex for some time, and I am
afraid I have forgotten my manners. What I meant to say,
of course, is that taking into consideration your more ten-
der sensibilities as a weaker vessel—"

"No wonder history always put me to sleep!" I couldn't
help myself, I had to interrupt. If he kept yammering on,
I was going to jump out of my skin. Maybe the old guy
and Marjorie were related after all. That would explain
why they were both so boring. "It takes you so long
to answer a simple question, how did you ever get anything accomplished?"

"Oh, I got a great deal accomplished during my administration. Which is quite remarkable, you will agree, considering I was in office actively for only four months. I
ordered an investigation into corruption in the Post Office.
I presided over a Treasury refunding in which most hold-
ers of maturing six percent bonds agreed to replace them
with a three-and-a-half percent rate. I . . ." Maybe he was
starting to get the message that I didn't have the slightest
idea what he was talking about; he swallowed the rest of
what he was going to say.

I curled my hands into fists at my side. "So this small
matter you'd like me to take care of . . ."

"Oh yes. Certainly. It is not that I wish to inconve-
nience anyone, but I am, after all, the president and—"

Oh yeah, by this time, I was practically willing to beg
him to get a move on. Anything to get him to stop wasting
my time. "What do you want me to do?"

He finally gave in, but I don't think it had anything to
do with me. Jeremiah Stone was pacing not three feet
away, tapping that pile of papers of his and mumbling
something about how nothing could be accomplished
until the president put his signature on them. "There is a
great deal of commotion around here," the president said,
and something told me he wasn't talking about Jeremiah

Stone or the men at the table, who were looking a little restless.

"You mean because of the commemoration." I nodded. Believe me, I understood! "Well, there's not much I can do about Marjorie. I think she's a royal pain, too."

"It is all disturbing the important work I have to do." The president stared at me. "You do understand, I am sure. There is a great deal for a president to accomplish, and when he is interrupted by other things . . ."

It was obvious from the way he glared at me that he believed Marjorie wasn't the only one disturbing his important work.

Dismissed and dissed, all in the same morning.

I walked away, waving a quick good-bye to Marjorie, who was still on the phone, and at the front door, I turned around for one last look into the rotunda. There was the statue, the marble columns, the stained glass windows. Everything was back to normal, and there was no sign of the somber men around the table, of Jeremiah Stone, or of the president.

W hat with getting tag-teamed by Marjorie and the most long-winded guy ever to hold public office, I needed a break, and fast. I drove to the administration building and snuck in through the back door, the better to avoid Ella and any phone messages Jennine might have taken for me while I was out. I had the latest issue of *Marie Claire* in my desk and that salad I had brought for lunch. If I could buy myself an hour of quiet time, I could put up my feet and get down to what was really important. An article on the hottest fashions coming for fall sure beat an hour with Marjorie or a dead president any day. Smiling at the very thought of avoiding my coworkers and chilling out for a while, I walked into my office and found—

Flowers!

I swear I felt the blood drain out of my face. I was left feeling cold and clammy, and I stood riveted to a spot near the door and forced myself to take a good, long look around. There was no one there. I knew this for sure because even though my office isn't very big, I checked out every nook and cranny twice, even behind the door and under my desk. When I was one hundred percent certain that I was alone, I closed the door behind me and went over to the desk for a better look at the bouquet that had been left on my computer keyboard. It was a bunch of white roses and pink carnations with their stems wound with pink satin ribbon, and for I don't know how long, I stared down at the flowers, listening to the blood whoosh in my ears and my heartbeat pound out a deafening rhythm.

Yes, I admit this all sounds a little over the top and (dare I say it?) crazy, too. Actually, I had good reason.

See, as if I didn't have enough to deal with earlier in the summer when I was working on that cemetery restoration project and solving a twenty-five-year-old murder, I found out something really creepy—I had a stalker. And not just any stalker, one with bad taste in flowers, candy, and all-wrong-for-my-coloring lipstick. He'd been lying low since I'd wrapped up that last case, and always up for a good game of denial, I'd convinced myself that maybe I'd gotten lucky and he'd fallen off the face of the earth. It would have been nice to go right on believing it, too—if not for this bunch of flowers.

I scraped my suddenly damp palms against my shirt-dress and poked the bouquet with one finger. Nothing happened.

Realizing just how nutsy it was to think something might, I wasn't sure who I was angrier at—the stalker, who'd gotten to me so badly I was poking flowers to see if they'd blow up or something, or myself, for giving in to the fear. There was one thing I was sure of, though. I wasn't going to take it anymore.

The thought burning in my brain, I grabbed the bouquet and marched out to the reception area with it.

"Jennine." I don't think I could have possibly surprised her since I was flaming mad and my peep-toe sandals banged against the floor, but she was scribbling a note on a message pad decorated with kittens, and she jumped a mile when I called her name. I stood in the doorway between the hallway and the reception area and waved the bouquet of flowers. "I've had it with this. I mean, really. I. Have. Had. It. And you're going to help me put a stop to this horse hockey. I need to know who brought these flowers and I need to know it right now."

In her job as receptionist, Jennine sees plenty of people, but they are not routinely five-foot-eleven redheads in full anger mode. Her eyes wide, she stared at me like I was making a scene (which I was, but since it was justified, that didn't count). Then she simply blinked, and pointed a finger behind me.

I turned and saw what I'd been too hopped up to see when I stomped through the hallway—a man standing over on my right, his arms crossed over his chipped-from-granite chest, his shoulders resting casually against the wall.

"Quinn!" My voice was much too breathy and I cursed myself for giving in to the surprise and him for having the nerve to show up out of nowhere and pull the rug out from under me. At the same time I thanked the fashion gods for watching over me and making sure I looked as good as I did that day; I wondered if Quinn didn't have a direct line to the same deities. He was wearing a charcoal suit and a shirt so white, it nearly blinded me. His tie was colorful in an I-am-a-detective-with-excellent-taste-and-I-don't-need-to-prove-it-to-anyone way, a refined swirl of black, gray, and white with just enough red splashed in for good measure.

Delectability aside, this was the same man who'd walked out on me not three weeks earlier. I told myself not to forget it (as if I could), narrowed my eyes, and it was a good thing I had that bouquet of flowers. Hanging on to it prevented me from digging my nails into the palms of my hands. Quinn was taller than President James A. Garfield. I looked him in the eye. "What do you want?"

He shot Jennine a thousand-watt smile by way of excusing us, then took me by the elbow. "A little privacy would be nice," he said.

I yanked my arm out of his reach. "Why?"

"If I wanted to stand here in the hallway and tell you, we wouldn't need the privacy." He knew where my office was; he led the way.

I made sure I closed my office door behind me, then crossed my arms over my chest. "Well?"

He'd already taken a seat in the chair behind my desk and he looked up at me, as unruffled at the center of personal drama as I'd seen him at the scene of a homicide. "I missed you, too. Why don't you sit down."

"I don't need to be invited to sit down in my own office." I took a couple steps closer to my desk, the better to glare at him when I asked, "What do you want?"

"I thought we should talk."

"If you wanted to talk, you shouldn't have walked out on me. Then we could have talked."

"You're angry."

I tossed my head. "No wonder you're a detective. You're a real whizbang when it comes to getting to the heart of things."

"Which is how I know you wouldn't be angry if you still didn't care."

"Oh, no!" I backed off and backed away. It was better than daring to get too close and catching a whiff of the expensive aftershave he always wore. That stuff made my knees weak, and Quinn knew it. Rather than dissolve into a puddle of mush, I sat in my guest chair. "You're not going to pull that on me."

"What?" Quinn had a way of shrugging that empha-sized his broad shoulders. His eyes were the exact color of my emerald dress and they glittered at me across my desk. "You're being unreasonable."

"Me?" I was out of that chair in a flash. "You haven't seen unreasonable, buddy, not from me. I'm the one who was always up front with you, and you're the one—"

"Who's had three weeks to think about everything we said to each other last time we were together." He stood, too, and came around to the other side of the desk. A stronger woman might have backed away, or at least taken a swing at him in an effort to wipe that sexy smile off his face. But I am not a strong woman, not when it comes to Quinn, and I didn't move a muscle, not even when he settled his hands on my shoulders.

"I am about to prove just how very reasonable I am," he said, his voice honey. "I've done a lot of thinking in the past three weeks, Pepper."

I swallowed hard. I knew what he was talking about, because I'd done a lot of thinking in that time, too, and somewhere between the anger and the misery, I'd decided the only way I would ever take Quinn back is if he came crawling. He wasn't on his knees, not yet anyway, but I could afford to curb my temper and bide my time. I felt an apology of epic proportions coming on. Oh, how I was going to enjoy hearing it!

He leaned a little nearer, and I knew that if I gave in the slightest bit and moved a fraction of an inch closer, he would have kissed me. As much as I wanted it, it was too soon to surrender. I kept my place, just like I kept my mouth shut.

He skimmed both thumbs over my collarbone and said, "I've decided to forgive you."

Even I didn't know I could move that fast. I had his hands batted away and the desk between us before Quinn knew what had happened. And believe me, I wasn't at a loss for words, even though I was just about choking on my anger. "You? Forgive me?"

Maybe he looked a little uncertain because he'd never seen steam coming out of a woman's ears before. "Yeah, I've thought about it, and I realize when you told me all those crazy things you told me—"

"About talking to dead people."

"Well, yeah." He scraped a hand through his inky hair. "Me walking out on you, it was a knee-jerk reaction, and it's not like anyone could blame me. I had every right to ask what was going on with you, and when you made up that nonsense about ghosts—"

"Get out." The bouquet of flowers was the perfect prop, but I motioned toward the door with it a little too forcefully. A shower of rose petals rained down on my desk. "Get out of my office, and get out of my life, and if you ever think of forgiving me again, get that out of your head, too. I don't need your forgiveness, Quinn, and I don't need you."

"I thought you'd be happy."

"Oh, I'm going to be happy, all right. As soon as you're out of here and you close the door behind you."

He did, and guess what? I didn't feel any happier. Just to prove it, after he was gone, I winged the bouquet of flowers at my closed office door. The ribbon around the stems of the flowers came loose and unrolled, and I saw that there were gold foil letters glued to the ribbon.

Dearest Grandmother, it said in loopy letters.

"Oh, you forgive me all right," I mumbled to myself, giving the bouquet a kick across my office just for good measure. "And you proved it by bringing me a bunch of flowers you swiped off a grave!"

4

Never let it be said I don't have a social life.

There were plenty of things I could have been doing the next evening. Honest. For instance, I usually call my dad in prison out in Colorado on Thursdays, and when I'm done talking to him, I call my mom to fill her in. That particular Thursday, I also could have gone to a car show with none other than Absalom Sykes, one of the guys I'd worked with on the cemetery restoration project. Sure, Absalom is a car thief, and yes, I suspected he was going to the show mostly to case the joint, but that was beside the point. Even though he's big, and gruff, and scary looking (and he practices voodoo, too), I like Absalom. We would have had a good time.

Unfortunately, by the time Absalom called to invite me along, I'd already given in and given up to Ella's pleading about how much she needed my help with the whole goofy commemoration, and what a team player I was, and how much she admired my willingness to pitch in, and blah, blah, blah. As much as I didn't want to—and believe me when I say that was a whole lot—I agreed to go to Marjorie's that evening.

None of which means I was particularly happy about it.

Marjorie lived in a nondescript house in a nondescript neighborhood, and I stood on her front porch, rang the bell, and braced myself. Not even that was enough to prepare me. When she answered the door in her cheap jeans and her white T-shirt with a picture of President Garfield on the front of it, I couldn't contain myself. Everything I felt for Marjorie bubbled out of me, and the words just came pouring out of my mouth. "I'm here exactly why?" I asked. Marjorie was not put off. For one thing, she was wearing a pair of shoes with the highest heels I have ever seen except for the girls on stage at *The Thundering Stallion* (trust me, I was there in connection with an investigation even though the owner tried to get me to audition). This was a pair of sandals untastefully done in black and white patent leather with an ankle strap, a two-inch alligator green platform, and heels in a color to match. Just to make sure I noticed she was taller than me, Marjorie raised her head and pulled back her shoulders. She was on her home turf, and if I thought she was condescending, annoying, and just plain nasty back at the cemetery, she was twice as condescending, annoying, and just plain nasty in her home sweet home.

"I'm happy to see you've come to your senses in regard to the commemoration." Happy, huh? She didn't look happy. She didn't sound it, either, when she added, "I have to admit, it probably would have been simpler and far less irritating for me to just handle the entire thing on my own. But since you're here, I suppose we should try to make the best of it." When she sighed, the president on the front of her shirt jiggled. She ushered me inside with a sweep of one arm and finally got around to answering my question. "You're here to see my collection, of course."

And see her collection I did.

The second I was in her living room, I found myself inundated, surrounded by, and totally swamped with James A. Garfield. There was a portrait of him hanging above the phony, electric-log fireplace. There were glass figurines of him on the mantel. There were books piled on the pine coffee table that featured his stern, unsmiling face on their covers, and there were all sorts of Garfield-y things framed and hung on the walls, such as an invitation to his inauguration, and an eleven-by-twenty photograph of Lawnfield, his house. Like I'd seen Absalom do with one of his juju dolls, Marjorie touched a finger reverently to a framed item that caught my eye. "Ah, you noticed this, did you? Maybe you're not a lost cause after all."

I think that was supposed to be a compliment. I leaned closer for a better look. The item in question looked like an old, battered floor tile. There was a little brass plaque mounted underneath it that said it was—

"A piece of the floor from the railway station where James A. Garfield was shot by Charles Guiteau?" I read the words on the plaque, only there was no question mark except in my voice. "You have a piece of the floor of the railway station?"

Marjorie puffed with pride, so much, in fact, that she wobbled on her high shoes. "It's not just any piece of the tile. The presidential collector who sold it to me assured me that this tile was taken from the actual waiting room of the Baltimore and Potomac Railway Station where the president was shot. If you look really closely . . ." She did. I didn't. "It could be my imagination, of course, though I doubt it. After all, those who are related often feel an uncanny attachment to each other. I think . . . no, I'm sure there's the tiniest bit of his blood on that tile."

I backed away like . . . well, like somebody told me I was looking at something that had blood on it. "Let me guess," I said, and I wasn't really guessing. Unfortunately, I'd known Marjorie long enough to know the answer. "That's one of the things you'd like to put on display for the commemoration."

"Oh, that, and a number of other wonderful things. One especially. It's going to cause quite a sensation!" She said this in the singsongy way people do when they think they know some big secret, but since I really didn't care, I didn't take the bait, and Marjorie gave up with a sigh. She wobbled her way around the room, stopping now and then to admire some piece of Garfield memorabilia. "I've decided that we'll do a sort of revolving exhibit. There will be one main display inside the rotunda, and that will remain the same throughout the commemoration. After all, it will have some very important things in it!" There was that tone of voice again. Her eyes shone. When I didn't bite, she kept right on.

"We'll also have a display downstairs outside the crypt. That's the one we'll change each month. Of course, just the idea that there will be new and interesting things to look at each month will keep people flocking back to the memorial. And since I have so much I can share that has never been on exhibit before, it would seem . . . well . . . un-American to keep all these wonderful things away from the public eye. We can do inaugural items one month, then the next, something like national bank currency that features the dear president's picture. We could even do a display of modern items that honor him."

"Except I doubt there are any."

I should have known better. A weird sort of half-smile on her face, Marjorie led me through the dining room, where there was a vinyl tablecloth decorated with American flags on the table, and into a back room that she used as a den. She paused just inside the doorway and glanced at the items displayed all around the room.

"Garfield pen and pencil sets, Garfield salt and pepper shakers, Garfield teacups," she said, and believe me, she was not talking about that fat and sassy orange cat. The entire room was crammed with things like commemorative plates, and ashtrays, and bookmarks and napkin rings and keychains, all with the image of the president on them. There was even a President Garfield mousepad on the desk next to a computer. There was a credit card on it, covering the top of the president's head and his face, but I'd know that beard anywhere.

"Hey, look at this!" A photo hanging nearby caught my eye. It showed the president standing at the head of a table where eight men were seated. They looked awfully familiar. "Who are these guys?"

"Those guys"—Marjorie spit out the word as if it tasted bad—"are the president's cabinet." She pointed to the men I'd seen around the table in the rotunda. "Here's Chester Arthur, who was Mr. Garfield's vice president and became president after his death. And this is James Blaine and William Windom, and Robert Todd Lincoln. Yes," she added quickly, though I wasn't going to say a thing. "That other president's son. Then there's Wayne MacVeagh, Thomas James, William Hunt, and Samuel Kirkwood. Unsung heroes. Every single one of them. Then again, our dearest president wouldn't have chosen them for his cabinet if he didn't think of them as honorable, hardworking men."

"Where's Jeremiah Stone?"

"Well, it looks like I may have underestimated you after all, Ms. Martin. You've done your homework!" Marjorie practically smiled at me. It was kind of disturbing. "Mr. Stone was the president's personal aide and not a member of the cabinet so he, of course, isn't in this photograph. I may have one of him around here somewhere."

"That's OK," I told her because I didn't have the time or the patience to wait while she went off and looked for it. "I have a pretty good idea what he looked like."

She didn't ask how, which was OK, because I wouldn't have told her, anyway. "Mr. Stone, now there was a dedicated young man!" Her voice warmed to the subject. "Even after the awful incident at the Baltimore and Potomac Railway Station, Mr. Stone was always at the president's side. You see, though the president was shot on July second, he didn't die until September. He suffered the entire time, poor man, enduring the pain of the bullet and the ineptitude of the doctors who were supposed to be healing him, but really only made things worse. And the entire time, Mr. Stone took care of the day-to-day details the president needed to know about, made sure he was kept apprised of political news, handled correspondence. You know, the things that needed to be done to keep the ship of state afloat. I doubt there are many men these days who are as devoted or as trustworthy or—"

Marjorie's doorbell rang. It was clear she wasn't expecting anyone else, and she smoothed a hand over her T-shirt then tottered back into the living room and toward the front door. Rather than be left in the den with James A. Garfield staring at me from bowls and pencil toppers and the covers of old, framed magazines, I followed along, and got to the living room just in time to see her peek through the peephole in the door and step back, suddenly looking as gooey as a tweenager at a Jonas Brothers concert. There was a basket on a table near the front door filled with those goofy filmy head scarves of hers, and she whisked off the one she was wearing (apparently it was an everyday head scarf and not suitable for company, which told me exactly where I stood) and grabbed one with giant yellow mums on it. She tied it under her chin, checked her reflection in a mirror that hung nearby, and pasted a smile to her face before she opened the door.

"Why, Ray! What a lovely surprise."

The Ray in question was Ray Gwitkowski, another of the Garden View volunteers. He was a tall, burly sixty-some-year-old guy who was a high school math teacher before he retired. Ray had been a cemetery volunteer for years, and ever since the winter before when his wife died, he'd been spending more and more time at Garden View. Like Doris, he was one of the good guys; he was friendly to staff and visitors and he did whatever we asked. That night, he was wearing khakis, a blue button-down dress shirt, and a worried expression that cleared up the moment he caught sight of me.

"Pepper! Hey, kid, what are you doing here?" He zoomed right past Marjorie like she wasn't there and headed my way. "You're the last person I expected to see here."

"This is the last place I expected to be," I admitted. "But—"

"Ms. Martin is going to be my assistant on the Garfield commemoration project." Marjorie wasn't the type who settled for being ignored for too long, or at all, for that matter. She teetered over to stand at my side and I guess it was the first time Ray noticed her shoes. He shot me a look that said he thought she was as loony as I did. Yeah, I liked Ray a lot. "I'm showing her the items I think would be appropriate to put on display. But then, Ray . . ." Marjorie put a hand on his arm. "You know how many interesting things I have to offer!"

Oh yeah, that was as creepy as it sounds. So was the look Marjorie gave Ray.

I'm pretty sure Ray thought so, too. That would explain why he slowly drew his arm out of Marjorie's reach. "I

know all about your Garfield collection," he said. "There's
no need for you to show it to me again." He glanced around
as he said this, and stopped when he got to the invitation
to the Garfield inauguration.

Clearly, he was surprised, and just as clearly, Marjorie
couldn't have been more pleased. Especially when Ray
blurted out, "You bought it? That invitation you talked
about seeing in the on-line auction? I thought you said it
was too expensive to even bid on."

"Sometimes the cost of an item is of no account." She
simpered and stepped to the side, the better to put herself
in too close proximity to Ray. "Sometimes a woman just
has to take a chance. Go for it. You know what I mean,
Ray?"

My guess is that he did. That would explain why Ray
looked a little green and ran a finger around his collar.

Marjorie wound her arm through his. "Ms. Martin will
be back another time to pick up the memorabilia I want to
display." She shot me a look as sharp as a laser. "You were
just leaving, weren't you?"

I had no intention of arguing, and maybe Ray realized
it. Seeing that I might walk out and leave him there—
alone—with Marjorie, a look very much like panic filled
his eyes, and he got right down to business.

"No, no. I refuse to interrupt whatever you two girls
are up to," he said, drawing away from Marjorie. "I'll
just be a minute and then you two can get back to work.
Marjorie . . ." He would have been taller than her if
she hadn't been wearing those goofy shoes, and he
pulled back his shoulders. "Marjorie, we need to talk. In
private."

She grinned—it was not a good look for her. "Of
course," she purred, and she led Ray toward the den.

Left to my own devices, I sat down on the red, white,
and blue plaid couch, but staring at all those books with

James A. Garfield's face staring back at me made me nervous, so I got up and poked around. I checked out a framed memorial card issued when the president died, and a glass case chock-full of campaign ribbons and buttons. There was an old photograph hanging above it of my newest ghostly contact in his Civil War uniform, and curious to see what he looked like when he was younger, I leaned closer to it. OK, I admit it, I wasn't paying attention. If I was, I would have noticed the round-bellied oil lamp at my elbow, the one with the president's face painted on it. Or at least I would have noticed it before it was too late.

The way it was, I bumped the lamp with my arm, and as if it were happening in slow motion, I turned just in time to watch it skid to the edge of the table, tip, and teeter.

Believe me, I knew what was going to happen next, and it wasn't going to be pretty.

My heart bumped, my adrenaline pumped, and I reacted as fast as I could. I stretched, grabbed, and saved the lamp from ending up in a million pieces on the floor.

Trouble is, when I did, I also knocked into a tall skinny vase (yes, Garfield's face was painted on that, too). It was filled with a bunch of those really long, old-fashioned metal hat pins, and the vase tipped, but lucky for me, it didn't fall and break. The hat pins fell out, though. Every single one of them bounced against the table on the way down. Except for the rumble of Ray's voice and the murmur of Marjorie's, it was deadly quiet in the house. The hat pins *ping, ping, pinged* like gunshot.

I cringed and froze, and that's how Marjorie found me when she came . . . well, it wasn't exactly running, seeing as how she was still wearing those high shoes.

"What on earth!" She looked at the hat pins scattered across the floor, so upset, the tight knot of the head scarf under her chin quivered. She tottered over, picked up the hat pins one by one, and set them back where they belonged. "Really, Ms. Martin, you need to learn to be more careful around precious objects. One would think you would have learned that working in a place as full of treasured things as Garden View. Sit down, why don't you." It was more of an order than an invitation. "And keep your hands to yourself. I'll be right back."

She marched . . . er . . . tottered back the way she came, and afraid she might be right and I might get in serious and possibly expensive trouble if I tried to look at anything else, I did as I was told. I plunked down on the couch and waited.

I would have stayed right there, too, if Ray's voice didn't float out from the back room. It was louder than it had been before, and more insistent. I couldn't catch exactly what he said, but let's face it, that made me more curious than ever.

I got up and sidled my way into the dining room.

"I don't know why you're getting so upset. Mistakes happen. And that's all it was, just a mistake." This was Marjorie speaking, and even long distance, I could hear that she was trying so hard to sound honest, there was no doubt she was lying. "I was confused. I spoke before I should have, before I had all the information. Now . . . well, now I know things aren't going to work out the way I thought they would. I was sure you'd understand. I never dreamed you'd hold it against me, Ray. I can't believe you're that kind of man."

"This is the last straw, Marjorie!" I didn't know people ever really said that, I mean, not in real life. I tipped my head to try and catch every word. "So what you're telling me is that you've been leading me on. Is that it? This whole thing . . . it's been nothing but a charade. And now this!" Ray paused like maybe he was showing something to Marjorie. "This just about proves it. You don't care about anyone's feelings but your own. You act like I'm some sort of trained monkey."

"But, Ray . . ." Marjorie must have known how desperate she sounded. She swallowed so hard, even I heard the gulp. When she started up again, she tried so hard to sound sexy, it was pathetic. Not to mention nauseating. "You aren't going to ruin a perfectly good thing just because—"

"There is no good thing. Don't you get that? There never has been. Whatever relationship we have—"

"It could be good. It could be better than good." Maybe she saw that trying to reason with Ray was getting her nowhere fast. Marjorie's voice iced over. "I simply can't believe you're getting upset about such an insignificant thing. If you'd just give me a chance—"

"I've given you all the chances you're going to get. I've been patient. And I've been willing to believe you'd come through with what you promised. And all I get is the runaround."

"That's not it at all." Suddenly, Marjorie's voice sounded closer, as if Ray had walked out of the room and she was following. I scooted back into the living room. "It's just that I want things to be good for us, to go smoothly. If you can't see that—"

"It doesn't matter, don't you get it? I've had it with this whole thing. I've had it with you." Ray's voice was louder, too. I sat back down on the couch, and grabbed one of the books off the coffee table, the better to look like I was busy reading—and not eavesdropping.

Just in time, too.

His cheeks flushed, Ray walked into the living room. I think that's the first he remembered I was there. He stopped long enough to acknowledge me, then headed to

the door. "I'll . . . I'll see you around Garden View, kid,"
he said, and he didn't wait for me to answer. He was
out the door in a flash.

"So, where were we?" Marjorie was either very good
at pretending or a complete idiot. Her hands clutched at
her waist and her chin high and just about steady, she acted
like nothing had happened. "Oh, of course. We were getting together some things for the exhibit. Here." She tilt-o-
whirled around the room, grabbing books and magazines
and a couple framed pictures off the wall. She glanced
around, caught sight of an open carton next to the front
door, and stowed everything in it. "There are some other
items in this box that I'll want to exhibit, too," she said.
When she dumped the whole thing into my arms, I couldn't
help but notice that she might act like Ray walking out
on her was no big deal, but her bottom lip quivered. "You
can bring it all to the cemetery tomorrow and we'll sort
it out. And remember, Ms. Martin, even though I've made
sure to entrust you only with things that memorialize
the president and never actually belonged to him, even
these small things must be well cared for. You can do that,
can't you?"

And before she even gave me a chance to answer, I
found myself with box in hand, standing out on the front
porch.

Too bad she closed the door before she had a chance to
see me sneer.

But not so bad that I was finally free.

Cheered by the thought, I headed for my car at the same
time I wondered what was up with Ray and Marjorie.

I might have had a chance to come up with some sort
of theory, but just as I got to my car, a hand clamped down
on my shoulder.

5

Stalker!

Like anyone could blame me for thinking it?

My brain and muscles froze. My heart raced. My pulse pounded. But never let it be said that Pepper Martin is a wimp.

My instincts for self-preservation kicked in, but since I was carrying that box filled with Marjorie's junk, I couldn't start throwing punches. With no options and no other way to defend myself, I twirled around and shoved the box of Marjorie's memorabilia right into the face of the person standing behind me.

I almost knocked down a little old lady wearing a pink chenille bathrobe and blue fuzzy slippers.

She scrambled to stay on her feet, too startled to say anything. The ugly little pug-faced dog she was carrying wasn't as shy. It snarled. I backed away.

"Oh my gosh! I'm so sorry." I set the box on the trunk of my Mustang, and since the dog was showing its crooked teeth, I made sure to keep my distance. It was then that I saw that the dog was wearing a pink chenille robe, too. "I thought you were someone else, and you snuck up behind me, and there's been this stalker after me all summer, see, and I didn't know you were there, and you scared me. I hope I didn't hurt you."

The woman had stick arms and loose skin under her chin that shimmied when she shot a look toward Marjorie's house. She hoisted the dog up under one arm, pulled a pack of Camels out of the pocket of her robe, and lit up. While she took a drag, then let a long stream of smoke escape from between her lips, she looked me up and down.

"You from the city?" she asked.

"The city?" Yes, I know it's annoying to answer a question with the same question, but I was trying to get things organized in my head. It wasn't easy. The dog's top lip was curled, and it was giving me a beady-eyed once-over. "Do you need to talk to somebody who works for the city?"

I guess it was a sore subject because both the woman and the dog growled. "Need to get that damned crazy woman out of the neighborhood. Thought maybe the city finally sent somebody to take care of it. I've been calling, you know. I have every right. I'm a citizen same as she is. Just in case they need to be reminded, I've told them over and over: Gloria Henninger is a taxpayer. She deserves to have her say. Been calling them every single day for the last six months. You know, ever since . . ." Gloria tipped her head in the direction of Marjorie's driveway and the backyard beyond. The dog *harrumphed*.

When I arrived, I'd parked out on the street and headed straight up the front steps, so I hadn't paid any attention to Marjorie's backyard. Now, I leaned to my left for a look. What I saw took my breath away. "Is that—"

"A statue of President James A. Garfield. You got that right, sister. I've never been to that memorial for him. Never even been to that cemetery where Marjorie spends all her time, but I hear it's a replica of the statue there."

I checked again. It was. Down to every last detail.

The statue stood on a cement pad off to the side of Marjorie's garage. It was surrounded by two-foot-tall bushes and pots of flowers. From the front yard, there was no way to tell it was there, but I imagined that whenever Marjorie's neighbors—on this street or the one that backed up to it—walked out their back doors, it was the first thing they saw. Yeah, it was that hard to miss. Especially this time of the night when there was a spotlight shining right on it.

"It's—"

"Ugly." The woman spit out the word, dropped her cigarette, and ground it beneath the sole of one slipper. She switched the dog from one arm to the other. "That's exactly what I told that crazy Klinker woman last spring when she had it trucked in here. Told her that statue was an eyesore. Told her it needed to be moved. Told her the neighbors weren't going to stand for it."

Like I needed to ask? I did anyway. "And Marjorie said . . . ?"

It was Gloria's turn to *harrumph*. "Gave me a lecture about her rights as a property owner, that's what she did. Told me to mind my own business. Just kept right on doing what she was doing. Put that statue right there and that was bad enough, but then last week she put up that spotlight. It's too much. That's what I told the city. I told them neighbors have to put up with some things. I understand that. But this? This is too much. Even little Sunshine . . ." She gave the dog a squeeze that made its already bulging eyes pop a little more.

"Sunshine won't even walk out into our backyard to do

her business. That's how afraid of that statue she is. That's what I told the city. Told them little Sunshine is terrified and that it's just not right. You'd think they'd care. I'm a taxpayer, after all. You wouldn't hear it from either of my ex-husbands, but I'll tell you something else, honey: I'm a reasonable woman. And I've been reasonable. I've asked that crazy woman nicely. I've begged her. I've pleaded. When that didn't work, I wrote letters to the newspapers and to the TV stations, and I've called my councilman. Nobody cares. That Marjorie Klinker acts like she's better than everybody else." Both Gloria and Sunshine aimed venomous looks at the house, and Gloria's eyebrows slid up her forehead.

"You know what we do?" She lowered her voice and looked back at me, sharing the secret. "Every single night before we go to bed, Sunshine and me, we say our prayers. And you know what we ask for? We pray for Marjorie Klinker to die. Hasn't happened." She was disappointed; her shoulders drooped. "Nothing's happened. The city doesn't care. The TV stations don't care. The newspapers don't care. There are times I think I'm going to live until my dying day looking at that eyesore of a statue." Disgusted, she shook her head. "I guess if anything's going to change, it's up to me. I'll just have to kill her myself."

It was hard to argue with logic like that, and I never had a chance, anyway, because Gloria turned and shuffled into the house next door.

Watching her, a shiver snaked over my shoulder. I didn't pay any attention to it. What I did instead was load that box of junk into my trunk and get in my car. Right before I drove away, I took one last look at the house.

I was just in time to see Marjorie race across the living room, tossing books and magazines every which way.

I didn't pay any attention to that, either, except to think

that Gloria and Sunshine were pretty good judges of character: Marjorie Klinker was one strange cookie.

I wasn't surprised to find Doris Oswald in the cemetery administration building the next morning. It's not always easy to keep people happy, especially when they're volunteering their time, but Ella has a magical gift for smoothing ruffled feathers. Of course she talked Doris out of quitting! What she'd talked Doris into, I didn't know, but I saw that whatever project Doris was working on, it must have been overwhelming for the elderly woman. She was flustered and short of breath when I bumped into her in the hallway.

"Oh, Pepper!" Doris's cheeks were rosy pink. "I was just . . . That is, I just . . ." Doris waved toward the copy room.

I suspected there was a problem with our cranky copier, and I so didn't want to get dragged into it. I pointed Doris toward Jennine, who was way better at taking care of all things technical than I would ever be, and zoomed into my office before I could get waylaid by anyone else.

Once I had the door shut firmly behind me, I turned on my computer and checked my e-mail. I had a message from a suburban teacher who wanted to schedule her class for a tour, and since I had nothing better to do and knew that it was better to get these sorts of things over with than obsess about them, I picked up my phone to call her. It beeped, the way it does when I have a voice mail message.

My voice mail only kicks in when Jennine isn't there to take my calls, and trooper that she is, Jennine is always there during business hours so this struck me as a little weird.

Unless Quinn had gotten a serious case of "I'm sorry" in the middle of the night.

My spirits rose. Yeah, I was still plenty mad at him, but that didn't mean I wasn't willing to cut him some slack. If he was appropriately penitent.

Anticipation buzzed through my bloodstream. Well, for a second, anyway. Until I reminded myself that if Quinn wanted to talk in the middle of the night, he wouldn't call the office. He had my cell number.

Grumbling at the thought that whoever wanted me must have wanted something to do with a cemetery tour, I punched in my code, and waited. According to the computer voice that kicked in right before the message started, the call had come in the night before, right about the time I'd left Marjorie's.

"Ms. Martin? Marjorie Klinker here."

I cringed.

"Ms. Martin . . ." Marjorie huffed and puffed, trying to catch her breath. "There are so many Martins in the phonebook, I don't know which number might be yours. Otherwise I would have called you at home. Or on your cell phone. That, of course, is a very good idea. Remind me to bring it up with Ms. Silverman tomorrow. Volunteers should have employees' cell phone numbers, so that they could call them day or night in case of an emergency."

I rolled my eyes.

"That is what this is, of course. An emergency. I certainly wouldn't have called you . . ." She put just enough emphasis on that last word to make me feel as insignificant as she intended. ". . . if it wasn't. Ms. Martin, I must see you in the morning. The instant you get to Garden View. First thing. It is extremely important. Please!"

Hearing Marjorie say *please* was a little like finding out a goldfish can talk. I gave the receiver a questioning look at the same time I deleted the message.

"The instant you get to Garden View!" I repeated the words in the same overly dramatic tone of voice Marjorie had used and made a decision right then and there: Marjorie Klinker wasn't the boss of me. Just so she wouldn't forget it, I took my good ol' time. I called that teacher and scheduled a tour for the next week, and since just thinking about spending a couple hours with fourth graders made me weak in the knees, I knew I had to fortify myself with a cup of coffee. Since it was Friday and Ella usually brings donuts in on Fridays, I was hoping for a bit of a sugar high, too.

Donuts weren't the only things I found in the break room. Ray was there, too, and I tried to make small talk mostly because I wanted to find out what he and Marjorie were going at it about the night before, but he would have none of it. He looked up long enough to say hello when I walked in, but that was it. He was preoccupied with the newspaper open on the table in front of him, though since he kept turning the pages and never once stopping to read any of the articles, I don't know why.

I grabbed my coffee and a glazed donut and took it back to my office. When I was done with both, I was also out of things to do so I gave up and headed for the memorial. Marjorie's black Saturn was parked on the road that circled the monument, but there was no one else around. Too bad. At least if there were tourists to keep Marjorie busy, she'd have less time to annoy me.

Determined to show her who was in charge and that it wasn't her, I left the box of Garfield memorabilia in the trunk, fully intending to tell her that if she wanted it, she could make the long trek down the memorial steps and out to the car for it. All about attitude, I went into the memorial.

The lights were still off.

"Hello!" I stepped into the entryway and looked around.

Even in the semidarkness I could see that Marjorie wasn't in the office, and I remembered that the last time I stopped in, she'd been upstairs. No way I was walking the narrow, winding steps. It would be far easier to head into the rotunda and call to her from there, so I did. I flipped on the lights—and stopped cold.

Marjorie lay at the foot of the statue of the president. There was a pool of blood behind her head, and her arms were thrown to her sides. Her legs were twisted in ways legs are never meant to move. She was wearing one tall, tacky black-and-white patent leather sandal. The other one was on the other side of the marble dais, its two-inch alligator green platform split in two.

I looked up at the railing surrounding the balcony above the rotunda.

I looked down at Marjorie's crumbled body.

It didn't take a genius to see that she had fallen, and that she was dead.

And honestly, I couldn't help myself. All I could think was that it was no big surprise.

Marjorie never should have worn those weird, high shoes to work.

By the time she got over to the monument, Ella was in such a tizzy, I made her sit at the desk in the office, put her head down as far between her knees as she was able, and take a few deep breaths. She tried her best to regain the self-control she hadn't had since I called and told her what I'd found. I stood at her side and watched a couple uniformed police officers bustle into the rotunda while the paramedics who'd arrived just before the cops stowed the equipment they realized there was no reason to use. There was no use even trying to revive a victim who was as dead as a doornail.

I'd made the 911 emergency call right after I told Ella the news, and just like I hoped they would, the cops were taking care of the details. They'd already gone up to the balcony to check things out up there, and they'd talked to me about what I did and what I saw when I got to the memorial. I'd heard one of them make a call and assumed they were having someone come over from the nearby coroner's office to cart away Marjorie's body.

I was expecting them to close the memorial until all that was done and everything (and by this, yes, I do mean all the blood) was cleaned up, but I wasn't expecting them to pull out their yellow crime scene tape and cordon off not only the rotunda, but the stairway leading up to the balcony, and a wide swath of the grassy hillside outside the memorial.

Since the cops had already told me not to touch anything, and not to get in the way, and not to bother them with questions, and not to leave the building, I knew I wouldn't get anywhere asking them why they were being so careful about investigating Marjorie's death. When I looked toward the winding marble staircase that led down into the president's crypt and saw the light that poured in from a small stained-glass window shimmer and shift, I knew it didn't matter. I told Ella to keep breathing, and headed to the staircase to talk to the one person who might have actually seen Marjorie take that tumble over the railing.

"What exactly has transpired here?" President Garfield asked the question before I could, only I never would have used a word as stuffy as *transpire*. "More commotion! Precisely what I do not need. My cabinet is convening in exactly . . ." He pulled a gold watch from a little pocket in his vest. It wasn't ticking. "We are scheduled to meet in less than fifteen minutes. I simply will not tolerate so many people coming and going when we have important business of state to discuss. What has happened here?"

"I was hoping you could tell me." I stepped to the side so that the paramedics and cops couldn't see me and kept my voice down. "Marjorie Klinker, you know, the volunteer who thinks you're the greatest president ever? She's dead."

"Dead?" The president was honestly surprised. And me? I was honestly disappointed. I was hoping to get the inside track on the accident.

"You didn't see anything?" I asked him. "You didn't hear anything? She took a header over the railing. You'd think she would have screamed or something."

"I neither saw nor heard a thing. But then, I have more important things to do than worry about what goes on here."

"But you are worried about it. You said you didn't like the comings and the goings."

The president threw back his shoulders and I was reminded of the photo I'd seen of him in his Army uniform. He sniffed. "I should not be discommoded in any way. I have a country to run!"

"Only you're not running it. You're dead." I leaned in as close as I dared and looked at him hard. "You know that, right?"

"Of course I do," he muttered, and he might have said more if the door to the memorial hadn't swung open. A streak of morning sunshine poured inside. Quinn Harrison wasn't far behind.

"Shit." It was my turn to grumble, and it wasn't just because the one man I didn't want to deal with happened to be standing not ten feet away. If Quinn had been called in, it could only mean one thing: Marjorie wasn't just dead. The cops thought she'd been murdered.

If I was going to get any answers that might help with the investigation, I knew I needed to do it quick, before

Quinn cornered me and started asking the same boring questions his brothers in blue had already asked.

"All right, so you didn't see what happened to Marjorie," I whispered though I guess I didn't have to. By that time, Quinn was already in the rotunda and talking to the patrol officers. "Did you hear anything? I mean, after the cops arrived?"

"One of the police officers mentioned signs of a scuffle." The president looked toward the stairway that led to the balcony. "Up there."

"Which means . . ." I groaned and checked on Ella. She was finally sitting up and looking just a little less pale than the ghost at my side. It was bad enough that she'd have to face the media and explain a death in the cemetery. It would be worse when she found out that the death wasn't accidental.

I knew I had to be with her when she heard the news. I turned to the president before I went into the office. "Why don't you just float on up there and check things out," I suggested. "You know, listen to what they're saying. I have no doubt Mr. High-and-Mighty Quinn is going to be heading up there to look around. Follow him and let me know what he says."

President Garfield's eyes flashed blue lightning and he pulled himself up to his full, imposing height. "Young lady," he snarled, "I do not do such things. I am, after all, the president."

I knew it wasn't polite to say *whatever* to a president— dead or alive—but it's not like anyone could blame me. Then again, the way the president looked at me, his nose wrinkled and his eyes narrowed, I had a feeling he wouldn't know what I was talking about, anyway.

6

After that, everything happened pretty quickly. The media arrived complete with sound trucks and satellite dishes and reporters who saw the yellow crime scene tape and pounced on its implications like bees on the sugar cubes at a garden tea party.

To her credit, Ella was helpful enough to keep everyone happy and just evasive enough to avoid answering any direct questions about murder. Understandably, by the time she was done, she was wiped. I couldn't blame her. She trundled back to her car so she could get to the administration building and start answering the phone calls we knew were sure to start pouring in. I, remember, had been told not to leave.

Like I was going to let that stop me?

I was in the office and already had my Juicy Couture purse in hand and my car keys out when Quinn walked in.

"Pepper Martin and murder. Why am I not surprised to be saying those words in the same sentence?"

"It's not like I killed her." I'd never even considered the fact that the cops might suspect I had, and just thinking about it made my blood run cold. Rather than let Quinn know it, I dropped into the chair recently vacated by Ella. "I suppose you want to ask me all the same questions the other cop asked me."

"Maybe." I'd seen Quinn in action before—work action, not *that* kind of action!—and I knew that when he was operating in detective mode, he could be as intimidating as hell. I refused to cave even when he took his time gathering his thoughts, the better to put me on edge.

After what seemed like forever when I did not check out (at least not too much, anyway) his navy blue suit, his spit-shined shoes, or the trace of a morning shadow on his chin that told me wherever he'd spent the night, it wasn't at home, I traded him look for look.

He took a small, leather-bound notebook out of his pocket and flipped it open. "Officer Gonzalez tells me you found the body."

There was no use repeating myself. I put down my purse and my car keys and folded my hands on the desk, waiting for more.

"She was already dead?"

"Her head was smashed on the marble floor, her blood was everywhere, and she wasn't breathing. I'm no expert, but I'm pretty sure that means she was dead."

"You didn't touch the body? Move anything? Pick up anything that might be evidence?"

"Oh come on, how stupid do you think I am?" I had a feeling I didn't want to hear his answer, so I barreled on. "Like I told that other cop, I was supposed to meet Marjorie here this morning to talk about a commemoration the cemetery is planning. I showed up. I found her. She was dead. End of story."

"Was there anyone else around?"

I thought back to when I arrived at the memorial. "Marjorie's car was parked outside. There was nobody else here."

"Could someone have come down the steps after you arrived?" Though he didn't need to, he waved in the general direction of the stairway that led to the balcony. "Could they have gotten past you without you seeing?"

"Only if I was blind and deaf. If somebody was up there when I got here, they're still up there."

"We've looked."

"Then whoever that somebody is . . ." I gave him time to jump in and maybe supply me with a little information, and when he didn't, I kept on going. "They were gone before I walked in."

Quinn took his time flipping the page of his notebook before he asked, "You knew the victim?"

"Since you're going to hear it from everybody who works here, you might as well hear it from me first. Yes, I knew her. She was a volunteer here at Garden View, and the biggest pain in the behind I've ever met. Well . . ." My smile was so sweet it hurt. "The second biggest."

He ignored the dig. Too bad. I thought it was a pretty good one. "So what you're telling me is that you think there might be someone here in the cemetery who wanted to see her dead."

I laughed. Let's face it; it was the only logical response. "I said she was a pain, I didn't say anyone wanted to kill her. Oh . . ." I thought about Gloria Henninger of the pink bathrobe and the dog. I thought about how Marjorie made Doris cry and almost leave a volunteer job she loved, and I thought about Ray, who wasn't smiling when he left Marjorie's house the other night. I thought about me. Oh yeah, I'd wanted to kill Marjorie plenty of times. This wasn't the proper occasion to admit it.

"Don't tell me you have a theory."

Quinn must have read the look in my eyes, but even though it was kind of what I was going to tell him—that I didn't have a theory so much as I had a couple interesting snippets of information to tell him about—I didn't. That's what he got for rolling his eyes.

I kept my smile firmly in place. "No theories."

"You could always ask one of those dead people to help out. You know, the ones you claim you talk to."

I got up, the better to let him know that his big, bad interrogator persona didn't scare me in the least. "Already have. He didn't see a thing."

Inside his starched shirt, Quinn's shoulders stiffened. "Right."

"He didn't hear anything, either."

His smile was so brittle I waited for it to shatter. "I'm grateful you took the time to talk to him for me. If he's here . . ." He glanced all around the office, and of course, he didn't see anything. Then again, I didn't, either. The president and his cabinet were MIA. "I really shouldn't leave without talking to every witness."

"He won't talk to you. And you can't see him. You don't have the Gift."

"And you do?"

I shrugged like it was no big deal, but of course, it was.

"Is he here now?"

"Nope. He told me he has more important things to do. By that, I assume he meant more important things than talking to you. Come to think of it . . ." I took a step toward the door. "I'm pretty sure I have more important things to do than talking to you, too."

"More important than a murder investigation?"

I grabbed my purse, the better to let him know that he was boring me and I was out of there. Just in case he missed it, I stepped around him when I said, "Looks like you're the only one who cares."

"You think?" The office was small and it didn't take me long to get to the doorway. I stopped there and looked at Quinn over my shoulder just as he added, "You're the one who's always getting involved in investigations. So apparently, you care, too. Maybe we could actually get somewhere with this conversation if you'd tell me why."

"Why I care? Or why I get involved? I've already told you why."

"Oh, that's right! The Gift. Well, this time, I'm going to tell you something." He closed in on me so fast, I didn't have a chance to move, and when he looked me in the eye and lowered his voice, I swear, I knew exactly how the bad guys felt when Quinn nailed them. He had a scary side. I was supposed to quake in my open-toe mules. Which was exactly why I yawned.

"I'm serious, Pepper." When I made a move to walk out of the office, Quinn grabbed my arm. The familiar heat of his skin against mine was almost enough to melt my composure. No way I was going to let that happen. Not right in front of him, anyway. I yanked my arm out of his grasp. "I don't want you mixed up with this case, you got that?"

"That's sweet." I batted my eyelashes. "You're concerned about me."

"I'm concerned about my case. I don't want you getting in the way and screwing anything up."

My chin came up. "Like I ever have."

"Like you always have." He beat me out of the office and over to the door of the memorial and stopped there just as he was about to open it. "Consider yourself warned. I don't want you anywhere near this case. Mind your own business. And leave the mystery solving up to the professionals."

* * *

" Leave the mystery solving up to the professionals."

Oh yeah, that was me grumbling to myself and sounding all bitchy and bitter. Like anyone could blame me? It was an hour since Quinn had left with that parting shot, and even though he and his cop buddies and the paramedics were gone, I was still at the memorial. That's because Ella had called and asked me to stick around. Apparently, a couple reporters were being pretty pushy about getting the inside track on the murder, and photos to go with it, and she wanted to make sure no one snuck around that crime scene tape and got into the building. Why didn't I just lock up the memorial and get the hell out of Dodge? My thoughts exactly, especially once the coroner came and left with Marjorie's body. No such luck. See, Ella also wanted me to wait for the cleaning crew that would be by to clean up . . . well, everything that needed to be cleaned up. For now, the place was as quiet as the tomb it was. Except for my grumbling. With time on my hands and nothing better to do, I did what I always do best: I obsessed as only a woman can who's been insulted, minimized, and irritated beyond reason by the man she'd once loved.

I was trying to keep myself busy and focused by looking through the latest issue of the employee newsletter, but let's face it, reading about landscaping plans for the fall and the upcoming holiday schedule would never be enough to get my mind off Quinn. I side-handed the newsletter across the office and watched the pages hit, scatter, and skid down the wall.

Even that didn't make me feel one bit better.

But never let it be said that Pepper Martin is not self-aware. I was plenty pissed at Quinn, sure, but I knew there was one—and only one—way to make myself feel better. Not incidentally, what I had in mind would also make him feel worse. I am hardly the type who's into revenge, at least except in the most extreme cases (which this was), but as soon as I thought of the plan, things started looking up.

I rooted through the desk for a pad of paper, and when I didn't find one, I went over to the door and the visitors' book we keep there for people to sign. I ripped out some of the pages in the back of the book where nobody would notice they were gone, grabbed the nearby pen, and got down to some serious self-healing. The cure for my obsession was obvious: if I was going to silence Quinn's voice inside my head and rid myself of the memory of that condescending look he gave me when he said, "Leave the mystery solving up to the professionals," I would simply have to solve Marjorie's murder before he did.

Who Wanted Marjorie Dead?

I was writing on top of the first piece of paper almost before I sat back down. I underlined the words and tapped the pen against my chin. It didn't take me long to fill in the blank below my heading right between the lines that asked visitors for *address* and *e-mail*.

Everyone who ever met her, I wrote in big, bold letters.

Obviously, this train of thought would take me nowhere, and I forced myself to focus and started again.

Gloria Henninger, I wrote, because after all, that's exactly what Gloria had told me, that she'd like to kill Marjorie herself. I didn't add Ray's name since I didn't know what he and Marjorie were fighting about that night I'd visited her so I had no way of knowing if it was serious. I did write down *Sunshine,* and I know it sounds crazy but then, I was getting kind of punchy from being locked up in the memorial all morning. Besides, as far as I could see, if the dog had the opportunity, she would have been all for offing Marjorie.

This, of course, did not get me very far.

I plinked the pen against the desktop, thinking while

I listened to the *rap, rap, rap*. That's when I remembered that frantic message Marjorie had left on my office phone the night before.

"The one you erased," I reminded myself. I consoled myself with the fact that anyone in their right mind would have erased a phone message from Marjorie. Especially when the anyone in question couldn't have possibly known that Marjorie was going to go and get herself killed.

I grabbed another sheet of visitors' book paper and wrote down as much of the message as I could remember. Marjorie said it was an emergency, I was sure of that. Marjorie said she needed to see me the instant I got to work. Marjorie said it was extremely important.

My only question now was if her extremely important issue had anything to do with her murder.

There was no better way to try to figure it out than to go to the scene of the crime.

With that in mind, I left the office, ducked under the crime scene tape draped across the stairway, and headed up the winding, narrow steps to the balcony. It didn't take a crime scene investigator or any special "professional" (yes, even in my head, the word had a sarcastic ring to it) to see why the uniformed cops had called in Mr. Big Guns Harrison. There were stuttering black scuff marks all across the floor. They started over near the doorway that led onto the balcony and zigzagged all over the place. They stopped abruptly at the railing.

Like Marjorie had locked her legs and fought like crazy to keep from getting dumped over the side.

A shiver raced up my back and over my shoulders, and though it wasn't especially chilly in the memorial, I hugged my arms around myself and took a few careful steps closer to the railing. From up here, the pool of Marjorie's blood against the marble floor below looked bigger than I'd ex-

pected. It was dark and sticky looking, and it was starting
to dry in streaks where the team from the coroner's office
had lifted Marjorie's body to haul it away.

"We were forced by circumstances and this intolerable
ruckus to postpone our meeting. I am particularly put out
by this most incommodious turn of events."

Yes, I was startled by the voice behind me, and yes, I
did squeal. I also pressed a hand to my heart and whirled
around.

"Don't do that to me!" I ordered the president. "Especially not when I'm standing on a balcony where somebody just took a header."

It took him a moment to process the unfamiliar word,
but he got it, finally. He nodded and looked over the side,
too. "It is truly a terrible way for any person to die," he
said. "All that blood, it reminds me of the Battle of Shiloh.
That was in '62, and I was a brigade commander under
Major General Don Carlos Buell. We had just . . ."

He rattled on. I didn't listen. That was 1862 he was
talking about, but even if it had been 1962, I wouldn't
have been interested. Ancient history is not my thing,
and I wasn't going to remember any of it, anyway. Afraid
he'd go on and on (and on) if I didn't stop him, I just
jumped right in.

"It would be nice if I could figure out what exactly
happened to Marjorie. You know, to satisfy the whole bal-
ance of the Universe, right and wrong thing and all that."
I figured it was the kind of argument that would appeal to
a politician, even a dead one. Which was why I focused
on the justice angle and completely left out the whole
Quinn/revenge factor because, really, it was none of his
business. "It sure would help if you could fill me in on
what went on here this morning."

"Help? Who? Most certainly not that unfortunate
woman. Nothing I tell you will bring her back."

"Then could you just pop over . . . wherever . . . and talk to her? Ask her what happened and who dun it? That sure would make things easier."

"Who *did* it," he grumbled. "And no, I cannot accommodate you in this matter. It is not the way these things work." When he turned and marched toward the stairway, I followed. "I've already told you I am unable to help. I was preoccupied this morning with matters of state. The single thing I noticed was that the woman was here early. Far earlier than you arrived."

"Was she alone?"

"When I saw her, yes. Most assuredly."

"Where did she—" We were almost at the stairway and I stopped for a moment. There were sections of the memorial where visitors weren't allowed, and those sections were roped off and had signs nearby that said, CLOSED TO THE PUBLIC. The sign at the bottom of the stairway that led up to the old ballroom on the third floor was upside down. Automatically, I righted it and kept on with my questions. "Where did she hang out?" I asked the president.

I swear, his cheeks got red. No easy thing for a ghost. "I . . . I beg your pardon!" he sputtered. "I assure you, I certainly saw nothing hanging out, and if I had—"

OK, I had a laugh at the old guy's expense. When I was done, I explained. "Hanging out. It means, like, the place she was when she was wherever she was when she was here."

His eyebrows dipped. "Your grammar is deplorable." He floated down the stairs.

I took the more conventional route and got back down to business. "So Marjorie . . . she was . . . ?"

"On the balcony, of course. You know that. But earlier, she was downstairs."

"In the ladies' room? Or in your crypt?"

I expected another lecture that included some nonsense about how indecent it was to even mention the ladies' room. Instead, the president shook his head. "As I said earlier, I was preoccupied. I paid her no mind. I really cannot say where she went."

He stopped floating at the main floor. I kept on going. If Marjorie had spent even a few minutes of the morning downstairs, I wanted to know why. I checked out the ladies' room, and knew right away that she hadn't been in there. The fixture above the sink had one of those curlicue, energy-saving lightbulbs in it. After it's switched on, it takes forever for the bulb to brighten. Every employee and every volunteer knows to turn it on just once in the morning, then turn it off again right before the memorial is closed. It was still off.

When I stepped back into the hallway between the ladies' room and the crypt, the president was waiting there for me.

It was more than a little creepy glancing from the President Garfield at my side to his flag-draped casket.

Rather than think about it, I went into the crypt. The crypt below the rotunda is shaped like an octagon. The president's coffin along with that of his wife, Lucretia, are on display behind an iron fence at the center of the room. So are two urns. I knew from working at the cemetery that they contain the ashes of his daughter and son-in-law.

I did a circuit around the caskets and stopped right back where I'd started. "I don't know what Marjorie could have been doing down here."

"Paying her respects?"

I think it was a whatcha-call-it, a rhetorical question, but I was too deep in thought to care. "She's got pictures of you everywhere. And books and all these weird sorts of trinkets. I don't see why she'd have to come down here to pay her respects." Like it might actually help me think, I went around again and my gaze traveled from the coffin of the president to that of his wife.

"You know . . ." I edged into what I knew could be a touchy subject. "I've been wondering . . . about that girl, Lucia Calhoun. If there really were any children—?"

I never got as far as even finishing the question before President Garfield started rumbling like a thundercloud. "Young lady," he growled, "I understand that society these days is far more casual and less structured than it was back in my day, but really, I do not think that excuses a complete lack of decorum, do you?"

I wrinkled my nose. I wasn't sure when we'd gone from discussing his love life to talking about decorating.

"It is simply not appropriate for you to be asking about such things," he snarled.

"But Marjorie thought you were related." My guess was this wasn't news since Marjorie talked about it all the time, and Marjorie spent all her time in the memorial. "And now Marjorie is dead and—"

"Then it really cannot possibly matter, can it?"

I would have argued the point if Jeremiah Stone didn't poof onto the scene. He was carrying a stack of papers and he tapped one finger against it. "You really must get these papers signed, Mr. President," he said. "They are quite essential."

"Yes, of course." The president turned to me. "As you can see, I have matters of import to deal with. The ship of state cannot captain itself, and I must provide Mr. Stone here with the proper example. It is my high privilege and sacred duty to educate my successors and fit them, by intelligence and virtue, for the inheritance which awaits them."

Like there was anything I could say to that?

They vanished and I stood there alone in the crypt, wondering what to do next. I mean, besides wait for the

cleaning people. In the hopes they might show up sometime soon, I went back upstairs and thought about everything that had happened and all I didn't know and couldn't
figure out.

"But Mr. President . . ." Jeremiah Stone was nowhere
to be seen, but his voice floated on the air from the nothingness he'd disappeared into. "We must get your signature on these papers, sir. It is imperative."

Signatures made me think about Marjorie and all that
stuff—including the Garfield autographs—she had in her
house.

And thinking about visiting Marjorie that night made
me think about Ray.

And thinking about Ray . . . well, I knew Ray might not
have all the answers. When it came to my investigation,
he might not have any of them. But something told me
that a guy who had the nerve to actually visit Marjorie at
home just might be a good place to start.

7

I would much rather save my empty calories for the occasional martini than waste them on fast food. Which was why, though the rest of northeast Ohio was flocking to a new franchise called Big Daddy Burgers, I had never been inside the front door of one of the distinctive purple and white buildings. The next day was Saturday and apparently a whole bunch of people were out for lunch celebrating the weekend. It took me a while to find a parking place at the BDB nearest to the cemetery, and even longer to get up to the front of the line so I could ask one of the harried-looking teenagers who was packing the orders and ringing the register if Ray Gwitkowski was working that day.

"The old guy?" The girl's eyebrow was pierced, and the little silver stud in it jumped when she gave me a look. Clearly, she was trying to figure out why someone as young and stylish as I was needed to speak to Ray. She poked a thumb over her shoulder toward the kitchen behind the counter and I noticed Ray flipping burgers at a grill. He was wearing an apron that matched the purple shirts of the kids taking the orders. "It's not his break time. I know, because he goes right after me, but, well . . ." She glanced around, and since none of the workers looked as if they were old enough to drive and nobody seemed to be in charge of the chaos, she shrugged. "I don't think anybody would notice if you went back there. If anyone sees you, they're going to think you're from the main office, anyway, since you're old, too."

So much for young and stylish.

Insult aside, I managed a tight smile and ducked behind the counter before anyone could tell me I didn't belong. I'd like to say Ray was happy to see me, but truth be told, he was so busy flipping burgers about the size of a playing card, adding cheese, and stirring the chopped onions browning nearby, he didn't exactly have a chance.

"I checked your file at the cemetery," I said by way of explanation, even though Ray didn't have time to ask for one. "I saw that you have a part-time job here and—"

One of the kids at the counter interrupted me with a shrill, "Big Daddy special. Hold the onions. Extra cheese."

"Hold the onions. Extra cheese," Ray mumbled under his breath. He tossed a few more frozen squares of meat on the grill and flipped like his life depended on it.

"It's just that I've been thinking about everything that happened at the cemetery and—"

"Baby Big Daddy! Extra onions. No cheese. Extra well done."

"Extra well done." Ray slid a burger nearer to the center of the grill, where it sizzled like mad.

"It's just that—" I dodged out of the way of a skinny kid carrying a box filled with hamburger buns. "With everything that happened, you know, I thought—"

"Wish I could help you, kid." Ray took his eye off the

grill long enough to shoot me a smile. "I don't have time to talk. Dang!" Ray stabbed his flipper under the burger at the center of the grill. The patties were paper thin, and that one had already gone from raw to crispy. "I hate when that happens," he grumbled. He tossed the burger into a nearby trash can and moved another one over to take its place. "If the owners weren't so cheap and would hire a few extra people around here, I wouldn't have to worry about burning food and wasting it. As it is, I'm the only grill chef at this time of the day, and Saturdays are always busy." Expertly, he whisked a couple burgers off the grill, slid them onto buns, stepped to the side where he could better reach the pickles, lettuce, and tomatoes in plastic containers, and grabbed a squirt bottle of ketchup.

"Waiting on that Big Daddy!" the kid up front called out.

Ray grimaced, torn between the burgers that needed to be dressed and finished and the ones still cooking on the grill.

And I knew an opportunity when I saw it. Even when it was one I would rather not have recognized.

There was a purple apron like Ray's hanging from a hook next to the grill, and I grabbed it, looped it over my head, and took the squirt bottle out of his hand.

I hope it goes without saying that I have never worked in a fast-food restaurant. No matter. The work was just as interesting as I always imagined it would be. After a couple minutes, my brain turned off and my hands moved automatically over the buns.

Ketchup. Squirt.

Mustard. Squirt.

One slice of tomato. One piece of lettuce. Three pickles.

Ketchup. Squirt.

Mustard. Squirt.

"Too much mustard," Ray critiqued while he stirred the

onions. "Not enough ketchup on that one. Here." He thrust a plastic container of grilled onions at me. "Add those. No! Not to that one." I stopped with my hand suspended in midair above a square of meat. "That's the Big Daddy special. No onions. Extra cheese."

"No onions. Extra cheese." I was beginning to sound as mindless as all the other Big Daddy workers, and I snapped myself out of it and slid Ray a look, all the while not missing a squirt-squirt-lettuce-tomato-pickle beat.

"I need to talk to you," I said.

He didn't look especially happy about it. Which he should have considering I was doing condiment duty. "What about?" he asked.

I thought he would have figured that out by now, but since he didn't, I supplied him with the Reader's Digest Condensed version. "Marjorie."

Ray's spine stiffened. The burger on his flipper slipped off and hit the floor. He stared.

Worried he'd gone catatonic on me or had some kind of age-induced stroke or something, I waved the ketchup bottle in front of his face. "Earth to Ray! I said I needed to talk to you about her, I didn't say I was raising Marjorie from the dead or anything."

He shook himself back to reality. "Of course. Yeah. Sure." Though no one called out another order, he went to the cooler, came back with a stack of burger squares, and carefully arranged them on the grill. "I figured someone from the cemetery would be talking to all of us, taking up a collection for flowers," he finally said. "If you're look-ing for a donation, Pepper, of course I'm willing to con-tribute. Only it's kind of hard right now in the middle of the lunch rush."

I didn't bother to point out that if I'd been looking for a donation, I could have found a way better place to solicit it. Besides, I didn't have a chance. A local suburb's senior citizen bus pulled up outside, and a collective groan went up from the kids behind the counter when a group of blue-haired grannies trooped in.

Oh yeah, we were plenty busy before, but I learned soon enough that *busy* meant zip in the fast-food business. Not compared with being slammed.

"Thanks for helping me out, kid." Ray slipped into the purple booth across from where I sat and plunked a medium diet cola in front of me. "After six months at this racket, I'm good at the grill, but not good enough to keep up with a crowd like that on my own. I couldn't have done it without you."

Any right-minded person who'd learned the intricacies of squirt-squirt-etc. in so little time would have been rightly proud of herself. I would have been, too, if I wasn't so bone-tired I could barely sit upright. It was an hour-and-a-half later, the crowds had finally thinned, and Ray had invited me to join him for his break. Since I was never planning to go near a Big Daddy Burger franchise again, it was the perfect opportunity for me to make my escape from the kitchen. Not to mention a chance for me to ask Ray all the things I hadn't had a moment to talk to him about while he flipped and I squirted.

"This is what the owners of this joint think of as good employee relations." There was a purple plastic tray on the table in front of him, and Ray tipped it my way so I could see it better. "Every day we get one free Big Daddy burger, an order of fries, and all the soft drinks we can swallow. I wish they'd just add another twenty-five cents an hour to my minimum wages. The food, it's OK for the first week. Then your stomach starts reminding you that too much Big Daddy is not a good thing." He pushed the tray away.

The sight and smell of food reminded me that I hadn't eaten a thing that day. Empty calories be damned! I made a grab for the burger.

"I wouldn't eat that if I were you." Ray shook his head in warning. "I know what they put in those things."

I set the burger down, then let my hand hover above the fries. When he didn't offer another warning, I popped one fry into my mouth and grabbed a few more. I waited until I swallowed before I said, "So here's what I'm doing. I'm trying to figure out what happened to Marjorie. And so far I'm not getting anywhere and I'd really like to solve her murder because . . ." Big Daddy Burgers wasn't exactly the kind of place I wanted to discuss my relationship with Quinn, and Ray wasn't a person I wanted to do it with, either. He reminded me of my grandfather, and Grandpa wouldn't have understood. Not about Quinn. I was beginning to realize that when it came to me and Quinn, even I didn't understand.

I twitched the thought aside. It was then that I noticed I had ketchup stains on the sleeves of my new black tunic shirt. It was cotton, sure, but it was dry clean only, and I promised myself I could pout about it later. For now, I couldn't afford to waste time. "Every time I try to think through what happened to Marjorie," I said, "it doesn't make sense. That's why I've been wondering . . . you know, about that night you stopped at her place. The two of you were fighting."

"Were we?" Ray didn't blink. In fact, except for the fidgety tap of his fingers against the purple tabletop, he didn't move a muscle. His face was suddenly as pale as if he'd already swallowed a couple Big Daddy burgers before someone bothered to tell him what they were made out of.

Oh yeah, I knew Ray was a lousy liar. I recognized all the signs. He looked exactly like my dad always did back in the day when he swore up and down that he didn't have anything to do with the Medicare fraud that landed him in federal prison.

I was so not in the mood to try and convince Ray that there was nothing to be gained from keeping anything from me. "Come on, Ray," I whined. "I know you might not want to gossip about it since Marjorie's dead, but it might be important."

"I don't see how it could be." There was a paper napkin on the table and he folded it with careful creases, then unfolded it again. "Marjorie and I, we hardly knew each other."

This time, I didn't need the lie-o-meter to see the writing on the wall. All I had to do was think back to that night. I propped my elbows on the table, the better to stare Ray down. "Hardly knew each other, huh? Is that why the minute you walked into her place, she was all over you like white on rice?"

Ray's cheeks got red. "You noticed that, huh?"

"I noticed that Marjorie seemed a whole lot more interested in you than you were in her."

"Yeah. Well . . ." He ran a thumb and forefinger up and down his throat. "Marjorie . . . well, I don't exactly know how to say this . . . Marjorie, she thought—"

"That you were a hot hunk?"

When he realized he didn't have to actually come right out and say it himself, Ray let go a sigh of relief. Now the tips of his ears were red, too. "Something like that," he admitted. "She's been after me practically since the day my Vanessa went into hospice. Once word of my wife's death went around to the other volunteers and Marjorie found out I was available . . ." Yeah, his cheeks and his ears were red. The rest of Ray's face turned an unflattering color that reminded me of olives. He fiddled with the straw in his diet cola.

"Marjorie was a pompous windbag, and I'm sorry she's dead, but really, there's nothing more to say about her and . . ." He glanced at his watch and slid toward the end of the bench, making it clear that it was time for me to get a move on. "You probably have better things to do on a Saturday afternoon."

Was I imagining it? I thought he looked disappointed when I stayed right where I was and said, "What I can't figure out is if the reason you stopped in at Marjorie's has anything to do with her death."

"No! Of course not. Not at all." All that color drained out of his face and left him as white as the napkin in his trembling fingers. "Marjorie and I, we were . . ." He creased the napkin again. "Well, this is a little hard to explain. And it's embarrassing, too."

He expected me to give in and tell him if that was the case, not to bother explaining. When I didn't, Ray swallowed hard and said, "A few months ago, Marjorie came to see me one day when I was working on a mailing project for the cemetery. I was in the copy room, sticking labels on envelopes. I knew she thought I was . . ." Another flush of color darkened his face. "Well, what you said. About me being a hot hunk. I knew she felt that way about me and I hope you know me well enough to realize I never thought of her like that. Not at all. Marjorie was a heck of a dedicated volunteer and an intelligent woman, but she wasn't . . . I wasn't . . . I didn't . . ."

Sure I was looking for the truth, but I hated watching him suffer. "She wanted you, but you didn't want anything to do with her."

He nodded. "I'd been avoiding her. Until that day in the copy room when she planted herself in the doorway and cut off my escape route. That's when she told me . . ." Ray leaned forward and lowered his voice. "Marjorie came to me and told me that she had a get-rich-quick scheme. It was a sure bet, she said. Can't miss. She told me she'd do me a favor and let me in on it."

Marjorie and money. The two words didn't jibe, not with her personality, and certainly not with a wardrobe that included those cheap, ugly shoes of hers. Maybe she was about to corner the market on filmy head scarves?

I batted the thought aside and asked Ray, "And did she? I mean, did she tell you about the get-rich-quick scheme?"

He sat back and chucked the napkin down on the table. "She didn't say any more than that. Not that day, anyway. But she promised she would. And I was stupid enough to believe her. It's not that I'm some kind of shallow jerk, Pepper. I don't want you to think that. I don't buy lottery tickets and I don't bet on the horses. I don't even play poker. And I don't light up like a Christmas tree anytime somebody just mentions money to me. It's just that Vanessa was sick for a long, long time and the bills really piled up. If I didn't have those medical bills to pay, believe me, I wouldn't be working here four times a week."

He didn't need to convince me it would take an act of desperation to don the purple apron.

This was all interesting, but I knew there was something he wasn't telling me. Ray was as jumpy as if he were one of those burgers sizzling away on the hottest part of the grill. "Why was Marjorie being so generous?" I asked. "She liked you and you'd been avoiding her. I can't believe she didn't get the message. So why was she willing to let you in on the scheme?"

"Don't you get it, kid? It was her way of getting her claws into me." His shoulders drooped. "And I was so desperate, I let it happen."

It was pretty pathetic (not to mention totally disturbing), but I couldn't afford to get distracted by that. It was my turn to lean forward, the better to pin Ray with a look. "So this get-rich-quick scheme of hers, what was it? And do you think it had anything to do with Marjorie's death?"

My hopes had been riding high that I could find some answers. They thudded to the ground when he shrugged. "Wish I knew. You see, Marjorie wasn't the kind of woman who was going to make this thing easy. That day in the copy room, she told me about this scheme, and she said she didn't have all the details yet, but she would soon. She promised she'd tell me as soon as she knew more."

"And did she?"

"She called a week or so later. She told me we had to talk. I wanted to do it right there, right on the phone. But she said she needed a couple more hours to get all her ducks in a row. She told me we could talk that night over dinner. That I could pick her up at seven, and that she'd already gone ahead and made reservations at one of those places in Tremont."

I knew the area. Old neighborhood, new bars and restaurants and clubs. A few of them were local hangouts, but some of the others were of the candlelight-dinner variety, pricey, and with reputations for excellent food and ambiance galore. Something told me Marjorie wouldn't have gone out of her way to plan dinner at one of the shot-and-a-beer bars. Something else told me I knew where Ray's story was going.

He confirmed my worst suspicions when he said, "That night at dinner, she put me off. She told me she still didn't have all the details. After that it was always the same thing. She'd tell me she had more information for me, and that she'd tell me all about it if I'd just take her to a movie, or to hear the Cleveland Orchestra, or if I showed up to act as her date for a party or something like that." Ray's shoulders rose and fell.

"I should have told her to get lost. I would have, too, but

she was always dropping little tidbits about this money-making scheme, telling me it was can't-miss, and that she even had a financial planner check into it and he assured her it was a sure thing. I needed the money so bad, it got to the point where I just couldn't wait to talk to her again. I kept hanging on, and I kept hoping. I kept telling myself that maybe this time, Marjorie would stop stringing me along. Maybe this time, she'd finally tell me everything I wanted to know. Gosh, Pepper . . ." He gave me a hangdog look.

"Listening to me now, you must think I'm an idiot. I know *I* think I'm an idiot. I should have seen what she was up to, but all I kept thinking about was that pile of bills, and the calls that were coming in from the hospital and the doctors and the collection agencies. I was holding out hope that, eventually, Marjorie would come clean and tell me what was up."

"But let me guess, she never did, right?"

He didn't confirm or deny, just went right on. "When I stopped at her house . . . well, I'd never done that before. I mean, I'd been there to pick her up for dinner or a concert of whatever, but I'd never just stopped in to socialize. I didn't want to socialize with Marjorie! But what happened that afternoon, it was the straw that broke the camel's back. You see, I knew Marjorie's nephew was getting married. She'd mentioned it more than a couple times, and I'd always just pretty much ignored her or changed the subject. I didn't want to go to that wedding with her. I knew if I did, she'd parade me around in front of people and show me off and act like there was more to our relationship than there ever was. I know it might not sound like it, but I have my pride. I wasn't going to let that happen. Then that day—the day before she died—I got a copy of the wedding invitation in the mail. The one for Marjorie's nephew, Nick. It was from Marjorie, of course, and she'd written across it with red magic marker: *It's black tie, don't forget to rent a tux.*" Ray slammed his fist on the table.

"That's when it hit me. She was treating me like a trained monkey, and I'd had enough of it. That's why I went to see her that night, and I was so relieved to walk in and see you there, I can't even tell you. The thought of being alone with Marjorie . . ." He shivered inside his purple shirt, and he didn't meet my eyes. "When we excused ourselves and went into her den, that's when I told her I wasn't going to take it anymore, that she had to tell me right then and there what this moneymaking scheme was all about. That if she didn't, she could find another patsy to put up with her nonsense."

"And did she?"

"That's the real kicker." Ray scrubbed a finger behind his ear. "That's when she told me it was all a mistake. She told me the whole thing fell through, that there was no surefire moneymaking plan because she'd done some digging and she found out it was all a scam. Can you believe it? Marjorie had the nerve to tell me she never should have mentioned the whole moneymaking scheme to me in the first place."

I drummed my fingers on the table. "Which means you'd been pimping yourself out and you weren't going to get anything for it."

"That's not exactly the way I'd put it," he admitted, "but I guess it's true. What a sucker I was! And I'll tell you something else, Pepper, I'm not sure she was telling the God's honest truth, not even then."

My drumming stopped. "Because . . ."

"Because Marjorie had that invitation. Not the invitation to her nephew's wedding, the framed one, the one for James A. Garfield's inauguration. I'm sure she showed it to you. Marjorie never missed a trick. Everybody who walked in the door, they had to see all that presidential crap of hers. She told me about that inauguration invitation about a month ago, said she saw it in an on-line auction and that she wanted it bad, but there was no way she could afford it. But there it was, hanging on her living room wall, right?"

Right. I turned this thought over in my head. "So you think she really did have some magic way of suddenly making money?"

Ray started with the *tap, tap, tap* against the table again. "It's the only thing that explains it," he said. "I think she was holding out on me. And all that time . . ." Disgusted with himself, he shook his head. "The worst part of the whole thing is that I just started dating someone, a really nice woman, you know?"

I did, I just couldn't get past the whole unnatural thing about old people dating.

Thank goodness, before I had a chance to consider it for long, Ray went right on. "A couple times, I've had to make excuses to this other woman about why I couldn't see her. You know, because Marjorie had me going here or there with her. I was too embarrassed to just tell my new lady friend the truth. Now . . ." This time when he sighed, it was with relief. "Well, now at least I don't ever have to lie to her again. So you see, kid . . ." Ray looked at his watch again, and this time when he slid out of the booth, I knew it was because he had to get back behind the grill. "That whole thing about me and Marjorie fighting, well, it was just me standing up for myself finally. It doesn't have anything at all to do with her dying."

"Of course not." It was an incredibly corny comeback, but I didn't have time to question him further, and besides, my head was suddenly spinning with possibilities. After I downed the rest of the fries, I headed to my car, thinking about everything he'd told me and wondering about that get-rich-quick scheme of Marjorie's. Could the money have anything to do with her murder?

Or was there more to Ray than the sweet, old guy he pretended to be?

Like a man who was tired of being Marjorie's love monkey and who'd had it up to his eyeballs? Sure he was angry at having her string him along. Angry enough to meet her at the memorial and give her the heave-ho off the balcony?

And then there was that new woman in Ray's life who he'd mentioned. Could she have been jealous? Was it possible she didn't want to share him with Marjorie?

Could there be enough passion in an old-people romance to account for murder?

8

My gut told me Ray didn't kill Marjorie, but my gut had been wrong before. Sometimes, it's hard to tell the murderers without a scorecard.

Still, even though I was sure Ray was lying about something (and even though I couldn't figure out what that something was), I just couldn't imagine a nice old guy like him tossing Marjorie over that balcony. Believe me, I was in the right place to try to picture it. The following Monday, I was standing in the rotunda of the memorial doing my best to look like the expert-in-residence. The why is no mystery: without Marjorie there to be the Garfield know-it-all, Ella needed someone to handle the day-to-day duties over at the memorial. Naturally—at least to Ella's way of thinking—she turned to me.

Back in the day, I wouldn't have minded. At least not too much, anyway. But then, back in the day, James A. Garfield wasn't exactly a tourist magnet. The memorial had a couple visitors now and then, but for the most part, the place was quiet and empty. Quiet and empty I could deal with. In fact, it would have suited me just fine. Then maybe I would have had a chance to sort through what I knew about my case. But it's funny, isn't it? And not in a ha-ha sort of way. Murder adds notoriety to a place, and the memorial was no exception. What with the publicity Marjorie's murder had generated in the media—local, national, and sensational tabloid—it was no wonder that there was a line waiting to get inside the memorial even before I unlocked the door.

"So this is where it happened, right?" A woman twice my age and half my height had the nerve to step into my path. "Where was the body? Was she beaten and battered? Was there . . ." The woman shuddered. "Was there a lot of blood?"

"No hablo inglés," I told her, and left her to figure out why if that were the case, I was wearing the standard-issue khakis and the yellow polo shirt with GARDEN VIEW embroidered over my heart. Before she could question me, I backed away from her and sidestepped a group of teenagers who were wondering if the memorial was haunted. If they only knew!

I slipped into the office, but even there I found no peace. There was a man standing near the desk with his back to the doorway. He was middle-sized and average height, and even when he turned around, I couldn't see his face clearly. That was because he was wearing a baseball cap tugged low over his eyes. Something told me I wasn't missing anything. He was fifty, maybe, and as bland as an outfit right off the rack at WalMart.

As much as I didn't feel like it, I put on my cemetery employee face. "May I help you?"

"Pepper!" The man's cheeks were pale and doughy. His chin was weak, his hands were plump. He fingered the unpatterned gold tie he wore with a blue shirt and faded

black pants, and even though his eyes were shaded by the
brim of his ball cap, I could feel his stare. Everywhere it
touched me, I felt a chill. "I saw you," he said, and I swear,
he must have run up every single one of the couple dozen
steps that led to the monument's front doors. He was
breathing that hard. "On TV."

I'd hoped *Cemetery Survivor* had been forgotten by
everyone who'd ever bothered to watch the reality show
based on the cemetery restoration we'd done earlier in the
summer. It was that bad. Still, it was kind of a kick to be
recognized. I sidled past him and slipped behind the desk,
and no, I didn't feel like it. I mean, I was stuck in the memorial and I had all those ghoulish people out in the
rotunda who kept asking me about Marjorie, and I had a
murder to solve. I gave the man a smile, anyway. "You
want an autograph or something?"

"I want . . ." His fingers worked over his tie, faster
and faster. He licked his lips. He shuffled his feet. "I
want . . ."

I am nothing if not a good sport, but being stared and
stammered at has a way of making even the most self-
assured woman lose her legendary cool. Still, I managed
to keep smiling. And waiting.

He, however, couldn't get out of the "I want" loop.

Still standing, I tapped my fingers against the desktop.

He shuffled forward. He scuffled back.

I tapped some more.

"I saw you on TV," he mumbled. "I watched. Every
week."

"That's terrific. Really. But if you want to talk about
Cemetery Survivor—"

"Talk? No. I want . . ." He shuffled another step closer
to the desk.

By this time, I'd pretty much had it. I mean, it was one
thing being a TV sensation. It was another thing to have

my time wasted by someone who probably just didn't have the nerve to ask what it was really like to find Marjorie's brains sprinkled all over the rotunda.

I pointed at the desk. "Work," I said. It might have been a far more effective strategy if there was actually something on the desk, but since the guy was so busy staring at me, I don't think he noticed so I went right on. "I've got a whole bunch of work to take care of. So if you really don't want anything . . ."

He jumped like he'd been slapped. His tongue flicked over his lips. "I want . . ." He shambled to the door, and the closer he got to it, the faster he moved. "I want . . ." I heard him say one last time, before he rocketed into the entryway and out the front door.

"Well, that was weird." I dismissed the thought—and the guy—with a toss of my head, and I was all set to plop down in the chair behind the desk and pretend I was actually working, the better to avoid the crowds outside the office.

It was then that I noticed the single red rose on the desk chair.

OK, call me slow on the uptake. I'd been so busy dealing with his weirdness, I never even thought that Ball Cap Guy and my stalker might be one and the same person.

My knees turned to rubber, and before they gave way completely, I swept the rose from the chair with shaking hands and plunked down. I lectured myself about letting my imagination run away with me. I reminded myself that just because someone was a little . . . well . . . a lot odd . . . that didn't mean that same someone was dangerous. Or threatening.

"He was just a tourist," I told myself. "And this is a public place, and anyone can come in, and sometimes, people are just a little strange, and that doesn't mean he's your stalker or anything. Does it?"

Brave words. They actually might have made me feel better if I didn't keep remembering the way his eyes had been glued to me.

When I reached for the phone to call cemetery security, my hands trembled. I guess that's why it took me a couple tries and I still couldn't punch in the right numbers. Before I had a chance to give it another go, I heard the front door of the memorial creak open, and yeah, my head told me it was probably just another harmless visitor come to ooh and ahh over the murder scene. My instincts weren't so sure.

My heart pumping a mile a minute, my stomach somewhere up in my throat, I watched a thin stream of sunlight sneak through the front door and pool on the floor of the entryway. It was followed by a shadow that paused for a moment, then pivoted toward the office.

He was back!

I swallowed down the sour taste in my mouth and reminded myself that Pepper Martin is no namby-pamby wallflower. Just to prove I was listening, I braced my hands against the desktop and pushed myself to my feet at the same time I tried to issue a warning. My mouth was filled with sand; the words wouldn't form. I gulped and tried again. "Get lost!"

"Wow, I'd heard people in Cleveland were tough, but I didn't think it would be this bad."

He came around the corner.

Not doughy Ball Cap Guy.

No way. No how.

This guy was tall. Blond. Gorgeous.

Really. I mean it. Absolutely, drop-dead gorgeous.

Strong, square jaw dusted with golden stubble. Eyes the exact color of the robin egg's blue in the golf shirt he wore with dark, tight jeans. Loose-limbed, rangy body. The greatest smile I'd seen in a long time.

Oh yeah, he was the total package.

And I felt like a complete idiot.

"I am so sorry." I was moving toward him even before I realized it. "I don't usually tell visitors to beat it. Honest. It's just that—"

"No apologies necessary." He stuck out his hand and it took me an instant to realize he meant me to shake it. "Jackson McArthur," he said. "My friends call me Jack."

When our fingers made contact, my heart thumped, and my words whooshed out of me. "Mr. McArthur, I—"

"Jack."

"Jack." It wasn't intimate. It wasn't anything but a name, an introduction. Which didn't explain why my insides buzzed like a hive full of bees. "I'm Pepper. I work here. I guess you can see that. Who else but someone who works here would wear one of these polo shirts!"

"You wear it very well!" He held on to my hand just a nanosecond longer than was polite, but I was so busy staring up into those electric eyes, I didn't have the sense to care. "You're the one in charge, right?" he asked.

"I guess I'm supposed to be." I figured I'd better start acting like it, so I stepped back and away from the magnetic pull of his personality. He was older than me, thirty-five, maybe even forty. I don't usually cave in to the whole maturity thing, but on McArthur . . . er . . . Jack, those years were as attractive as the relaxed charm he wore like a second skin. "Can I help you with something?"

"Well, there's a loaded question if I ever heard one." One corner of his mouth lifted into a smile that was a little more personal than the one he'd given me a moment earlier. "Actually, I'm here because of—"

"Marjorie." I figured I might as well beat him to the punch. "You want to know about the murder."

He moved a couple steps farther into the office. "Well, I have read a thing or two about it. And I have to admit, it's pretty bizarre. It's not every day that a woman gets murdered in a presidential memorial. Your cemetery's famous because of it."

I made a face. "It's not the kind of famous anyone around here ever wanted. Ella . . . she's my boss . . . she's pretty tired of fielding questions about what happened and when and—"

"Shouldn't the media be asking you those questions?" I was baffled, and I guess he knew it, because he shrugged and added, "You're the one who found the dead woman, right? You did say Pepper. And Pepper, that's a hard name to forget." He took his time looking me over, from the top of my head to the tips of the open-toed ballet flats I'd been smart enough to wear because I had a feeling I'd be running all over the memorial that day. When doughy Ball Cap Guy looked at me like that, I felt like I needed to shower. With Jack, it was a whole different feeling, and maybe he knew that a tingle raced up and down my spine, because his smile inched up a notch. "There's no way I could ever forget you. I'm sure you were mentioned in the on-line article I read about the murder."

I guess the fact that I hadn't realized I was an Internet celebrity said something about how good Ella was at her job. She was deflecting the media and the questions. I was grateful. And suddenly a little suspicious, too. Tingling aside, I narrowed my eyes and looked Jack over. It was no hardship. "You're a reporter, aren't you?"

"Honest. Not." He held up one hand, Boy Scout style as if that would prove it. "Though I have to admit, I'm just as curious as everyone else. You really are the one who found the body, right?"

It's not like I could deny it or anything.

I braced myself for more questions, but Jack just shook his head. His eyes were troubled. "That must have been awful."

Aside from Ella, he was the first who'd acknowledged that finding a body, especially one that had been smashed against a marble floor, isn't anything near glamorous. Believe me, the fact that this complete stranger sympathized and Quinn never had was not lost on me.

He took another step closer and he was tall, so he had to cock his head to look into my eyes. "Are you OK? You know, there are counselors who specialize in this sort of thing. Trauma counseling, grief counseling. Have you talked to anyone? A professional?"

"No. I mean . . ." His gaze was so intense, so downright concerned, the only thing I could do was pretend I hadn't spent the weekend not sleeping. It was either that or admit that every time I closed my eyes, I saw Marjorie's brains and Marjorie's blood and Marjorie's broken limbs. "I'll be fine," I said.

His serious expression was relieved by the smallest of smiles. "I know that. But promise me you'll talk to someone, anyway."

I managed to smile back. "No. Really. I'm cool."

"Well, obviously!" Jack laughed, and just that easily, all the tension drained out of me. I smiled, too, and realized that for the first time since I'd walked into the memorial the Friday before and found myself at the center of a murder investigation, I felt the knots in my shoulders loosen and the ice in my stomach melt. "So . . ." He took a quick look around the room and nodded, confirming something to himself. "This is it. The famous Garfield Memorial. It's just as impressive as I thought it would be."

"This is just the office." I guess he knew that, but I figured it didn't hurt to point it out. I was the cemetery's one-and-only full-time tour guide, after all. "The rotunda is bigger and fancier. The president and his wife—"

"Lucretia, yes." Jack's eyes lit. "I can't wait to see the crypt."

"Really?" I couldn't have sounded more skeptical. Or less like somebody who was supposed to be proud of the place she worked. I cringed. "I mean, really! You're actually here to see the memorial?"

He leaned back and took a quick look into the rotunda. "You're telling me that all these other people . . . Let me guess, they're all here because of the murder." His sigh rippled the air between us. "There are always new and different ways that people disappoint me. I guess I shouldn't be surprised. They're probably trying to get the facts firsthand from you since you were the only one here when the body was discovered. You were the only one here, right?"

I nodded.

"You were the only one here so everybody assumes you saw something. But you didn't, right?" He brushed aside his own question with the lift of one shoulder. "Of course you didn't. If you had, you would have told the cops, and somehow, the media would have gotten wind of it. From what I've heard, the police don't even have a suspect."

"They wouldn't tell me if they did." It was the truth, though I failed to mention the Quinn component. There was no use muddying the waters, and besides, there was no way Jack would care. "All I told them is what happened. I came in here. I found the body. I called the cops."

"And there was nothing else? Nothing suspicious? Of course there wasn't, and I bet I'm sounding just as morbid as everyone else. I'm sorry. It's hard not to get caught up in the sensationalism. I should know better, and I should have known to stay away for a while, too, out of respect for the poor woman who was killed. But this was my only opportunity to see the memorial. What with earning a few continuing education credits, I've been busy all summer, and school's going to be starting again soon."

"You're a—"

"History teacher. Lafayette High School. Hammond, Indiana."

"I never had a history teacher who looked like you." I hadn't meant to say the words out loud. My cheeks got hot. "I mean—"

"No problem. Believe me, I didn't expect a cemetery worker who looked like you, either." There was that smile again, as bright as the sun and just as hot. "So you'll give me a tour, right? If you have time? I've always been a huge admirer of James A. Garfield."

Sheesh!

That's what I thought. What I said was, "Of course, but we've got a time limit. Marjorie's funeral is this afternoon, and in her honor, the memorial is going to close at one and stay closed for the rest of the day. That gives us . . ." I glanced at the clock on the wall and so did Jack.

"Plenty of time," he said. Like the hero in a swashbuckling movie, he made a dramatic gesture toward the doorway, but before I could walk out with him, he caught sight of the red rose on the floor. He scooted over and picked it up. "You drop this?" he asked, then looked again. When I threw the flower from my stalker onto the floor, I hadn't exactly been careful about it. Its petals were mooshed and the stem was bent. Jack twirled the flower between his fingers. "You learn a lot teaching high school," he said. "You know, watching students and teachers and parents, dealing with their dramas and their moods. I'm going to go out on a limb here and say that somebody . . ." He gave me a look that was only half-teasing. "Somebody is in the middle of a lovers' spat."

Just the thought of the word *lover* associated with the creepy man in the baseball cap made me shiver. I hugged my arms around myself. "No way."

Maybe Jack was the basketball coach at Lafayette High, too. He tossed the rose across the room. It arced over the desk and splatted into the wastepaper basket without ever touching the rim. "Good." He grinned. "That means I don't have any competition."

Oh yeah, a girl's head could get turned by a man like Jack McArthur. This girl's head sure did. By the time we were out in the entryway and he was deciding if he wanted to hit the rotunda or the crypt first, I didn't even care that he was a fan of James A. Garfield. Don't get me wrong! I still knew it was lame. I just didn't care.

"So . . ." He drew in a breath and glanced around, taking in the marble, the stained glass, and that statue of the president, his right arm bent and his hand resting against the vest pocket where I'd just recently seen him take out his nonticking watch. "Where to first? What do you think is the most important aspect of the memorial, Pepper? You probably know the building better than anyone, you must have your favorite spots. Certainly, the fact that Garfield isn't buried here, that his casket is on display . . . that's unique in and of itself." His eyes glinting, Jack waited for me to comment, and when I didn't, he sailed right on.

"Refresh my memory. When was the memorial built?"

So far that day, I'd done a pretty good job of avoiding questions. Now I was trapped. I blinked up into Jack's brilliant blue eyes. I smiled my most competent and cemetery-visitor friendly smile. I stalled, wondering as I did how easy it was to pull the wool over a history teacher's eyes.

"The building was begun in 1885, and dedicated on Memorial Day in 1890. The architect was a fellow named George Keller."

At the sound of the deep, booming voice, I turned just in time to see the president materialize at Jack's side. He

stood with his shoulders back and his chin up and his right
arm cocked, just like the statue inside the rotunda. I repeated what he'd just said, except I left out the *fellow* part.
There was no use sounding as fuddy-duddy as he did.

"And he wasn't even quite fifty years old when he
died." Jack shook his head sadly. "Fifty. It's sounding
younger all the time, isn't it?"

I couldn't say I agreed so I was glad he didn't wait for an
answer. "President Garfield was in the House of Representatives, I know that," he said. "But for how many terms?"

"Nine," the president rumbled. "I was elected in 1862
while still on active duty with the Army. I attended my
first congressional session in 1863."

"Nine." I parroted the information to Jack. "I . . . that
is, *he* was elected in 1862 but he was in the Army then, so
he didn't go to Washington until the following year."

I wasn't imagining it; Jack was impressed with my
knowledge. His eyes lit up. "And he was elected president
in 1880." He was on a roll now, but then, I couldn't blame
him. Thanks to the quick answers the president had pro-
vided, Jack mistakenly thought I was a kindred spirit in
the Garfield geek squad. "He was shot in July of that year
and died in September. Such a loss to our country. Such a
waste."

"Humph." The president agreed without actually coming right out and agreeing. "I advocated civil service reform, you know."

"Civil service reform," I told Jack.

"I directed a special subcommittee to modernize the
census-taking process."

"Census."

"When I was a congressman, I even went around and
visited various government agencies so I could see firsthand how they were spending the people's money. Once I

assumed the presidency, I ordered an investigation into
widespread corruption in the Post Office."

"Post Office," I said.

The president frowned. "It is truly a shame there wasn't
time to accomplish more. And a calamity that I didn't
have time to teach my successors to pay more attention to
the past in their search for solutions to the problems of the
present. Alas, the lesson of history is rarely learned by the
actors themselves."

I couldn't follow most of that, so I just glommed on to
the last part. "The lesson of history—" I began.

"Is rarely learned by the actors themselves!" Jack
grinned. "You can even quote the president. Pepper . . ."
He took my arm, and together, we headed into the crypt.
"Something tells me this is a match made in heaven."

Was it?

I couldn't say. I only knew that for the first time since
Quinn walked out on me, I felt pretty, and smart, and more
than competent in my job. Of course, the president helped
me out every step of the way. But Jack didn't know that.
And Jack didn't care. Jack was funny and he was friendly,
and yes, OK, he was also incredibly hot. But there was
more to my attraction to him than that. Take, for instance,
the way he talked about history and actually made it seem
not nearly as boring as I always thought it was. We ex-
plored the memorial top to bottom, and an hour-and-a-
half flew by.

I'd already gone into the rotunda and told the gawkers
there that the memorial was closing for Marjorie's funeral. Now, standing outside the office together, Jack and
I watched those visitors file out the front door. He leaned
close. "You'll be here again tomorrow?" he asked.

I hoped it meant he was planning to come back, but I
knew the rules of the game. If I wanted to keep him inter-

ested, I had to play it cool. "I'm on permanent assignment
here in the memorial," I told him. "At least until Ella can
find a docent to take my place."

"Take your place? Impossible," he said, and humming,
he walked out of the memorial.

When the door closed behind him, I realized I was
humming, too. The president was hovering outside the office and I smiled at him. "You want to come along?"

"To that woman's funeral?" I didn't know ghosts could
look green, but he did. "I have business of state to take
care of," he blustered. "Important matters. Things essential to the workings of the government. I—"

I cut him off with a laugh. "I was talking about a walk
around the memorial." I swirled a finger in the air. "I've
got to make sure there's no stragglers left behind."

"Oh." He blew out a breath of relief. "Well, really, I'd
best get back to my cabinet. We are discussing those Post
Office reforms, you know, and . . ." Even as I watched, he
stepped into the rotunda and poofed away into nothing.

I took one last look around, and everything was ship-
shape.

Well, just about everything.

Upstairs, just outside the roped-off doorway that led
into the old ballroom, that CLOSED TO THE PUBLIC sign
was upside down again.

9

Believe me, when it comes to the men-and-romance department, I have more than enough experience, some of it good, some of it is disastrous. I knew better than to have my head turned by Jack's smile, or Jack's charm, or Jack's gorgeous body.

That didn't mean I wasn't grinning—just a little —when I locked up the memorial and headed to the other side of the cemetery for Marjorie's funeral.

Or that I didn't have to remind myself that standing at the edge of an open grave and grinning probably wasn't the most politically correct thing to do.

I wiped the little glowy aftermath of my encounter with Jack from my expression and did my best to concentrate on what the minister was saying about Marjorie. No easy thing considering it was all about how dedicated she was, how wonderful she was, how knowledgeable she was about all things James A. Garfield, and blah, blah, blah.

To my way of thinking, it would have been way more

interesting if the plump, bald minister could have given me some insight into who tossed her over that balcony.

With that in mind, I took a careful look around the crowd of mourners. It was no surprise that most of them were familiar, Garden View employees and volunteers. I mean, really, did I expect Marjorie to have friends?

I gave the people I knew a quick once-over. Ella and Jim Hardy (our big boss) both looked appropriately solemn. So did Ray Gwitkowski. He was just behind Ella, next to Doris Oswald, and both Ray and Doris had their eyes cast down, looking at the simple, but tasteful, program we'd all been given that listed the bare essentials of Marjorie's life: birth date, death date, and the plot number where her copper-colored casket would soon be lowered into the ground. It also included a note of gratitude from her nephew, Nick Klinker, who said, as Marjorie's only relative, he was grateful for all the kindnesses shown to him in his hour of need.

Or maybe the program wasn't what Ray and Doris were looking at.

I'm tall, remember, so I sometimes get an interesting perspective on things. I craned my neck for a better look, and from where I stood, I could see what a lot of the other mourners couldn't: Ray and Doris didn't have their eyes averted out of grief, or even respect. They weren't reading the program. Both of them had their gazes focused on where their fingers were entwined.

Old people, holding hands like lovestruck teenagers?

I would have been grossed out if I wasn't so busy wondering what it meant and if it could have anything to do with my case.

Ray had mentioned that he was dating someone new, but I never expected it to be Doris, and talk about a new perspective! Suddenly, ideas weren't just niggling at the back of my mind, they were jumping up and down, shouting out the possibilities. Here's pretty much the way my thought processes went:

Marjorie made Doris cry. Marjorie made Doris think about leaving the cemetery. And Doris loved her volunteer work at the cemetery.

This told me there was no way Doris could have been all that fond of Marjorie.

Marjorie blackmailed Ray into taking her to concerts and movies and parties. Marjorie demanded his time and his attention. She dangled the promise of a get-rich scheme in front of him like a fat worm on a hook, and because of it, she expected him to jump at the drop of a hat. She had not only stolen Ray's time—time he could have been spending with his new honey, Doris—she'd also humiliated him and played him for a chump.

This meant that Ray wasn't a big fan of Marjorie's, either. In fact, I knew this to be true, because Ray had gone to her place that night I visited to throw that wedding invitation back at her.

Could old-folk love run deep enough to spark jealousy? The kind that resulted in murder?

I didn't know, but I did remember that both Ray and Doris were in the cemetery the morning Marjorie was killed. If I recalled correctly (and yes, I usually do), when I ran into them, they both looked a little flustered. And I hadn't forgotten that back at Big Daddy Burger after all the flipping and the squirting was done, Ray lied to me about something. Nobody was that jittery when they were telling the truth.

I tucked all this away for further consideration, and since the minister was now saying something about Marjorie's dedication to always looking her best (yikes!), I continued to study the crowd. I'd gotten there a couple minutes before the service started and talked to Ella, so I knew the man standing closest to the minister was Marjorie's nephew,

Nick. He was in his thirties, and not bad looking, considering he was related to Marjorie. He had eyes that were a soft shade of blue, mousy brown hair, and a high forehead. He was wearing a dark suit that was just outdated enough for me to think he only pulled it out of his closet for weddings and funerals. Ella said he was a software engineer, and I wasn't surprised. I pegged him as a geek.

Nick's wedding was the one Marjorie had tried to browbeat Ray into attending, so I assumed the petite blonde who stood at Nick's side was his fiancée. She, too, was wearing a dark suit. Every strand of her shoulder-length hair was in place and her nails were perfectly manicured. One look, and I knew that Marjorie and her soon-to-be niece-in-law did not share the same good taste, especially when it came to shoes. No alligator green platforms for this woman! She wore a pair of Dolce & Gabbana pointed-toe slingbacks made from a combination of earth-toned patent, suede, and snakeskin, and I experienced an instant pang of shoe envy.

"Amen!"

I was jolted out of my thoughts when the minister finished his prayer and the folks all around me mumbled, "Amen," in response.

Before the mourners scattered back to the cars parked along the winding road, I knew I had to talk to Nick. For one thing, I had a trunkful of Marjorie's Garfield memorabilia I was anxious to get rid of. For another . . .

Well, experience has taught me more than just what's what where men are concerned. I knew that when it came to murder, it wasn't out of the realm of possibility to suspect the victim's nearest and dearest. I also knew it would be stupid not to take this opportunity to question Nick. After all, if anybody knew Marjorie, it was probably her only living relative.

I was all set to close in on Nick when I saw him approach Ella. I didn't want to butt in. He might have been doing something sappy like thanking the staff on behalf of the family for all their concern and support. Or he could have actually been as nutsy as his aunt and eager to talk about President Garfield and his supposed connection to the family. Either way, I wasn't taking any chances. I waited until Ella walked away before I made my move.

"I'm Pepper," I said by way of introduction. "I'm the one who—"

"Found her. Yes, of course." Nick's expression softened. "I can't tell you how grateful I am—" He stopped short and glanced at the woman at his side. "I can't tell you how grateful Bernadine and I are for all you did for my poor, dear Aunt Marjorie."

I carefully avoided pointing out that by the time I found her, there was nothing I could have done for Marjorie even if I'd wanted to. She was that dead. I sloughed off his gratitude. "All I did was call the cops. It was nothing."

"It was the final act of kindness for a woman who was nothing but kind herself."

See? I was right. He was getting all mushy. Funerals do that to people. I knew this for a fact when this total stranger reached over and gave my arm a squeeze. I guess it was a good thing I was so distracted by the gesture, since it kept me from saying what I was thinking, and what I was thinking in relation to this horse hockey about Marjorie being kind was, "Huh?"

Instead, I tried to keep myself—and my investigation—on track. "Speaking of cops . . ." We weren't, not exactly, anyway, but I wanted to, and this was my perfect opportunity. "I've been wondering if you have any theory about what might have happened to your aunt?"

"Theory?" Nick and Bernadine exchanged glances. "It seems pretty obvious what happened. She went over the railing of the balcony. The police say she was pushed."

The *what* was all pretty straightforward. It was the *who* I was worried about. There wasn't exactly a good way to inch closer to the subject so I jumped in with both feet. "Do you know anyone who disliked your aunt enough to do that?"

Nick's nose scrunched. His eyes scrinched. If I didn't know that Quinn had already asked him the same question—and believe me, I knew he had; there was no way a guy as thorough as Quinn would let something so obvious get away from him—I would have said that Nick was surprised by the very thought.

"You work here," Nick said. "And Aunt Marjorie spent so much of her time here. I have to imagine you knew her well. So it shouldn't come as a surprise when I tell you exactly what I told the police when they asked me that question. No one disliked Aunt Marjorie. How could they? She was sweet and compassionate. She truly cared about other people, about their interests and their ideas and their feelings."

"Right." I hoped I looked more enthusiastic than I sounded, and when I was afraid I didn't, I settled for hoping Nick wouldn't notice. "But someone did throw her off that balcony," I reminded him. "If we could figure out who—"

This time, he patted my arm. "Aunt Marjorie was a big believer in law and order, and so am I. I have faith that the police will find the real murderer. Until then, all we can do is wait, and hold Marjorie in all our hearts."

Actually, there was something else we could do. "Speaking of that . . ." I hoped I wasn't stepping into something I couldn't easily get out of, and braced myself in case Nick started babbling on about the long-gone president and I had to make a quick exit. "I was at Marjorie's the other night, and she has all that memorabilia and—"

"Of course! Aunt Marjorie told us all about that com-memoration she was in charge of for the cemetery, didn't she, Bernadine?" His fiancée's nod was a reflection of his. "I just told Mrs. Silverman . . ." He looked back to where Ella was chatting with the minister. "None of her collection means anything to me. I don't want any of it, and we certainly don't have room for it, do we, Bernadine? I'll be liquidating every bit of it as soon as I'm able. Now, if you'll excuse me." The minister had turned toward his car and I knew Nick had to catch up with him so I backed off. Good thing I did, too, or I would have missed out on the most interesting thing that happened that day.

Well . . .

I remembered Jack, and now that the funeral service was over, I allowed myself a smile at the same time I cor-rected myself. This was the second most interesting thing that had happened that day.

Because just as I turned around, I saw Ray head toward his car.

And as soon as his back was turned, I watched as sweet, fluffy Doris kicked dirt on Marjorie's grave.

J ust for the record, one o'clock is a lousy time for a fu-neral. By the time it was over, it was too early to head for home, and too late to get much accomplished back at the office even if I was inclined to go over there. My wis-est course of action seemed to be to head back to the me-morial. After all, it was officially closed for the rest of the day, and that meant I could officially take my time, free of the gawkers, and try to get a line on my investigation.

I parked and walked around to the front of the building, and it wasn't until then that I second-guessed my plan. But then, that's when I noticed a movement in the huge rhododendron bushes over on my right. And that's when I remembered the creepy guy with the baseball cap and the chilling gaze.

As if he was looking at me right then and there, I froze, watching the branches of the bush twitch. My heart in my throat and my knees already starting their morph into Silly Putty, I thought about how alone I was, and gauged the distance back to my car. I'd already taken a step in that direction when the rhododendron branches parted and Jack walked out.

He looked just as surprised to see me as I was to see him.

"I'll bet this looks weird, doesn't it?" He strolled up to me and poked a thumb over his shoulder and back toward the bush. "I wasn't doing whatever you think I was doing."

"Since I can't imagine what you were doing . . ." Baffled, I shrugged. "What were you doing?"

His answer was simple enough. "Communing with President Garfield."

I wasn't sure if I should be relieved or worried. If Jack and I shared a Gift and he really was talking to the president, it would save me the trouble of maybe someday having to explain the whole I-see-dead-people thing to him. That being said . . .

I glanced around.

I didn't see any sign of President Garfield.

Which meant maybe I should be worried that Jack was as weird as the weird guy who'd weirded me out earlier in the day.

Something told me Jack could read the cascade of worries and doubts that filled my head. He laughed. "Communing with the president. Up there," he said, and because from where we stood I couldn't see what he was talking about, he grabbed hold of my hand and gently pulled me to the side of the building. "I was trying to get a better look at the bas-relief sculptures."

Bas-relief. It's one of those terms I should have learned when I got my degree in art history. Since I didn't, I had to learn it when I started taking visitors around the cemetery. *Bas-relief* describes a sculpture that's made from chipping away stone so that the picture stands out from the background. In the case of the memorial, there are five of them, high up on the walls. Each one shows a different aspect of the president's life: Garfield as a teacher, a soldier, a congressman, the president, and at his death. The figures on each of the reliefs are life-size.

"I was trying to get a better look," Jack explained. "And then I realized that from down there . . ." He glanced toward the bushes. "I was just trying to see the sculpture from a different perspective. I know it's hard for you to understand. You're surrounded by all this incredible history all the time."

I think that's the first we both noticed that we were still holding hands. My brain flashed back to Ray and Doris at the graveside. My body was focused on something else. Like the heat that intensified when Jack tightened his hold on my fingers and grinned. Still hand in hand, he led me over to one of the nearby picnic tables and we sat down.

"I'm so impressed with this place, I can't even begin to tell you," he said. "I just can't get enough of it. That's why I hung around, even after you closed up the memorial and left for the funeral. How was it?"

I'd been so busy staring up into Jack's incredible blue eyes, funerals were the last thing on my mind. I shook myself back to reality. "Funerals are never fun. And when the person getting buried is a murder victim, it's even worse."

"Was the family very upset?"

I thought back to everything Nick had said about his

aunt, and mumbled, "Delusional more than upset," but when Jack didn't catch what I said and asked me to repeat it, I told him it was nothing.

It was just as well since he was staring up at the Garfield sculptures again. On the relief he was looking at, the president was posed just like the statue inside, with one arm bent and his head high. He was surrounded by other figures. Some of them looked like the men I'd seen around the table when I got a glimpse of the ghostly cabinet meeting.

"It's the kind of beauty money can't buy," Jack said on the end of a sigh, and I was all set to bat my eyelashes and make some half-baked protest about how I'd been blessed by good genetics and a better-than-average understanding of skin cleaners, moisturizers, and really good sunscreen, when I realized he wasn't talking about me, he was talking about the monument.

I was appropriately peeved, but I didn't let on. After all, he *was* a history teacher, and from Indiana to boot. Maybe he just didn't know any better.

Or maybe he did. When he looked back at me, he grinned, and whether he meant it as an apology or not, I decided to cut him some slack. He was too cute to get pissed at. At least this early in our relationship. "It doesn't seem right to even be talking about money in a place like this," Jack said. "Garden View is so impressive and so historic. It's incredible, and they're lucky to have a woman as classy as you on staff. Something tells me . . ." He cocked his head and gave me a slow look that spread fire every place his gaze touched.

Of course, I couldn't help but think about Quinn. I mean, what woman in her right mind who'd been sleeping with the sexiest detective in town wouldn't? Hot-as-hell smiles tend to do that to me.

Unlike Quinn, who was all about smoldering looks and

pent-up emotions, Jack was much more aboveboard. He was open and honest and said what he was thinking. There was a concept that would throw Mr. Sexy Detective for a loop! It all made me think that, in addition to being as hot as a firecracker, Jack might also be a whole lot of fun.

"Let me guess, you live in a fancy condo in some trendy part of town."

That was Jack talking, and I'd been so busy letting my imagination run wild, I hadn't even been listening. Maybe he didn't notice because he went right on to say, "And I suspect you have a great wardrobe, too." He glanced over my khakis and polo shirt, which obviously weren't anybody's idea of a great wardrobe, and his golden eyebrows rose. "You vacation in fabulous places, right? Cancun? Rio? Punta Cana? No way you're the skiing type. I picture you on a beach, palm trees swaying overhead and a drink in your hand. One of the ones with the little umbrellas in them."

"I picture me on a beach, too, and in that fancy condo, but that's not going to happen anytime soon. Do you have any idea the kind of money a cemetery tour guide doesn't make?"

He laughed, but only for a second. "Not to sound morbid or anything, but funny you should mention that. I was walking around here in the quiet and thinking about you over at that funeral, and that got me thinking about that woman who was killed. I wonder how it all looks to her now? You know, life. I think about how I'm always trying to stretch my paycheck so I can make my mortgage payment, and my car payment, and have a little extra every week to go out for a burger and a beer with my friends. And I was just wondering, you know, how if once you're dead, it all doesn't seem really stupid. All that scrimping and all that saving, and what does it really come down to? Maybe once you're dead and up there . . ." He pointed a finger up at the puffy white clouds that floated overhead. "I wonder if you don't look down on the world and think, 'I should have bought that fancy condo when I had a chance.' Or 'I should have gone to Cancun when I was young. I should have enjoyed life because now it's over and—'" This time, Jack's grin wasn't as hot as it was just plain sheepish. He was as cute as a button.

He got up from the picnic table bench. "Sorry, I sound like a crackpot! I'll warn you, I tend to be introspective, but I swear, I'm not usually this focused on death. Honest. I was just thinking, that's all. You know, about how I hope that poor woman enjoyed her life, how I hope she didn't nickel-and-dime her way from year to year and miss out on the things she really wanted. Because now she's dead, and she'll never get to enjoy any of it again."

I waved away his concerns. "Not to worry. One thing Marjorie apparently never did was scrimp and save. She had more James A. Garfield memorabilia than a museum."

"Really?" He dropped back down on the bench, all excited in a very history-teacher-like way. "I would have loved to see it. She'd probably been collecting for years. I mean, I read how old she was and that she used to be a librarian, and I'm thinking that once she retired, she would have had to cut back on her spending."

"Apparently not. I was at her house and . . ." No, Jack had never met Marjorie. I still assumed he would think I was a loser for visiting her at home. Rather than even try to explain, I smoothly turned the attention away from that particular incident. "Ray—he's another one of the volunteers— he told me that Marjorie just bought an original invitation to the Garfield inauguration. It was something she talked about buying a few months ago and said she couldn't afford. But then she turned around and did it, anyway. So I guess that was a good thing. She did just what you said all of us should do, she used her money to buy the things that brought her happiness."

"Well, good for Marjorie. I hope she rests in peace."

Don't ask me why, but it was the first time I even considered that she might not, and the very idea sent a claw of icy terror clear through me. If Marjorie dead was anything like Marjorie alive . . . well, if her ghost ever spooked its way into my life, I was going to have to figure out a way to turn in my Gift club membership—fast.

I guess the thought made me look just as panicked as it made me feel, because Jack leaned closer and automatically tried to comfort me. "It was just a figure of speech. You know I'm kidding, right? You don't think I believe in—"

"Ghosts?" I hopped off the picnic table bench. A tiny portion of my brain advised me to get it over with here and now. Tell Jack about my Gift. Lay it on the line. Before I had any emotions invested and anything to miss once he determined I was crazy and walked out on me.

Would I have done it? Fortunately, I never had a chance to find out.

His cell phone rang, and he hauled it out of his pocket and took a look at the caller ID. "Gotta go," he said. "But I'll be back tomorrow to see more of the memorial. You'll have lunch with me?"

He didn't give me a chance to answer; he just smiled in a way that told me he was looking forward to it.

And maybe that was a good thing. Just like telling him about my ability to communicate with ghosts might not have been a smart thing, jumping up and down and yelling *yes, you betcha, absolutely!* probably wasn't the best course of action for a woman who was trying to play it cool.

10

I may have been wondering what on earth I was supposed to do next as far as my investigation was concerned, but believe me when I say I had no such reservations about choosing an outfit the next morning. I was going to lunch with Jack, so no khakis and polo shirt for me. Instead I picked out a sleek little cotton dress: square-necked, sleeveless, form-hugging. I grabbed a matching, kiwi-colored bolero on my way out the door of my apartment just in case the memorial was cool. Since Jack was hot (and oh, how I was counting on that!) and I didn't want to look too dowdy, I could strip off the bolero before he arrived.

What I wasn't counting on was getting down to my car parked behind my apartment building and finding that two of the tires had gone flat. I grumbled, sure, but never let it be said that Pepper Martin isn't a woman of action. I called AAA on my way back up to the apartment, where I took off the kiwi-colored dress, carefully folded it, and stashed it in a carry bag so I could change back into it at lunchtime. That done, I pulled on the dreaded khakis and polo shirt and, as long as I was at it, a pair of sneakers, too. Sure the open-toed slingbacks I'd been wearing were adorable, but just as sure, I could never walk the mile from my apartment to the cemetery wearing them, even if it weren't all uphill. The slingbacks, too, got tucked into the bag. Thus prepared, I started out for the monument.

It was a sticky morning, so even if it was born of necessity, bringing clothes to change into was an act of pure genius. Just like cute shoes with high heels aren't meant for walking, perspiration stains on a gorgeous dress make such a bad impression. Especially when the fabric is dry clean only.

By the time I had climbed all those stairs that led up to the front door of the monument and stuck the key into the lock, I was breathing hard and desperate to sit down.

So one can only imagine how much I did not want to be greeted by a certain dead commander in chief.

"This is impermissible." President Garfield paced the entryway like a caged lion. He'd obviously been waiting for me; he was so worked up, the great orator actually sputtered. "I simply will not tolerate . . . I cannot abide . . . these sorts of interruptions are unconscionable, not to mention rude. Comings and goings and—"

"It's Tuesday. I'm supposed to be here." I was sweaty and tired, remember. I couldn't afford to stand on ceremony, even with the president. I trudged into the office, set down my purse and my carry bag, and flopped into the chair behind the desk. It was blessedly cool inside the monument and I fanned my fiery cheeks and wished I could enjoy a few moments of peace. You'd think a man who'd made it all the way to the White House would have been smart enough to pick up on that.

"I have been patient," the president said, coming into the office and sounding anything but. The way he huffed and puffed, it was like he was the one who'd had to slog to work that morning. "I have been forbearing. I have been as a man who is adrift on a stormy sea, and who sees that there is no beneficial result to be had from raging against the conjunctive forces of Fate and Nature. He must stay his time, and excogitate his plans. He must—"

With a sigh, I pushed myself out of the chair. "He must get to the point?"

The president flushed. He had a high hairline and the color flowed over his cheeks and all the way up his forehead. "The point is, young lady, I can no longer abide such disturbances. I have a country to run!"

It was early. I was hot and tired. There was no coffeemaker in the memorial like there was in the administration building, where I would have stopped first thing if I was in my car instead of on foot, and the caffeine from the cup I'd had back at home had been sweated out of me. I was a little nervous about having lunch with Jack, and a little annoyed that, so far, my case wasn't coming together. I was a little worried that Quinn was making more progress when it came to Marjorie's murder, and more than a little sure that if he was getting somewhere more promising than my nowhere, he wouldn't share any information with me and that he would, in fact, gloat about it the first chance he got. Oh, how I didn't like the thought of Quinn gloating!

Like anybody could blame me for blowing a fuse?

I pounded out into the entryway and flung open the door, stepping back so the president could get around me. "You want to run the country? Fine! Get out of here and go run it. You certainly couldn't do a worse job than all the other goofballs who think they know what they're doing." When he didn't move fast enough to suit me, I stomped one sneaker-clad foot and waved him toward the outside world. "Go!"

The president threw back his shoulders and marched to the door. "I will do exactly that," he rumbled, and he stepped outside.

If we were in some TV drama, or one of those romance novels my mom likes to read so much, I would have slammed the door behind him and brushed my hands together in a good-riddance sort of way. I was all set to when I looked out to where the president stood on the flagstone veranda and saw his jaw go slack. His shoulders dropped, and he turned as pale as I'd always pictured ghosts would be before I met one and found out they don't look any different from anyone else. His eyes bulged and he jerked forward and threw his arms out to his sides—right before he let go a cry so gut-wrenching, it rattled my bones.

I rushed outside, but remember, the living can't touch ghosts. If any of us do, we'll freeze up like Popsicles. If I could have put a hand on his shoulder, or given him a shake, I might have been able to get through to the president. The way it was, all I could do was stand there, helpless and panic-stricken, while he writhed in pain and screamed as if he were burning from the inside out.

"What's going on? What's happening?" By this time, I was jumping up and down in front of him, and he was flickering, like a strobe light. On, then off. On, then off. My eyes filled with tears of desperation and a lump of terror in my throat, I realized that each time he flicked off, it took him longer to come back. "What do you want me to do?" I screamed.

He vanished before he could tell me, and I waited. One second. Two. Three. This was not good. I'd seen ghosts disappear from this world to go into the next before, and aside from one who got dragged to hell and deserved it (the bitch), I had never seen one pass over so violently.

I waited, my pulse beating out each second, wringing my hands and wondering what to do and how to do it and—

The president poofed back onto the wide veranda outside the front door, and I let go a breath I hadn't even realized I was holding.

"Something's wrong," I said. As if he needed me to tell him that. "What do you want me to do?"

Slowly, as if each move he made was painful, he turned to look at the door. "Inside." The word didn't exactly come out of his mouth. It hissed through the air like the wind and chilled me from head to toe. "Must . . . get . . . into . . . the tomb."

It was the first time I realized that when we came outside, the massive wooden front door had slammed closed behind us. I prayed it hadn't somehow locked, too, and I grabbed for the handle, but though I was icy on the inside, my fingers were slick.

My hand slipped.

The president flickered.

"Hold on!" I yelled, and made another try for the door. My fingers wrapped around the iron handle, and once I had a hold of it, I hung on tight and wrenched open the door. A whoosh of air from inside the memorial rolled over us. The president stopped flickering.

"Quick. Inside," I told him. I didn't have to. One step at a time, he dragged himself back into the memorial. Once he was in the entryway, I slammed the door closed behind us and stood with my back braced against it, breathing hard.

"What the hell—"

"Really, Miss Martin." The president puffed like a faulty steam engine. "A woman should never—"

A laugh burst out of me. "You almost disappeared. Or dissolved. Or exploded. Or something. And all you can worry about is my language?"

"I am afraid it is a product of my upbringing." He laughed, too, but then, I guess I couldn't blame him. I didn't know what happened there outside the front door, but whatever it was, he was lucky to have escaped. He knew it, too. I could tell because though he tried to keep a stiff upper lip, his eyes were troubled and his expression was clouded. "I am grateful for your assistance," he said, snapping himself out of the uncomfortable memory. "As you know, I cannot touch things of this world. If you had not been here to open the door for me and allow me back inside—"

"You could have just poofed right through it." I nodded to convince him, and myself. "I've seen ghosts do that. They can disappear on one side of a wall or door and pop up on the other side."

"Certainly, if they have the strength."

"And you didn't." Just thinking of the way his features had twisted with pain made my stomach swoop. I hugged my arms around myself. "What happened?"

"You angered me."

I was about to tell him no way any of it was my fault when he held up a hand to keep me quiet.

"You angered me, yes, with your taunting and your insistence that I should take my place in the world rather than keeping to myself here in my tomb. But I should have known better than to give in to so unproductive an emotion. I was weak, and that failing within my character made me act with brazen disregard for all that is true."

Like this was supposed to explain things? I leaned forward. "And all that is true is . . . ?"

The president *harrumphed*. He grumbled. He muttered. When he was done doing all that, he turned and walked into the rotunda. Just like the first time I went in there with him, the marble pillars around us were suddenly enveloped in sparkling fog. It drifted around my feet and curled up my arms. When a blast of air cleared the mist around us, we were back in the room with the fireplace and the long wooden table with all those portraits of all those presidents staring back at us from the walls.

"I was president for only four months," Mr. Garfield said. "You know that, of course. You must pardon me if I sound far too self-absorbed, but really, like all my countrymen, you must be aware of my singular history."

I really wasn't, and I doubted too many other people were, either. I mean, honestly, how many Americans know anything about President James A. Garfield? Though I'd grown up in the area and had attended public schools not all that far away, none of my teachers had ever even mentioned him except in passing. We'd never come to his memorial for a field trip, either, and now that I thought about it, that was a shame. There was a president of the United States entombed practically in our backyard, and I bet thousands of Cleveland-area schoolchildren didn't even know it.

After all I'd seen him go through outside, I didn't have the heart to make the president suffer any more. Hearing that practically no one but a history teacher like Jack or a nutcase like Marjorie remembered him . . . well, there was nothing to be gained from that. I scrambled to think of everything Ella had told me about the president before she assigned me to his memorial.

"You were the twentieth president."

"Yes." He nodded, pleased. "That is most certainly true."

"You took office in March."

"March of 1881."

"And you were shot in . . . July?"

"Yes. Exactly. I was shot by a man named—"

"Charles Guiteau." I was pretty proud of myself for remembering it. "But you didn't die right away. You lived until—"

"September. September nineteenth, to be exact." His

shoulders rose and fell. "So little time, and so much important work that needed to be accomplished. I could have done so much."

I scurried through the mental notes I'd made in case someone who visited the memorial actually wanted to talk about the president instead of Marjorie's murder. "But you did. There was civil service reform. And that investigation of the Post Office. And—"

"And all of it important, yes. But I had years stolen from me. Years, and achievements I can still, to this day, only dream of. All taken from me by a man who was brainsick. You see, by his own authority and with no knowledge or encouragement from any member of my staff, Guiteau gave a speech or two on my behalf during my presidential campaign. Once I was elected, he thought himself solely responsible for my success and insisted he should have a post in my administration as a show of my appreciation. Again and again, he wrote to me, and to members of my cabinet. He insisted I should send him to Vienna and name him consul general. Needless to say, I ignored his missives, as did the members of my staff, but that did not stop him. He kept up his incessant supplications. He wrote letters. He waited outside my office at the Executive Mansion. He finally gave up on Vienna and demanded that I name him ambassador and that he be posted to Paris. Imagine the audacity of the man!"

The president snorted his outrage. He turned and stomped to the table, his footsteps muffled by the thick Oriental carpet at our feet. His back was to me, so I couldn't see his expression, but I could hear the anger simmering in his voice. "You know, this Guiteau fellow once stole into a presidential reception and actually managed to insinuate himself close to the First Lady. My poor Lucretia! If I had sensed she might be in any danger, I would have pummeled this Guiteau fellow myself, right then and there." His face purple, he whirled around and slammed his fist into the palm of his other hand.

I think it was the first time he remembered that I was there watching. He blinked, and his eyes cleared. "You must pardon my anger," he said. "It is a fact that, in my younger days, I was a minister. Apparently I listened when I gave my flock advice, for aside from moments such as these when I allow my emotions to get the best of my nature, I have long ago forgiven Guiteau. He was unbalanced, after all. I do believe that these days, you would call him a stalker."

Stalker.

The word settled somewhere between my heart and my stomach and sent a cold wave through me that left me shaky. It was one of the times I was actually grateful to be a detective because, well . . . I wasn't very content with unanswered questions. As disturbing as it was to watch President Garfield suffer when he stepped outside the memorial, thinking about that strange incident sure beat thinking about the doughy-faced man who'd showed up at the office the day before.

"You haven't explained," I said, and because I knew he was going to pretend he didn't know what I was talking about, I stood my ground and refused to let him change the subject. "I want to know what happened outside the front door, and why."

"Ah, the why of it. That is what I have been trying to elucidate for you. You see, I did not have my chance to be president here on this earth—"

"So you're president here! Inside the memorial!" The bits and pieces of everything he'd said and everything I'd seen in the rotunda that wasn't the rotunda when he was with me suddenly made sense. So did the reason why, after all these years, his ghost was still hanging around. All of the ghosts I'd met since I'd discovered my Gift had unfin-

ished business, but not this one. The president's assassin
had been punished. Justice was done, and that should have
been the end of that. Yet he was still haunting the memorial. Note: I said *memorial*. In fact, I'd never seen him
anywhere else in the cemetery. In light of everything he
said, that made sense. "So what you're telling me is that
you're making up for lost time."

He nodded. "I was offered a trade, you see. My time on
the Other Side for time here. As president. I was denied so
many productive years by my untimely death. Now, as
long as I stay within the boundaries of my memorial, I
continue to exist in this form. If I leave—"

"You go up in a puff of smoke."

"Not exactly the way I would have worded it, but yes.
That is exactly what would happen should I leave the
confines of this tomb for too long. I would cease to exist,
in this world or in the next. I have no regrets about making the decision to stay on here. Here . . ." He spread his
arms, taking in the elegant room. "Here I am president.
I continue the work I started all those years ago. I make
decisions. I meet with my cabinet. There is a great deal
that needs to be done. So you can see why it is of the ut-
most importance for me to be left undisturbed. With all
the ruckus of late—"

"Well, I'm guessing we're still going to have the commemoration, with Marjorie or without her. So there's no
way you're going to get away from that. And no way to
avoid the tourists who keep showing up to check out the
spot where she bit the big one, either. That will die down,
I'm sure. And the commemoration won't last forever.
You'll get your peace and quiet eventually."

"Yes, yes. Of course those things will come to an end,
and it is all for the better. But really, that is not at all what
I'm talking about. I'm talking about the comings and goings at all hours."

I must have looked as baffled as I felt because he shook his head, disgusted. "Really, I have been attempting to tell you about these disturbances since the day we met. I cannot believe you are not aware of—"

"What?" I closed in on the president. "You said *all hours*. Are you telling me—"

"That there are people coming and going when there shouldn't be. Yes, yes. Exactly. There are people in parts of the memorial where they have no business."

"Like?"

"The ballroom, certainly."

A memory sparked inside my brain and I hurried out of the rotunda and hung a right in the entryway. Good thing I was wearing my sneakers, I made it up to the roped-off doorway outside the stairway that led up to the ballroom in record time. President Garfield was already there waiting for me.

I poked a finger at the printed sign, the one that said CLOSED TO THE PUBLIC. That day, it was exactly where it was supposed to be, and right side up, too. "A couple times when I've been up here, this sign has been upside down. I thought maybe someone on the cleaning crew was just being careless. Or some visitor was being a smart-ass. But if you've seen people going into the ballroom . . ."

"It may be a signal of sorts," the president said. His brain and mine were working on the same track, which was kind of scary, but helpful, too, since we didn't have to fill each other in about what we were thinking. "Perhaps the inverted sign tells these intruders when they should go in. Or that they should stay away."

I looked beyond the rope to the closed ballroom door. "But why?"

I don't think he had the answer, so it was just as well that Jeremiah Stone popped up out of nowhere. He cleared his throat. "Mr. President, there is work to be done," he said. He pointed to the ever-present bundle of papers he carried in one hand and backed away. "And papers to be signed, sir. It is really quite important."

"Yes, of course."

When the president moved to follow him, I stopped him. "Wait! What about the ballroom? What about the people who are hanging around who shouldn't be hanging around? What's going on?"

I swear, there was actually a twinkle in the president's eyes when he answered. "Remember, young lady," he said right before he vanished. "Things don't turn up in this world until somebody turns them up. You're the detective!"

It wasn't very encouraging. Especially since now, I was more confused than ever about what the hell was going on. Before I had a chance to think about it, though, a couple things happened. The front door opened and three middle-aged women walked in and started oohing and aahing. I didn't know if they were gushing over the monument or the murder scene, but either way, I had to get down there and play hostess. Just as I got to the stairway, my cell rang and I fished it out of my pocket, saw it was the guy who'd gone to take care of my flat tires, and figured I'd better talk to him before he did something that was too expensive for a cemetery tour guide's wallet.

"Hey, did you take a close look at those tires of yours?" he asked. Obviously, though he'd done some repairs and maintenance on the Mustang, he didn't know me well. Tires are just about the last thing I'd waste brain cells thinking about. "Those tires of yours weren't just flat, Miss Martin. They were slashed."

I was on the winding staircase and I paused, one hand on the railing and one foot dangling above the next step. "Slashed? What on earth are you talking about? Why would anybody—?"

"Don't ask me, honey. All I can say is that it was no

accident. Either some punk was out getting his kicks with a little vandalizing, or . . ."

It wasn't what he said, it was the way he said it. That one little *or* and suddenly I felt like I'd gone one-on-one with one of my ghostly contacts. My stomach turned to a block of ice. Goose bumps shot up my arms.

"Or?" I asked.

He clicked his tongue. "Well, if that's the case, then I'll tell you what, sweetie. There's somebody out there somewhere who doesn't like you a whole, big bunch."

11

Every time I heard the front door of the memorial open, I thought about Ball Cap Guy, and every time I thought about Ball Cap Guy, my heartbeat sped up at an impossible rate and my imagination raced right along with it.

There's somebody out there somewhere who doesn't like you a whole, big bunch.

The words of the auto mechanic swirled inside my brain and left me lightheaded. Oh yeah, there's nothing like thinking about a stalker with a knife sharp enough to slash tires to make a girl jumpy.

Preoccupied, I twitched my way through the early morning, and a dozen or so visitors. Joy of joys, Ball Cap Guy never showed his doughy face. It wasn't much consolation. Not with the words *not yet* echoing in my head.

The good news in all this was that apparently it was a slow day around Garden View. Doris showed up at the administration building to do whatever it is volunteers do, and since Ella couldn't find anything to keep her busy, she sent the little old lady over to the memorial. Not that I thought Doris would be much help in a fight, but I had to admit, it was nice to have someone else around. At least if my stalker showed, I had some backup.

With no emergencies in sight, Doris was busy with a group of four ladies who were asking more questions about Marjorie than they were about the president. After watching her kick dirt on Marjorie's grave, I was itching to know how much—exactly—Doris knew about Marjorie (and more important, Marjorie's murder), but unfortunately, I was stuck dealing with a visitor who was actually there to tour the memorial. He was a half a foot shorter than me, a pudgy guy wearing a suit that was too dark and too wooly for a sticky summer day. He had an impenetrable Eastern European accent and a scraggly beard that was the same salt-and-pepper color as his hair. No matter how hard I tried to avoid him, he dogged my steps, and once he had me cornered, there was no getting away from him. Even when I finally gave up being polite and just blatantly tried to eavesdrop on what Doris was saying, he kept pestering me with questions.

"This president of yours, this James Abram Garfield . . ." He carefully read the name from the brochure he'd picked up outside the office. "He must have been your bestest of presidents, to have a place in which he is buried such as this. I am thinking he must have done many big great things, yes?"

I half expected the president to show up and start listing them, and when he didn't, I was on my own. "There was something about the Post Office," I mumbled. "And the Civil War and—"

"Murder."

I heard Doris say the word, and in hopes of catching more, I quickly stepped closer to where she and the four other women were standing.

The little man had other things on his mind. "These mosaic tile pictures, they are very marvelous." He looked up to the dome high above our heads and the head of the statue of the president. Since Doris and the ladies she was talking to turned around and headed in the other direction and the only way I was going to hear any more from her was to take off after them, I gave up with a sigh and I looked up, too. The last time I'd been in the rotunda, it was so full of that swirling, sparkly fog, I couldn't even see the dome.

The entire inside of the dome is decorated with a background of gleaming gold mosaic where mosaic angels with wicked big wings and wearing flowing white robes mark the directions: north, south, east, and west. Between each angel are more mosaic pictures, swirling scrolls that burst into blooms of pink stylized flowers. The whole shebang is bordered at the bottom with red and white stripes and glistening golden wreaths. It's all pretty spectacular, and I would have allowed myself to be impressed if the wreaths didn't make me think of wheels, and wheels didn't make me think of tires, and tires didn't make me think of—

Never mind.

"I am inquiring is all what I am doing." I snapped out of my thoughts to find the little man with one finger pointed straight up. "How do you say this? I am asking yourself as the representative of the cemetery in which all this is possessed, if it is possible to get a more better look?"

Since I only speak English, it took me a bit to work this through. "Oh, you want to go up there? Upstairs?"

He nodded, and relieved to finally be getting rid of him, I showed him the way to the stairs.

Unfortunately by that time, Doris and the four visitors she was working with were up on the balcony, too. I went back into the rotunda, but from where I was standing, I couldn't catch a word of what she was telling them. I could, however, see them, and I watched Doris (all sweet-faced and as fluffy as one of those mosaic angels) gesture wildly toward the balcony railing.

The ladies looked appropriately horrified.

All three of them.

I'd been a little busy wondering when and if Ball Cap Guy was going to jump out from some shadowy corner and attack me, but believe me, even that wasn't enough to make me forget what I'd learned from the president earlier that morning. He said there was commotion in the memorial. At all hours. He said he'd seen people near the ballroom door, people who weren't employees or volunteers. And I remembered that CLOSED TO THE PUBLIC sign that seemed to have a way of getting turned upside down when no one was looking and how the president had suggested that it might be some sort of signal to the intruders who were disturbing his peace.

Intruders like the woman who was suddenly and suspiciously missing from Doris's group?

I backed up a step, the better to take a closer look at the balcony above my head. The little man with the beard was up there snapping pictures with a digital camera. And Doris was still talking away to the three women who were hanging on her every word. But there was no sign of their friend.

Curious, yes? And being curious, too, I scampered up the corkscrew stairway to the floor above the memorial hall. The balcony up there loops around the rotunda, and from where I was standing, I couldn't see any sign of the bearded man, or Doris and her tour group. I scooted around to the blocked stairway that led into the ballroom. That CLOSED TO THE PUBLIC sign was exactly where it should have been, and not upside down, and I was about to chalk up the whole silly thing about the sign as a signal to an imagination that was running way too wild when I thought I heard a noise from inside the ballroom.

"Hey!" I reached for the door. "If there's somebody in there, you're not supposed to be. The ballroom isn't open for tours, so why don't you just—"

"Aha! There you are."

At the same time I heard the voice behind me, someone touched my shoulder and I jumped about a mile. One hand pressed to my heart, I whirled around.

"Jack!" My blood kept right on rushing a mile a minute, and believe me, it had everything to do with being surprised and not with Jack's hotness (though in jeans and a faded blue T-shirt with a picture of Kurt Cobain on the front of it, he looked plenty hot). I thought about my own outfit and the absolute unhotness of khakis and a polo shirt, and the blood drained from my face. "It's not . . . it can't be . . ." I gulped down my mortification. "Lunchtime already?"

"Looks like you're busy today. I saw some people just leaving as I was coming in. I guess your morning must have flown by. That's why you didn't realize what time it was." He glanced around the balcony. "I heard voices up here, too. You're not giving someone a tour, are you? Am I interrupting?"

I thought about that sweet little kiwi-colored dress down in the carry bag in the office. And I thought about the noise I thought I'd just heard from inside the ballroom. I glanced at the door at the top of the stairway, beyond that CLOSED TO THE PUBLIC sign. As always, it was shut, and I could tell it was locked. When it wasn't (which wasn't very often, only when a cleaning crew went in or the maintenance guys had to visit), it had a way of sagging so that a strip of light showed all along the side of the door.

"Interrupting? No." I looked back at Jack. "It's just that—"

"I brought sandwiches." He held up a paper takeaway bag and I recognized the name of the place printed on the side of it. It was from Presti's, one of the restaurants in the Little Italy neighborhood where I lived, just down the hill from the cemetery. Good food, great prices. Leave it to a history teacher to find quality and thriftiness in a strange town.

"Hungry?" Jack asked.

I was. But there were more important matters than my hunger pangs. I made a face. "I wanted to change before you got here. I have this really cute summer dress, and—"

"You look fine." He gave me a careful once-over that made my heart start thumping madly again. "Better than fine. You look—"

"What was that?" Another noise made me spin around. "Did you hear something?" I glanced at him over my shoulder. "From up there?"

He shook his head. "Can't say I did."

I knew he was probably right. The door was locked, after all; there could be no one inside the ballroom. Not someone alive, anyway. I didn't have a key, and it was just as well. If I went in there to check things out, Jack would follow me, and if my imagination was playing tricks on me and there was nothing and no one there, I'd just end up looking jumpy and paranoid. On the other hand, if there was a ghost prowling around, he wouldn't see it and I would, and I'd just end up looking jumpy and paranoid. Believe me when I say I did not want to look jumpy and paranoid in front of Jack.

I made a move for the door, anyway. At least I could jiggle the handle and satisfy myself that all was well and the door was locked tight.

I probably would have gotten there if Jack hadn't grabbed me, whirled me around, and kissed me.

Just like that.

He was holding the paper bag in one hand, and he still managed to pull me close. The bag scrunched between his body and mine, and the unmistakable smell of pizza sauce filled the air. His other hand was free, and he slipped it from my wrist to where the short sleeve of my polo shirt ringed my arm. His fingers were cool against my skin. His mouth was hot. He slanted it over mine, and even if I cared that one of our visitors might see us . . . well, let's face it, at that moment, I didn't care. Not one little bit.

"Sorry!" It's not the kind of thing I like to hear after a heart-stopping kiss, but when he pulled away, Jack softened the blow with a smile that melted my anxiety. "That was way too forward of me," he said. His voice bumped over his rough breaths. "I just couldn't help myself. You're so beautiful. I shouldn't have done that. I hardly know you and you work here and—"

"Yeah." I struggled to catch my breath, too. "My boss wouldn't be happy if somebody reported that they'd seen you and me here and—"

"Which means I won't let it happen again." He stepped back. Just as quickly, he moved forward again, dropped the takeaway bag, and scooped me into his arms. "Well," he said. "Maybe one more time."

There was nothing impetuous about this second kiss. It was slow and leisurely, and I tilted my head back, enjoying every scrumptious moment of it.

"No more kissing you while you're at work," Jack said when it was over, then proved himself a liar by giving me another quick peck. "You ready for lunch?"

I was ready for a lot of things. Lunch wasn't necessarily one of them. And this definitely wasn't the time or the place to think about it. I smoothed my hands over my hair. "You go on down," I told Jack. "I'll be right behind you."

With another sleek smile, he headed over to the stairway.

I took a careful step to make sure I could move, even though my knees were mush. When I was sure I could, I wiped the dreamy little smile off my face (just in case I met Doris or a visitor on my way down) and followed him. It was a good thing I looked back right before I got to the stairway. Otherwise, I never would have noticed that CLOSED TO THE PUBLIC sign.

It was upside down again.

OK, so Jack was delectable.
    Jack was charming.
Jack was one hell of a good kisser.

None of that was enough to turn me from a capable, self-confident, independent woman into a complete moron.

Was it?

I liked to think not, and I proved it to myself by smiling and chatting my way through lunch out at one of the picnic tables near the memorial like nothing was wrong. And when Jack left? Well, of course I told him I'd talk to him soon. I even agreed to meet him for drinks later in the week. That would certainly not be a sacrifice.

No, no . . . not because Jack was hot. Because now I knew he wasn't on the up-and-up.

See, I realized something the moment I saw that upside-down sign outside the ballroom door: luscious or not, that kiss was nothing more than a diversionary tactic. Any idiot could see that. While I'd been busy getting all melty and enjoying the sensations that popped through me like Fourth of July fireworks, Jack had turned over that sign.

Question number one, of course, was, why?

Question number two (not as important but way more aggravating) was, did he really think I wouldn't notice?

Unfortunately, I knew the answer to that one. Jack was a guy. He assumed women were dumb, and that I would be left so starry-eyed from getting kissed, I wouldn't pay attention to anything else.

How wrong he was!

Unfortunately, though I was itching to have at it, I got a little sidetracked in my quest for the truth. No sooner had Jack gone than a bus full of visitors showed up from the Rocky River Senior Center, and after that, the day was not my own. The old folks kept me running, and by the time four o'clock rolled around, all I wanted to do was go home and take a nap.

Unfortunately, a private detective's life is never that easy.

In an effort to satisfy my curiosity, I locked the front door of the memorial and headed up the winding staircase to the ballroom. I tugged on the door.

Yep, it was locked.

So it was my imagination that made me hear what I thought were noises coming from inside. But not my imagination about the CLOSED TO THE PUBLIC sign.

Thinking, I batted the little sign back and forth and watched it swing from the red velvet rope where it was hanging.

"Jackson McArthur, history teacher from Lafayette High School, Hammond, Indiana." I mumbled the words to myself, my mind racing and every one of my thoughts leading to the same place.

Within a couple minutes, I was at my desk in the administration building, asking myself the same question I'd asked myself back at the memorial. Namely, just how dumb do guys think women are?

Because for one thing, there was no Jackson McArthur in the Hammond, Indiana, phone book and I know, I know . . . he could have had an unlisted number, and for all I knew, a guy as gorgeous as Jack needed one or he'd have every woman in town panting at his front door.

For this, I was willing to cut him some slack.

But I wasn't done with my computer search, and what I found should come as no surprise.

See, that's the beauty of the Internet. It took me less than a couple minutes to find out there is no Lafayette High School in Hammond, Indiana.

I could have obsessed about the whole Jack thing.

I did obsess. At least for a while. Obsessing about who Jack really was and what he really wanted was a far better way to keep my mind occupied than thinking about Ball Cap Guy and looking out my apartment window every ten minutes while I muttered fervent prayers that I would not then (or ever) see him outside looking back at me.

But really, though I am very good at it, even I can obsess only so long. By the next morning, I'd convinced myself that worrying about the doughy, stuttering man who'd come to see me at the memorial would get me nowhere. I would be careful at work. I would be smart when I went out and pay attention to who was around. Thus assured that I would also be safe, I concentrated on the mess that was the rest of my life.

Every time I tried to sort out the facts, I came back around to the same three things:

President Garfield said there was commotion in the memorial.

Jack turned over the sign.

Marjorie was dead.

And detective that I am, I had to ask myself if those three things were related.

It was kind of hard to get my brain around the whole

thing, especially since I didn't have much help. The president was good about complaining, but he couldn't offer me any information as far as who was hanging around the memorial or what they were doing there. And certainly, Jack wasn't going to tell me what he was up to.

That left Marjorie.

The thought actually crossed my mind to try and communicate with her spirit. Truth be told, in the course of investigating other cases, I had tried this with a couple other victims, and never with any success. Which wasn't what kept me from trying again. I am, after all, a redhead, which means I don't give up easily.

But there was the little matter of Marjorie's not-so-likable personality. She was a total and complete pain, and I wasn't going to take any chances. I mean, just imagine what might happen if I was able to bring her back and then she wouldn't leave! Spending the rest of my life listening to her nattering on about how she was related to James A. Garfield was not something I wanted to even think about.

With the possibility of talking to Marjorie off the table, I knew I had only one choice: I had to think like her. Scary, yes? But once I convinced myself that there would be no filmy head scarves involved, my nausea disappeared and I carried on with my plan. The next morning, I called Ella and played up the fact that I had to pick up my car from the mechanic and how I'd be in to work only it wouldn't be until a little later. No worries, she told me, she would simply send Doris over to the memorial.

Thus relieved of my duties (at least for a couple hours), I picked up the Mustang and headed thirty minutes east of town to Mentor, Ohio, where President Garfield lived with his family. The place is called Lawnfield and it's now a National Historic Site. That means I had to pay five bucks to get in.

Was it money well spent?

For the first thirty minutes I toured the rambling Victorian house along with a couple of senior citizens, a homeschooling mom with two very uninterested preteens, and a pretentious guide named Tammi, I figured I'd been had. Sure, there was plenty of history all around me. And yeah, I suppose there are folks who would swoon over the Victorian kitschiness of it all. Or the historical significance. Or whatever. But even though I tried to put myself in Marjorie's place as I looked over the ornate parlor with a fireplace nearly as big as me, the family photos on the walls, and the library where a marble bust of the man I talked to back at the cemetery looked back at me, I was pretty much convinced I was spinning my wheels.

Until we stepped out into a hallway near where we'd walked in.

That's when I noticed a blank spot where a square of paint was a slightly different color than the wall around it. Like something had recently been taken down from the wall and not replaced.

The rest of our tour group had wandered off to look at the exhibits in the Visitors' Center in the old carriage house. That left me with Tammi, and thinking like Marjorie would have if only she were there, I said, "It seems funny you would change the exhibits here. I mean, if it's supposed to be a historic place and look like it did when the Garfields still lived here."

Tammi took her job very seriously, poor thing. Apparently anything that even smacked of criticism was a slap in the face. Inside her Park Service uniform, her shoulders shot back. "We strive for accuracy in our depiction of the history of this house," she said. "The pictures displayed on the walls are mostly the same ones that were here when the Garfields were in residence."

"Mostly. Except for this one that got taken down."

She was wearing orange lipstick and her mouth pinched. She looked around like she wanted to make sure one of her supervisors wasn't within earshot. "We had a problem," she said, leaning closer to me. "A couple months ago. It's never happened before, and it hasn't happened since. I mean, we are the Government, after all." The way she said it, I was sure that word, *Government,* was capitalized. "But every once in a while, someone slips up. I didn't work here then."

"What you're telling me is someone stole something. Right off the wall of the home of a president."

The pinch got tighter. "Fortunately, it was nothing the Garfield family themselves ever owned, certainly nothing that had any direct connection with the president himself."

"But somebody took it, anyway."

"It was donated."

"And then you hung it up, and then somebody swiped it."

She didn't say *yes* or *no.* But then, she didn't have to. Because what she said next was, "It was authentic enough, but there were people here who didn't think it belonged, that since it wasn't original to the house, it shouldn't have been here in the first place."

"So you think someone who works here took it down? Just to get rid of it?"

"I never said that." The look in her eyes was one of pure horror. "What I said was there are those of us who don't miss it. Not that we didn't report it as stolen. We did. Well, they did. Like I said, I didn't work here then."

"So it obviously wasn't your fault."

She liked my take on things. If we weren't standing in a site of National Historical Significance, I think she actually might have smiled. Instead, she nodded. "The tour guide got distracted. She left a visitor alone. When she came back, it was gone."

"And it was . . . ?" It was my turn to lean forward, urging Tammi to spill the beans.

She took another careful look around. "A framed floor tile," she said. "From—"

"The waiting room of the Baltimore and Potomac Railway Station, where the president was shot."

Tammi blinked at me in wonder. "How did you know?"

I didn't explain. I mean, how could I? I knew because I was thinking like Marjorie, and thinking like Marjorie made me think I would do whatever it took to get my hands on every bit of James A. Garfield memorabilia out there, even if it meant resorting to larceny.

Was it worth the five bucks I'd paid to get into the president's house?

Well, for five bucks, I'd learned something I didn't know before. Namely, that Marjorie had a dishonest streak. It didn't help me figure out who'd killed her, but it told me more about the woman than I knew before.

Cha-ching!

12

Sure, I've been known to fudge the truth a little once in a while. Usually in the name of solving a case. Or when doing so is vital to something important like my weight or my dress size. That doesn't change the fact that I am now and always have been a basically honest person.

I didn't say a word to Tammi the tour guide, but the idea that Marjorie had a purloined piece of property—stolen from a president's home no less—just didn't sit right with me. Even before I left Lawnfield, I knew what I was going to do. I didn't stop home, but I did make a quick detour to the library, long enough to use the Internet to find Nick Klinker's home address.

Nick, it seemed, had better taste than his aunt. At least when it came to neighborhoods and houses. Within an hour, I found myself clear on the other side of town in the chichi suburb of Bay Village. Big houses. Towering oaks. Views of the lake for the lucky few who were smart enough to scoop up waterfront property.

Nick Klinker was one of them.

I parked the Mustang on the circular drive that led up to a house with more windows than walls, and a sweeping backyard where I could see a garden with a fountain and one of those gazebos. Vine covered, of course. The house was situated high on a bluff overlooking Lake Erie, and though real estate is not my thing, I had been trained right early on; I knew—and appreciated—pricey when I saw it.

Recession? What recession? Obviously, things were just peachy in the software engineering world.

By the time I rang the bell, I had already practiced what I was going to say when Nick answered the door. There was no use beating around the bush, and no way to sugarcoat the truth: his late aunt wasn't just the most annoying individual I'd ever met; she was a crook, too.

Only I was going to put it in words nicer than that.

I would have, too, if Nick answered the door. Instead, when it swung open, Bernadine, Nick's fiancée, was looking back at me. At least I thought it was Bernadine. She couldn't have looked more different than the stylishly turned-out woman I'd seen at the funeral. The impeccable outfit was gone, replaced with a pair of ratty denim capris and a T-shirt that immortalized some 5K run everybody had already forgotten. The sleek hairstyle? There was no sign of that, either. Bernadine's blond tresses stuck up in weird spikes all over her head.

"Who are you? What do you want?" Bernadine's eyes were blazing. She looked me over, twisted a lock of hair around one finger, and pulled hard. "Do I know you?"

I did my best to smile. It would have been easier if she'd been wearing those sweet Dolce & Gabbana pointed-toe slingbacks. But she wasn't wearing any shoes at all, and half her toenails were polished garish pink. The others were done in a chocolately shade of maroon.

I looked back up to her face. "We didn't have a chance to talk on Monday, but I chatted with Nick. At Marjorie Klinker's—"

"Don't even mention that woman to me!" Bernadine threw her head back and groaned. When she turned around and padded down the hallway, she didn't close the door and she didn't tell me to get lost, so I followed her, closing the door behind me. By the time I found her in the cavernous house, she was in a kitchen with a floor-to-ceiling view of the lake. She had a bottle of Black Velvet in one hand.

She poured a healthy couple inches into a glass and downed them in one gulp. "Do you know something about what Nick's up to?" she asked me.

I was a tad confused so I didn't say anything. She was a tad busy pouring herself another drink so she didn't notice. As jittery as a double jolt of caffeine, she went over to the stainless steel, industrial-sized refrigerator and got a handful of ice cubes. She dumped them in with the whiskey and swirled the drink, studying me over the rim of the glass.

"Well, do you?" she asked. "Because I'll tell you something, I don't know what the hell's going on, and it's making me crazy, and I don't have time to mess with this kind of nonsense. My wedding is in exactly . . ." She glanced at a calendar almost as big as the refrigerator it was stuck to with magnets. The days of the month that had already passed were marked off with thick red X's, and the Saturday just one week away was circled. There was a big yellow star on the date.

"I'm getting married a week from this Saturday," Bernadine said. She took a couple quick sips of her drink. "And do you see my groom here helping me get ready?" She spread her arms and looked around the kitchen, demonstrating.

Point made. We were the only two people there.

"I've got wedding favors to make," she wailed. "Three hundred and forty-seven little porcelain picture frames, and every single one of them needs a photo of me and Nick put in it. But is Nick here to help?" Another swig, and she was rarin' to go. The panic in Bernadine's voice climbed right along with her anger.

"Was he here last night when the florist stopped by for one final chat? Did he show up this afternoon when I talked to the soloist about the songs for church?" She didn't wait for me to say anything, but then, she didn't need an answer and I wasn't about to interrupt. That old saying about hell hath no fury like a woman scorned? A woman scorned doesn't hold a candle to a bride whose wedding day is breathing down her neck.

"I know he's been distracted, what with Marjorie's death and everything," Bernadine said, doing her best to be understanding. "And I know he's nervous, too. His tummy's been acting up and he's not usually the high-strung type. That tells me he cares and knowing that . . ." She fueled her thoughts with another sip of whiskey and apparently her brief tiptoe into the land of the sensible was over. Her voice rose to a screech. "Has Nick done one damned thing to help me these past few days?" she asked no one in particular. "I'll tell you what, no, he hasn't! Does he think a bride can do all these things by herself? I mean, really. Is it fair to expect me to go to the tanning salon, try out nail lacquer colors, do a run-through on hair and makeup, and count out those little bags of pink and red M&Ms with *Bernie* on some and *Nick* on some and *Love Forever* on others? I ask you. Is it?"

I had once been engaged myself; I could empathize, if not with the Black Velvet, at least with the stress levels. Rather than get into it, I tried to keep her on task at the same time I struggled to make sense of everything she said. "Has Nick disappeared?" I asked. "Has something happened to him?"

"Happened?" Her laugh was maniacal. It echoed back at us from the high ceiling and bounced its way over the stainless steel stove, the matching dishwasher, and the glass-fronted wine chiller built in below the countertop. "Nick's lost his mind. That's what's happened to him. And it's all *her* fault."

Oh yeah, just the way she said that *her*, I knew exactly who she was talking about. "You mean Marjorie."

"Aunt Marjorie." Bernadine threw her hands in the air. She was still holding her glass of Black Velvet and it sloshed out and rained down on the white ceramic tile floor. She didn't bother to clean it up. "For years and years, Marjorie Klinker has ruined my life," she wailed. "Every holiday. Every birthday. Every vacation. Marjorie was always there with those little . . ." She wiggled her fingers over her head, and I got the message.

"Head scarves," I said.

"Those head scarves. Yeah. Those hideous head scarves! She was always there wearing those things and acting like God's gift to the whole wide world. And talking about family history." Her moan was worthy of a ghost in a horror movie. "Oh, how I hated listening to her talk about family history. I put up with it," she added, one hand out and her palm flat. "I tolerated her. I welcomed her into my home. I couldn't stand the woman, but I managed to swallow my pride and tell myself I was doing it for the sake of family."

"You didn't kill her, did you?"

Hey, I figured it was worth a try. Bernadine was so worked up, she just might be in the mood to confess.

No such luck. But then, I don't think she even heard me.

"And now . . ." She hiccuped. "Now, even after she's dead, Marjorie's ruining my wedding!"

There was a table nearby and I sat down. Just as I'd hoped, Bernadine did, too. It gave me the opportunity to look her right in the eye. The way I would if she was a dog and I was trying to get her attention.

"You're going to need to start from the beginning," I said. "Because I can't help you if I don't know exactly what's going on."

She tapped one bare foot against the floor. "It all started Monday. After the funeral."

I nodded, waiting for more.

She leaped out of her chair to refill her glass. "He never cared about any of it before," she said at the same time she took a long swallow. Her words were liquor-soaked. "Marjorie, she carried on about it all, constantly. Oh lord, how I was tired of hearing about it!"

I might be confused, but I was not insensible. I knew exactly what she was talking about. "James A. Garfield."

"You got that right." She returned to the table, slammed down her glass, and plopped back into the chair. "You knew her, right? You must have if you were at the funeral. It was the only thing she ever talked about, the only thing she ever cared about. Garfield this, and Garfield that, and how she was related and wasn't that just so special." Bernadine's top lip curled. "I was sick to death of hearing about it. If I wasn't so crazy about Nick . . ."

I was grateful she'd brought up his name. I needed to get her back on track. "So after the funeral on Monday, what happened to Nick?"

"I've known Nick for four years, and all that time, he pooh-poohed Marjorie like everyone else. He was only nice to her because she was his father's only sister, and the only living relative he had left. All those claims about how she was related to the president? Nick was sure they were nothing but a lot of bull. He never cared a thing about any of it. Not the books or the pictures or all that presidential crap she has all over her house."

"And then . . . ?"

"Then it was like someone flicked a light switch. You know what I mean? After the funeral, we went back to Marjorie's, and it was like watching someone take over his body. Like he got possessed with Marjorie's spirit or something."

Not a pretty thought. I shivered.

Bernadine tugged on her bangs. "All of a sudden, he's obsessed with President Garfield, too. He reads about him in books. He checks out websites on the Internet. He goes over to Marjorie's and he stays there for hours and hours and he doesn't come home. And he's not helping me with the wedding." She slapped one hand against the table. "The wedding is next Saturday. *Next* Saturday! And instead of worrying about the biggest day of my life, all he does is talk about all that junk of Marjorie's. He's going to bring it home. Here!" She tapped her fingernails against the table. She crossed her legs and uncrossed them again. She plucked at her hair.

"I can't believe it's happening. Not now. Not when the wedding's just one week away. But I'll tell you one thing . . ." Bernadine slugged down the rest of the Black Velvet and slammed the empty glass on the table. "It's going to stop. Or there's not going to be a wedding." Her outrage lasted only so long. The next second, her big blue eyes filled with tears and her bottom lip trembled. "Oh, my wedding! I don't want to cancel my wedding. It's the most perfect wedding in the world . . . and . . . and I want to marry Nick. I just don't understand what's hap-pened to him."

That made two of us.

Because if everything Bernadine said was true, Nick was suddenly as obsessed with James A. Garfield as Marjorie ever was. And the one and only time I talked to him . . .

Well, I knew I wasn't remembering it wrong.

The time I talked to Nick Klinker, he made it abundantly clear that he thought Marjorie's Garfield collection was nothing but a bunch of junk.

I was back in the car and driving to Marjorie's neighborhood in no time flat. The reason, of course, was self-evident: I needed to talk to Nick Klinker.

About his sudden and irrational interest in James A. Garfield.

About his aunt.

About his aunt's murder.

A full plate for a Wednesday afternoon, and there was still the little matter of how I was supposed to be at work that day. Not to worry, I called Ella and talked my way out of it with a story about my poor car and how there was more wrong than just the tires. I was stuck at the mechanic's, see, and with no way to easily get back to Garden View.

Ella bought it, hook, line, and sinker. Which she might not have if she'd been paying attention and had heard the traffic noise in the background.

That taken care of, I parked in front of Marjorie's nondescript house, hurried up the steps, and rang the bell.

No answer.

If what Bernadine told me was true, Nick had to be there. He was spending all his time there. He was suddenly a buff, a devotee, a Garfield maniac.

And I wanted to know why.

I tried the bell again, and when there was still no an-swer, I went over to the picture window that looked out over the front porch and pressed my nose to the glass.

There's something about obsession that sticks in the mind, and Marjorie's fixation was pretty far out there. Try as I might to forget it, the weirdness of everything I'd seen on my last visit was imprinted on my brain. I remembered exactly how the living room was arranged. That's why I knew things had been moved.

Moved being an understatement.

All the pictures had been taken down from the walls. (And just a reminder, all the pictures were of Gar-field.) They were stacked on the red, white, and blue plaid couch.

All the books were piled on chairs.

All the knickknacks were heaped near the fireplace, including the oil lamp I'd nearly toppled over while Marjorie and Ray were arguing in the den and the vase filled with those old-fashioned hat pins that I had knocked over.

It was obvious Nick had been through everything with a fine-tooth comb, sorting and inventorying and stashing away. It was not so obvious why.

Thinking about it, I turned—and nearly jumped out of my skin when I realized Marjorie's neighbor, Gloria Hen-ninger, was right behind me. So was Sunshine.

She (that's Gloria, not Sunshine) didn't bother to apol-ogize for nearly giving me a heart attack. "Oh, it's you," she said, the words leaving her mouth along with a stream of smoke from her cigarette. She had the dog in her arms and she gave it a little squeeze. "Sunshine told me some-body was sneaking around over here. Figured I'd better come have a look. It's what neighbors do for each other, you know." She dropped the stub of her cigarette on the porch and ground it with her sneakers. They were yellow and they matched the T-shirt she was wearing, the one that said, I KISS MY DOG ON THE LIPS. Her shirt, in turn, matched Sunshine's, except that the dog's said, I KISS MY OWNER ON THE MOUTH.

Since I didn't want to think about either of these possibilities, I was glad when she said, "At least that's how neighbors should treat each other. Not that the Klinker woman ever did. Didn't care about anybody. Anybody but herself."

I could have said something about how it wasn't exactly appropriate to criticize seeing as how Marjorie had just recently been murdered, but let's face it, I couldn't think of anything nice to say about her, either. And anyway, Gloria beat me to it. "Don't even give me that hogwash about speaking kindly of the dead," she growled. So did Sunshine. "I had nothing good to say about her when she was alive, and I'm not going to be a hypocrite now that she's gone. The woman was the curse of the neighborhood."

I remembered the glimpse I'd had of Marjorie's backyard. "Maybe now her nephew will get rid of the statue of President Garfield."

My suggestion wasn't met with as much enthusiasm as I'd expected. Gloria scraped a finger back and forth across the top of Sunshine's head. "Well, that's what I was thinking, too. And I got all excited about it. You know, when Nick started to move it. But it didn't last."

There didn't seem to be much point in asking her to explain, so I walked to the railing on the far side of the porch and leaned over. The statue of President Garfield was still there, but just like Gloria said, and like everything else I'd seen in the house, it, too, had been moved.

Instead of standing directly in the path of the beam of that spotlight, the president was now six feet over to the left. The pots of flowers from around the statue had been shifted in front of the garage, and the bushes that ringed the statue? They'd been dug up. They sat on the driveway, their roots withering in the sun.

"See what I mean?" Gloria poked me with one bony elbow. "Saw that Nick Klinker messing with the statue, and I thought, Glory be! He's going to get rid of it. No such luck. Now that he's messed with it, it just looks worse than ever. I've called the city. Told them I pay my taxes and I have the right to a neighborhood free of eye-sores. Nobody's listening. Nobody cares."

I did. But not for the reasons she thought.

I decided it was best not to mention this so instead I asked, "What's Nick up to?"

"Hell if I know." Gloria made a face. "All I can tell you is that he's been here all hours, and had people in and out, in and out. It's upsetting to Sunshine. She keeps a regular schedule. She doesn't appreciate the interruptions."

"People in and out. Like who? What people?"

"Well, I don't know all of them." Obviously, I should have realized this. At least that's what the look Gloria gave me said. "But I did recognize that one fellow. You know . . ." Trying to think, she snapped her fingers. "You know, the big guy. Bushy head of silver hair. He's on that show on PBS where they look at the antiques people bring in. Not the famous show that goes all over the country. The other one. The one they film right here in Cleveland."

"*Antique Appraisals*?" Don't get the wrong idea. I am not and never have been a faithful viewer. The show was on right before *Cemetery Survivor* so I'd seen a couple minutes at the end of a couple episodes right after I turned the TV on and right before I turned it right off because I couldn't stand to watch myself in the corny cemetery restoration show. "I know who you're talking about. Ted Something."

"Ted Studebaker. That's him." Gloria's face lit like a Christmas tree. "I know I'm right. It was him. I know it for a fact. And it's not just because I'm a sort of magnet for superstars. Met Jimmy Durante once. Live and in person. And Telly Savalas." She looked at me expectantly.

I stared at her blankly.

Maybe she was more perceptive than I'd given her credit for. Rather than belabor the point, she started down the steps. "Come on, honey," she said. "And I'll prove it to you."

I followed her next door to a house much like Marjorie's except for the lack of Garfield memorabilia and the addition of a gag-in-the-mouth doggy smell that mingled with the unrelenting stench of cigarettes.

Once inside, I stayed as close to the front door as politely possible, in hopes of catching the occasional whiff of fresh air. Sunshine still in her arms, Gloria rattled around in the kitchen.

"I know I've got it here somewhere." Her voice floated to me from the back of the house. "I'll find it. You'll see. You'll see that I met him."

Since I wasn't sure if she was talking about Ted the antiques appraiser or about those guys I didn't know, the ones named Jimmy and Telly (wasn't he a character from *Sesame Street*?), I waited. Left to my own devices, I had a chance to take a quick look around.

Gloria's furniture was cheap and not worth mentioning. The wall-to-wall carpet had seen better days. She had a big-screen TV next to an aquarium where a dead fish floated on top of the water. There were a couple magazines on her coffee table, and a couple pieces of mail. Curious, I took a deep breath, held it, and hurried over there. I shuffled through the mail, checking it out.

An electric bill. An ad from a local dentist. What looked like a birthday card.

Nothing interesting, and certainly nothing that would help with my case.

"Ah, here it is!" I heard Gloria say, and I dropped the mail back on the table before she got back to the room. It slid under a three-month-old *Ladies Home Journal*, and I quickly moved to put it back in place. When I did, something else slid out from under the magazine, too.

For a second, I simply stared. But I knew another second would be too long. I scooped up the paper, folded it, and stuffed it into the pocket of my khakis.

Just in time, too.

"Here it is." Gloria shuffled back into the room holding a business card. She handed it over. Sunshine grumbled when I got too close.

Gloria pointed at the name printed on the card in raised lettering. "See? See, right there. It was Ted Studebaker himself, all right. Just like I said. I saw a car pull up. Something slick and shiny. I knew it wasn't anybody who'd been here before so I went over to see what was going on. You know, the way a good neighbor would. Nick was just coming out of the house and he introduced me. That's when Ted Studebaker gave me that card."

I gave the card a careful look. It was printed on quality paper and embossed with an eagle in the background. Ted Studebaker Antiques, it said, was located in Chagrin Falls, a charming and highfalutin suburb to the east, and it said that Ted was a specialist in presidential "autographs, memorabilia, and ephemera."

"So Nick was talking to a presidential collector." I said this to no one in particular, but of course, Gloria assumed I was talking to her.

"That's right." She grabbed a plastic cigarette lighter from a nearby table and fired up another smoke. "I heard them. You know, when I was on my way over there. Nick

was telling Ted Studebaker to come on inside, telling him
he had lots to show him. Ted, he wasn't even through the
front door and Nick was asking about what stuff was
worth and if anybody would want it."

"Did Studebaker say anybody would?"

"Well, it never got that far. Not as far as I heard, anyway. Because that's when me and Sunshine, we showed
up to see who the stranger was and we introduced ourselves. Didn't we, Sunshine?" She kissed the dog on the
top of the head.

At least it wasn't on the lips. I took comfort in the
thought.

"I can tell you that Studebaker, just looking inside
the Klinker place from the front porch, he was practically foaming at the mouth. That's how excited he was
to get in there and start rooting through things. When
we were leaving, they went into the house, and I heard
Nick say something about how he wanted to sell it. All
of it."

I thought about the neat piles of Garfield kitsch in Marjorie's house. It made sense that Nick would have been
through it. Especially if he wanted to sell it all.

Well, maybe *all* wasn't exactly the right word. There
was still the matter of the floor tile Marjorie had stolen off
the wall at Lawnfield. And the box full of Marjorie's stuff
in the trunk of my car.

Those were problems for another day. So was Ted
Studebaker. For now, I had more important things to think
about, so I thanked Gloria for her help, got in my car, and
did that thinking.

Remember, at our first meeting, Gloria was the one
who told me she wanted Marjorie Klinker dead.

She was also the one who swore up and down that she
didn't really know what the statue of President Garfield at

the cemetery looked like, because she'd never been to
Garden View.

At the next red light, I reached in my pocket and pulled
out what I'd swiped from Gloria's coffee table.

It was a brochure from the Garfield Memorial. Yep, the
same brochure we hand out to visitors.

13

Every time I picked up the newspaper, I expected to see some screaming headline about how the cops (read that, *Quinn*) had made major strides in solving Marjorie's murder. Every time I turned on my TV, I held my breath, hoping against hope that I might not see You-Know-Who's gorgeous face looking back at me. I knew him well, see, and I knew that when the big moment came, when the lights were on and the cameras were rolling, he'd be his usual chilly as a frozen cucumber self in front of the crowd. Oh yeah, he'd be all about business. His jaw would be tight. His shoulders would be rock steady inside a suit no cop should be able to afford. His voice would be impassive as he told the world he had a suspect in custody.

His eyes, though . . . his eyes would spark with a message meant just for me: *Take that, Pepper. I solved it before you did!*

The fact that he didn't even know I was investigating

said something about how paranoid I was about the whole thing. And how determined.

Was it any wonder I was itching to get back to my investigation?

Too bad working at Garden View tends to get in the way of my real life. Perfect example: the next day. After missing work on Wednesday in the name of paying a visit to Nick's home, then darting off to Marjorie's, I couldn't very well call off again. So there I was, all day Thursday, stuck in the memorial. And all day, there were people in and out.

None of them was Jack. This was unfortunate, because it meant I didn't have a chance to satisfy my curiosity about either what he was up to or if he was really as good a kisser as I remembered. And no, the sign outside the stairway that led up to the ballroom wasn't moved again. I knew that for certain because I dragged myself up and down those darned winding steps five times that day, just to check.

So that part of my investigation was at a dead end.

There was no sign of the president, either, so even though I doubted he'd been paying enough attention to remember one tourist, I couldn't question him about Gloria Henninger's visit to the memorial. I wondered if she was part of the comings and goings he complained about. I wondered why Gloria lied about never being in the cemetery. I wondered what business she could have had there, and of course, considering how much she liked "that Klinker woman," I wondered if she'd murdered Marjorie.

I had no answers and no way to find them considering I was stuck inside catering to tourists like . . . well, like I was the cemetery's official tour guide.

And again, my investigation was up against a brick wall.

With nothing left to do, I actually worked like a dog

that day. I showed visitors around, and talked about presidential history and mosaics and marble and all that other
stuff, and even though I mostly didn't know what I was
talking about and made up half of what I told them, they
all seemed pretty pleased and left there thinking they
knew more than they did when they walked in. Even at
four o'clock when it was time to lock up, I still wasn't
done. At Ella's request, I headed to the administration
building to proofread the latest edition of her Garden View
newsletter. After bailing out on her the day before, I figured it was the least I could do. It was six o'clock by the
time I left the cemetery, and even then, I didn't head home.
I know, I know . . . a private detective's work is never
done. I had no choice. I went right back to Marjorie
Klinker's.

I still had all her junk in the trunk of my car, remember,
and a boatload of questions to ask Nick.

I parked in what was becoming my usual spot and hurried up the front porch stairs. At that time of the year, it
was still light in the evening, and I guess it was a good
thing it was. Otherwise, I wouldn't have screeched to a
stop when I noticed the gouges all along the front door
jamb. I bent closer for a better look. Sure enough, the lock
had been forced.

My first reaction was surprise. But I am ever practical.
Especially when it comes to danger. My second thought
was that I needed reinforcements. Obviously, when anything happened in the neighborhood, Gloria and Sunshine were the first to know, and I had already made a
move toward their house when I saw that there was no car
in Gloria's driveway, no lights on in the house, and no
signs of movement from inside. Didn't it figure, the one
time I needed the neighborhood busybody, she was out for
the day.

Left to my own devices, I put a finger to the door and

pushed. It had been closed, but not all the way, and it swung open. I'd seen my share of cheesy horror movies in my day; I knew better than to go inside alone. But honestly, I couldn't help myself. I took one look and caught my breath. I just had to step inside for a better look.

Close up, what I saw was even more astounding. The neat piles of Garfield pictures had been swept off the couch and were scattered all over the floor. The books were unstacked from the chairs and tossed all around. The pile of knickknacks near the fireplace looked like it had been hit full force by a tornado. Stuff was everywhere, knocked over, messed up, gone through.

Gone through. Yeah, that's what I said. Like somebody was looking for something.

I couldn't imagine what, so I guess it was a good thing I didn't have a chance to think about it. Then again, when I heard a noise from the den, I wasn't sure that was a good thing, either. Too late, I realized that just like what happens in all those B horror flicks, I wasn't alone in the house.

Something told me it wasn't Nick. From what I'd heard about his sudden change of heart, I knew he wouldn't have been skulking around in parts unknown. He would have been there in the living room, weeping over the mess and cataloging like a fiend even though he should have been home concentrating on those pink and red M&Ms.

The realization settled in my stomach like ice, and I held my breath and inched back toward the front door. I should have moved faster. That way, I would have been within getting-out distance when a man walked out of Marjorie's den.

I don't know who I was expecting, but it sure wasn't friendly-as-a-teddy-bear Ray Gwitkowski. I shot forward, surprised, sure, but relieved, too. "What on earth are you doing here?" I asked him. "And what happened to this place?"

"Don't ask me." As if I'd just told him to stick 'em up, Ray held up both hands, distancing himself from the mess. "It was like this when I walked in. Honest. And hey, kid . . ." He bent forward as if he needed a closer look to be sure it was me. "You're the last person I expected to make a return appearance at Marjorie's. What are you doing here?"

Don't think I didn't notice that he'd asked the same question I'd asked him.

Or that he'd never answered mine.

"It sure didn't look like this the last time we were here, did it?" Ray propped his fists on his hips and looked around. "You know, the night we both were here to see Marjorie."

"And it didn't look like this yesterday, either," I told him. "Yesterday it was all organized and neat. And today . . ." I looked back toward the smashed lock on the front door. "Did you do that? Did you break in?"

"Absolutely not. No way. I just stopped by and I wasn't even planning to come in. But then I saw that the lock was banged up, and the door was open and . . ." His shoulders sagged and he scraped a hand through his hair. "It's like this . . . I was hoping to get in and out of here and I was praying that nobody would notice. And now here you are." Ray was still wearing his Garden View volunteer shirt. It matched the one I was wearing except that mine had the word STAFF embroidered over the heart. His face turned as sickly yellow as the color of our shirts. "I think I might be in big trouble, kiddo."

It wasn't what he said that made me believe him. It was the way he looked. Miserable. Ray's arms hung limp at his sides. His eyes were tormented. I picked my way through the framed pictures of President Garfield and the books spread out all over the living room floor, sat down on the couch, and patted the seat beside me. "You want to tell me about what's going on?"

"I don't want to tell anybody. It's too embarrassing. And . . ." He shoved his hands in his pockets and looked up at the ceiling. "I'm pretty sure what I did was illegal, too. I don't . . ." When he looked at me again, his eyes were pleading. "I don't want to get in any trouble. I've led a good, honest life. It's a little late in the game for me to be going to jail."

Had I just invited a murderer to sit down beside me?

I admit, the thought crossed my mind. Too late to take back my invitation. Ray came over and plunked down on the couch.

I consoled myself with the fact that, number one, I was wearing sneakers and not high heels. Which meant I could probably get through the minefield that was Marjorie's living room pretty easily, even if it did mean crunching a couple pictures of President Garfield in the process. Number two, Ray was old, and he was visibly shaken. I was pretty sure I could outrun him.

Just to be sure, I glanced at the front door, gauging the distance and the best way to get there. Sure of my escape route, I got down to business. Obviously, I do not mean cemetery business.

"I know it doesn't seem likely," I said, folding my hands in my lap, the better to look professional and proficient. "But I've had some experience when it comes to things that are illegal."

He nodded. "I'm not surprised. You're one smart girl, and I heard Ella talking once. She said something about how you helped find out who killed somebody."

I sloughed this off. After all, if Ray was a murderer, I didn't want him to think I was too good. "Ella tends to exaggerate. But I have been . . . well, sort of involved in a couple investigations. That's why I went to Big Daddy Burger to talk to you the other day, Ray. I'm trying to figure out some things. You know, about Marjorie's murder."

I wisely did not mention that one of those things was who dun it. Just in case. Instead, I kept things cool and noncommittal. "I've just been wondering. That's all. You know, about everything that happened. I can't figure it out."

"Wish I could help."

I stared at him in a way that should have told him he could, if only he'd open up and tell me what was going on. But since Ray was so busy wringing his hands and looking at the floor, I guess he didn't notice. That's why I had to egg him on.

"What are you doing here, Ray?" I asked.

He cleared his throat. He tapped one foot against the carpet. Just when I thought he was going to spill the beans, he folded. "I can't," he said. "It's too embarrassing."

"More embarrassing than the way Marjorie strung you along so that you'd take her to dinner and the movies?"

It was a good move on my part. He had no choice but to shake his head. "Not more embarrassing than that," he admitted. "But still . . ."

I am not usually an ease-into-the-subject sort of person. It's a waste of time, and honestly, I don't have the patience for that sort of nonsense. But I could tell that Ray was going to need some coaxing.

I eased into the subject.

"Nobody liked Marjorie," I said, and sure it was an understatement and went without saying, but remember, I was easing here. "She was a bully."

"A self-righteous bully." Ray's shoulders rose and fell. "That's the worst kind."

"Which doesn't mean she should have died the way she did."

I was hoping he'd agree with me. Instead, he sat up straight and asked, "Do you think it's all right to pay somebody back for the bad things that somebody did to you?"

I turned in my seat, the better to keep both eyes on Ray. "You mean Marjorie."

He nodded. "Do you think revenge is all right? I mean, if it's justified?"

My throat was suddenly dry. I swallowed the sand. "If you're talking about murder—"

"Murder? Oh my, no way!" A touch of green added to the sallowness of Ray's complexion. "I hope you don't think—" He blanched because, of course, from what he'd just said, it was the only thing I could think. He slid me a look. "You gonna tell the cops?"

"Not if there's nothing to tell them."

"You gonna think less of me?"

"That, I can't say." I scooted just a titch closer. I was trying to establish some kind of rapport, after all. I needed every advantage I could get. "I don't know what I'll do or say until you tell me what's bugging you."

He laughed uncomfortably. "It's a biggee."

"Bet I've heard it before."

I was pretty sure my strategy wasn't working. Ray sat there like a lump, and I was all set to chalk the whole thing up to faulty psychology when he pulled in a breath and let it go along with a sigh. "That day when you came to see me at Big Daddy Burger, I wasn't exactly truthful with you, Pepper," he said. "Not completely anyway. And it wasn't like I wanted to lie to you. I just couldn't help myself. You see, when you asked me what I was doing here at Marjorie's that night—"

"You told me you came here to tell her to get lost. Because of that rude note she sent you about Nick's wedding."

Ray nodded. "Well, that's true insofar as it goes. That's why I came here. I wanted to tell her that I was tired of being taken advantage of. And I did. I wanted her to know that Ray Gwitkowski is nobody's patsy. And I told her that, too. I wanted to make her understand—loud and clear—that I was tired of her stringing me along. I did that, too. But I also . . ." He hung his head. "I did something else, too."

So he wasn't about to confess that he'd killed Marjorie. Not that night, anyway. Not unless he loaded her body into a car, drove all the way to the cemetery, dragged her into the memorial and up that corkscrew stairway just so he could hurl her off the balcony.

I breathed a sigh of relief. Whatever he told me, it couldn't come anywhere near murder.

"I never meant for it to happen," Ray said. "It was just . . . well, you remember, Marjorie and I went into the den to talk. That's when I was all set to tell her how I was tired of waiting for that get-rich scheme she promised me. I'd had it with her. I would have told her right then and there, too. If you hadn't knocked over whatever it was you knocked over in here."

I looked toward the fireplace. The day before, that vase with the long, old-fashioned hat pins in it had been set right next to it. Today, the vase was knocked over and lying on its side about five feet away.

"It was those hat pins," I told Ray, pointing. "They made a lot of noise when they hit."

He nodded. "And Marjorie came running. That's when I had a couple minutes alone there in her den and that's when . . ." Color shot up his neck, and even the tips of his ears burned red. "I was in there by myself," Ray said. "And I was waiting for Marjorie to get back and I was just standing there by the desk. And that's when I saw it."

"Saw—?"

Before I could even finish my sentence, Ray leapt up off the couch and went into the den. Apparently old people can move pretty fast when they want to. I told myself not to forget it, and just in case he was planning to come back into the living room with some kind of weapon, I got up, too, and edged over to the door.

He was back in a jiffy and he picked his way through the junk on the floor and handed me a—

"Credit card?" I turned it over in my hands.

Ray nodded. "It was on Marjorie's desk next to her computer along with a printout from an auction site. You know, one of those places that specializes in historical artifacts. You know she was addicted to Garfield memorabilia, and apparently, she always had her eye out for new things. This particular site had an auction in progress. Marjorie had one of their offerings circled. It was a paperweight and the bottom of it was etched with an excerpt of one of President Garfield's speeches. In Japanese."

"And she wanted to buy it?" Impossible to understand, but I couldn't let that distract me. "So you were in the den and Marjorie and I were out here. And you found the credit card and the listing about the paperweight and—"

"And I realized she was going to buy it. The paperweight, I mean. She had underlined the parts of the printout that said what time the auction closed. Exactly eleven fifty-nine that night we were both here."

"And so Marjorie had her credit card out, all set to get in on the auction at the last minute and scoop up the paperweight." It was pretty obvious, so I wasn't exactly happy when Ray shook his head.

"You almost got it right," he said. "But not exactly. I don't doubt she was planning on using that credit card to get in on the auction and buy the paperweight. But look at it, Pepper. It's not hers."

"Not hers?" I took another look at the credit card and my heart bumped against my ribs.

Ray was right. Marjorie Klinker's name was nowhere on the card. Somebody named Bernard O'Banyon's was.

I looked from the card to Ray. "So who's this Bernard guy?"

He shrugged.

"And why did Marjorie have his credit card?"

Another shrug.

"And do you suppose this has anything to do with her murder?"

This time, he didn't even bother to shrug, and I couldn't blame him. I was reaching. We both knew it.

"I want you to know, I never meant to do anything with the card. But there I was with it in my hands. And she was out here lecturing you. That voice of hers, that attitude, it was like a knife inside me, twisting and twisting. It brought up the whole, ugly situation all over again and I . . . well, I can't say what happened. I guess I went a little crazy."

Ray was too upset to stand still. He kicked the stolen framed piece of railroad station tile out of the way and paced out the distance to the den and back again.

"This is the first really dishonest thing I've done in my whole life," he said. "And the only explanation I have is that Marjorie made me do it. You see . . ." When he gulped, his Adam's apple bobbed. "I took that credit card. Slipped it in my pocket, just like that. Before Marjorie got back in the room. I don't know what I was thinking. I guess I just really meant it to be a joke, you know? I thought about how Marjorie would go into the den right before that auction was set to close. Then I pictured how she wouldn't be able to find that credit card, and how she'd be madder than a wet hen. It was cruel, I know, and a cowardly way to get even with her. But I figured she had it coming for all she put me through."

"So you swiped the credit card. That's what you were getting all tweaky about when I talked to you at Big Daddy that day. Every time I mentioned money, you looked like you were just about ready to jump out of your skin."

"I knew you didn't know I'd taken it. I mean, how could you? But I still felt plenty guilty. I was just going to string Marjorie along. You know, the way she did to me all that time with her promises. I was never planning to use it. In fact, I was just thinking that I'd stop by the memorial the next day and leave the credit card on the desk there where I knew she'd find it. By then, she would have missed the auction and that stupid paperweight she wanted. Would have served her right."

"And did you?"

Ray's cheeks got chalky. "You mean, did I stop by the memorial? Or did I use the credit card?"

"Ray!" I closed in on him, flapping the card in his face as I did. "You used it? Somebody else's credit card? Do you know how incredibly dumb that is?"

"I did. I do. I shouldn't have, but . . ." He went back over to the couch and collapsed, his head in his hands. "After I left here, all I could think about was the way Marjorie had lied to me all those months. She told me we were going to get rich together, and instead, all she did was lead me on and treat me like a fool. I didn't start out being angry, just disgusted with myself. But the more I thought about it, the crazier it made me. Finally I was so mad, I couldn't see straight. And then I thought about the credit card I put in my pocket, and how it would serve her and this Bernard guy right if I got back some of my own. I'd taken Marjorie out for so many dinners, waiting for her to tell me more about how much money we were going to make. So . . ." He sniffed. He coughed. He scraped a finger under his nose. "I went to Ruth's Chris on the way home and had myself a really nice meal."

Truth be told, I couldn't blame him. Even if I never would have had the nerve to do the same thing myself.

Instead of admitting it, I went for the obvious questions. "They didn't flag the card? You got away with it?"

"They never batted an eye. And I spent a lot of money. I don't get out much these days. Me and Vanessa, we used to go out to dinner once in a while, you know, for special occasions. But then she got sick and the bills started piling up, and . . ." He rubbed his eyes with his fists. "In my whole life, I never enjoyed a steak as much as I did the one I ate that night. Until I got home, that is. I was up all night with indigestion, and it wasn't the food, I know that. It was my conscience talking, telling me that I didn't deserve that expensive dinner, that I'd done something I shouldn't have done. The next morning, I checked the phone book, but I couldn't find anyone with the name that's on that credit card. So I did the next best thing. I worked three extra shifts at Big Daddy that week, got the money together, and sent cash to that restaurant, just to make myself feel better. Cost me a bundle, but at least I've been able to close my eyes every night."

He knew he did the right thing, he didn't need me telling him. Besides, I was too deep in thought to say much of anything. I tapped the credit card against my chin, thinking, and I was still wondering what it all meant when we left the house and closed the door behind us and when I stared at that credit card all night, unable to sleep.

Of course the solution hit me right around three in the morning when it was too late to do anything about it. I waited until the sun was up and hit the cemetery early, the better to get into my office and in front of my computer before anyone was around to bother me.

I found two Bernard O'Banyons listed, neither of them local, and made the calls.

As it turned out, the first Bernard O'Banyon was a bar in Wichita and the man it was named after? Well, he hadn't been around since sometime in the 1850s. I was hoping his descendants were, and tried the Bernard O'Banyon listed in the Topeka phonebook.

Credit card in hand, I punched in the phone number and started into my spiel. It was all about how I was from the credit card company, and I really needed to talk to Bernard.

"Well, you must have the wrong person." The woman on the phone sounded sleepy, but then, I didn't account for whatever time it was in Kansas. "My Bernard, he didn't believe in credit cards."

I felt my spirits deflate. "You're sure?" I asked.

"Sure as sure can be. He used to have one of them gas station cards. You know, for filling up the Buick. But he gave that up back in '04. That's when he got his identity stolen."

My deflated spirits perked up. So did my ears when she added, "That thief, he got it all. Even Bernard's Social Security number. Used it to rent an apartment in Denver. Imagine the nerve of some people."

I told her I couldn't and asked if I could talk to Bernard.

"Talk to him?" I didn't have to see her to know she held out the phone and gave it a look, like she could see me at the other end of it. "What do you mean, talk to him? Bernard, he up and died back last Christmas."

Did I thank her for the information before I hung up?

I honestly don't remember.

But that's because I was too busy thinking again. About credit cards belonging to dead people, and stolen Social Security numbers. About Marjorie.

And if maybe there was a lot more to her than any of us ever imagined.

14

To catch a thief, I had to think like a thief.

Only I wasn't trying to catch a thief, was I? I was trying to catch the murderer who killed the thief.

No matter. As one of my college professors used to say, it was all just semantics, though what the meanings of words had to do with Jewish people, I didn't know.

Maybe Ted Studebaker was Jewish. But that didn't matter, either. Unless he was Orthodox and his shop wasn't open on Saturdays. What did matter was that I had to wait until then, but once the weekend rolled around and I didn't have my pesky nine-to-fiver to worry about, I drove out to cute, picturesque, pricey Chagrin Falls.

Yes, there really is a waterfall. It's nowhere near the Niagara variety, but it's still pretty, in a picture postcard kind of way. The river that feeds the falls meanders through the village of charming cottages and gardens and spills over a twenty-foot drop right near an old-fashioned popcorn and ice cream shop. I swear, it's true. Like something out of a corny movie, only for real, and it brings in tourists by the droves.

There is also a main street (predictably called Main Street) that features a gazebo and a whole bunch of boutiques and gift shops where scrumptious-looking fall clothes were displayed in the windows. It was a shame I didn't have time to browse and shop. But then, I didn't have the money to shop, either, so unless like Marjorie, I was planning on using Bernard O'Banyon's credit card . . .

No worries. The card was safe at home, hidden in the bottom drawer of my dresser underneath the wool sweaters I had a feeling I would be taking out any day now.

It was barely September, and I was chilled to the bone.

An unseasonably cold wind whipped down Main Street, and I wished when I was getting ready to leave my apartment I had paid more attention to the weather than I had to fashion. I was wearing a short-sleeved white linen jacket. It was as cute as can be, but between that and the tank top I had underneath it and my skinny jeans and wedge sandals, it didn't offer much in the way of warmth. I was carrying an oversized leather tote, so I couldn't even wrap my arms around myself in the hopes of generating a little heat.

Good thing Ted Studebaker Antiques wasn't far from where I parked the Mustang.

I took a minute (no more, believe me, I was too cold to waste time) to look at the understated display in the front window of the shop. It featured a gigantic American eagle carved out of mahogany. It looked just like the one embossed on Studebaker's business card. In front of that was a table with fancy legs with a silver coffeepot on it and a tasteful sign in flowing script that said, PRESIDENTIAL COLLECTIBLES A SPECIALITY.

I sailed right on in like I had every right to be there. But then, I guess I did. I had questions to ask: about Marjorie's collection, about Nick's sudden interest in it, and about the fact that there must have been something in that Garfield lollapalooza that someone was desperate to find.

The shop was in a big, old building, and it had one of those tin ceilings, and walls that were painted muted gray. It smelled like lemony furniture polish in there, and it was no wonder. Every table and chair and elaborate china hutch was shined to within an inch of its life. Every plate and vase and oversized pitcher and bowl set gleamed so that every picture of every president on those plates and vases and oversized pitcher and bowl sets was shown off to perfection. There were bookcases all around and hundreds of books on them with titles like *Jefferson the Statesman*, and *The Kennedy Years*. There were presidential autographs framed and hung on the walls, and portraits, too. Dozens of them. They reminded me of the ones I'd seen in President Garfield's office—stern-faced presidents in old-fashioned duds, looking grim and important.

Ted Studebaker Antiques was impressive, all right. Even to me. I reminded myself not to forget it. When I finally came face-to-face with Ted, the last thing he needed to know was that, in reality, antiques give me the creeps.

And it's no wonder why.

If the people who shopped there could see what I saw—which was a whole bunch of ghosts hanging around, too attached to their earthly possessions to leave them behind—they never would have taken the chance of buying the stuff and dragging it (and the ghosts) home. Even so, it wasn't the spook-a-rama that turned me off. It was the idea of owning something—I mean, purposely—that someone else had owned before. Who in their right mind would want to do that?

When Ted himself stepped out from a back room, I recognized him right away. I'd seen him in those snippets of *Antique Appraisals* I'd watched on TV. He, apparently, had never returned the favor and caught even a moment of *Cemetery Survivor*. Otherwise I was sure he would have recognized me, too.

"Can I help you?" he asked, and even if I hadn't seen him on the show, I wouldn't have been surprised by his deep, baritone voice. It went perfectly with his barrel chest, his shock of wild, silver hair, and his impressive height. Though the window display may have been understated, and the shop was civilized and genteel, there was nothing unpretentious about Ted Studebaker, his two-thousand-dollar suit, his Italian silk tie, or his alligator shoes. He looked me over and grinned, not in a lecherous-old-man way, but in a very gay way that told me he appreciated my sense of style.

I could see that Ted and I were going to get along.

He eyed me and my tote bag up and down, and before I could say a word, he said, "If you're here for an appraisal, I'm afraid I'm going to have to disappoint you. I wish I could help, darling, but no can do. These days, my agent is in charge, and she insists I can't even think about an appraisal without a signed release form and a camera rolling."

"Then I guess it's a good thing I'm not looking for an appraisal." He had a dazzling smile, so it wasn't hard to smile back. "Actually, I was by here a couple weeks ago, and I saw your sign." I looked toward the front window. There was a roly-poly ghost standing in the way, hovering over a set of china with big pink flowers on it. Not that it mattered. Studebaker couldn't see the ghost. And I didn't need to see the PRESIDENTIAL COLLECTIBLES sign. "I was wondering, do you just sell presidential memorabilia? Or do you buy, too?"

Like collectors everywhere, Ted's eyes lit up at the prospect of discovering something new and different that wasn't on the market yet. He rubbed his hands together, and the heavy gold rings he was wearing glittered in the light. Unaware of the short, pudgy ghost wearing a mini-skirt she shouldn't have been caught dead in standing in the way, he ventured closer. When he got too close to her for comfort, a shiver snaked over his shoulders, but something told me he must have been used to the chilly feeling. With as many ghosts as were hanging around the shop, he must have run into their icy auras all the time. There was a glass case nearby chock-full of old jewelry and he came to stand near it.

Little did he know he had positioned himself right next to another ghost. This one was a skinny woman in a black Victorian gown. I shooed her out of the way with a look that told her I didn't appreciate getting flash frozen and joined him.

"You're interested in selling?" he asked.

I hoisted up the leather tote and held it in front of me in both hands. "Maybe. If what I have is worth selling. But if you tell me that, that would be like you giving me an appraisal, right? I don't want you to get in trouble with your agent."

"I'll handle her." He gave me a wink and looked at the tote. "You have it with you?"

I did. I set the tote on the counter.

"He's going to try to flimflam you, kid." The voice came from just over my right shoulder and I looked back to see a ghost wearing a suit and tie who looked like he'd just stepped out of one of those old black-and-white gangster movies. He had a pug-dog nose that sat a little crooked on his face and a nasty-looking scar that followed the outline of his jaw, all the way from his left ear down to his chin. "Don't let him con you, sweetheart. I seen him do it, see. To plenty of other suckers. Whatever you're selling, hold out for a good price. Before you agree to anything, make him hand over the cabbage."

It wasn't like I could tell the ghost the price Studebaker quoted didn't matter, that I wasn't there because I was looking for money, but for information.

I reached into the bag.

The ghost leaned forward. "Don't be a pushover, doll."

I ignored him and pulled out one of the pieces of Garfield garbage . . . er . . . memorabilia that had been in the trunk of my car since the night before Marjorie was killed. It was a framed front page from the *Kern County Weekly Record* in Bakersfield, California, dated July 7, 1881. PRESIDENT GARFIELD—HIS ATTEMPTED ASSASSINATION, the headline read. HOVERING BETWEEN LIFE AND DEATH.

If they only knew!

I presented the piece to Studebaker and waited, giving him my best look of eager anticipation.

Just like he did on TV when he was sizing up some piece of junk or another, he stepped back, his weight resting on one foot, and pursed his lips. He clicked his tongue. He turned the frame toward the light for a better look.

"It's interesting, surely," Studebaker said. He set the framed newspaper page on the counter and tapped one finger on the glass. "I'll give you twenty dollars for it."

"Told you he'd try to pull a fast one," the ghost in the suit hissed in my ear. "He does it all the time. You shoulda been here the day some dame waltzed in with a musty old book of poetry. Studebaker turned up his nose, all right, and offered the babe five smackers. She refused, and I was glad. If Studebaker woulda taken a closer look, he woulda seen there was a letter tucked in the pages of that there poetry book, signed by that Hemingway guy. Wish I could tell him. That would teach him a lesson!"

I tuned the ghost out and turned back to Ted. Truth be told, I wasn't surprised that the newspaper page was practically worthless. Marjorie had come right out and told me she wouldn't dare entrust me with much of anything that was valuable. Still, I couldn't let on. "I thought it might be worth a little more," I said. "It's pretty old."

"Oh, darling! Everything in this place is pretty and old. Including me! That doesn't mean anyone's going to pay big bucks to take me home." Studebaker's laugh boomed through the store.

My smile was anemic. But then, I was playing hard to get. "But you'll turn around and sell it for more, right? I mean, that is your business. So if you're going to sell the newspaper and get more for it than you gave me, I thought . . . well, I thought maybe you could up your offer a little."

I think he was just trying to let me down easy when he gave the framed newspaper page another look. "I'm being honest here," he said, at the same time the ghost at my shoulder muttered, "Don't believe it, sister. He don't know the meaning of the word."

"I'll need to have it looked at by an archivist to see if there's anything that can be done to preserve the old newspaper," Studebaker said. "And it will probably need to be reframed. Even once all that's done, the most I can ask for it here in the shop is sixty dollars or so. So you see, I'm being as generous as I can possibly be."

I pretended I was disappointed and scooped the newspaper page off the counter. After all, I couldn't really sell it. Somewhere along the line I had to get it and all the other nonvaluable stuff Marjorie had saddled me with back to Nick.

Studebaker watched the newspaper page disappear back into the tote bag. "You have more?" he asked. "At home? More old newspapers? More Garfield collectibles? The president was from this area, you know. There's a great deal of Garfield memorabilia left in northeast Ohio."

"I might have a little more. I used to think it was valuable, but after what you've told me, I guess none of it is worth very much." Rather than stand there and clutch the tote bag, I set it on the counter. "Tell me, Mr. Studebaker, what kinds of things are valuable? Are some presidential antiques worth more than others? And why?"

"Ah, you're being sly!" He shook a finger at me. Not like he was mad, more like he knew I wasn't as obtuse as I was pretending to be. I wasn't. But not in the way he thought. "You do have more collectibles at home. Tell me about them."

I thought back to Marjorie's house and how it had been neat and organized one day, and completely trashed the next. "All the obvious stuff couldn't be that valuable, because all the obvious stuff was overlooked," I mumbled. "And Nick—"

"Nick? Nick Klinker?" Studebaker threw back his head and laughed like a jolly Santa Claus. "Now I see what you're up to. You're Nick's fiancée, aren't you?"

Though I'm not sure what it means and I don't know who would want to look inside an animal's mouth in the first place, I am a firm believer in never looking a gift horse in the mouth. I stuck out my hand and shook Studebaker's. "You can call me Bernadine," I said. "I know you've been to . . ." I coughed, but then, it was kind of hard to get the words out without gagging. "To dear, sweet Aunt Marjorie's house to look things over. But really, Mr. Studebaker . . ." I leaned closer. "I'm sorry to be so secretive, but Nick has been acting so strange. He says not much of what dear Marjorie had is very valuable. I just can't believe that's true!"

He hesitated, weighing the wisdom of getting in the middle of a family argument. I liked to think it was my winning personality that helped him make up his mind. "Nick is right. About some of it," he finally said. "But Marjorie had a good eye when it came to Garfield collectibles. That tile from the railroad station!" His eyes glowed. "Now there's something I'd love to get my hands on. I saw something similar once on the wall at Lawnfield. You know, the president's home."

"And the tile?" I did a sort of slow-mo rerun through my last visit to Marjorie's. As far as I could remember, the framed tile was right there on the floor with everything else that had been left behind. "Is that tile especially valuable?"

"It doesn't have as much monetary value as it does historic value." Studebaker studied me closely. "What are you getting at, Bernadine? I've had a couple long talks with Nick and he assured me he'd been through everything and he was being totally up front with me. Is there something Marjorie had that he hasn't told me about?"

I could play coy with the best of them, and I went all out. I glided one finger back and forth over the glass countertop, then realized I probably shouldn't have. As sparkling as the whole place was, I hated to be the one who left fingerprints. I also couldn't take the chance of Studebaker noticing my definite lack of an engagement ring. "There are a few more things I need to look through. You know, boxes in the attic. That sort of thing. I'm not even sure Nick's seen them yet. I just wondered if I should pay more attention to certain things. You were saying, about how some things are more valuable than others. Like what?"

He thought about it. "Well, one-of-a-kind things, that's for certain. And if you're not sure if something's one of a kind, all you have to do is call me. I'll be glad to pop over and take a look for you."

"That's so kind." I smiled my thanks. "So what would be one-of-a-kind?"

"Well, certainly anything of national significance."

Studebaker made a face. "Obviously, you're not going to find anything like that. Marjorie knew her stuff when it came to the president. Anything like that, she would have donated to the government. You know, so it could be put on display."

"Display." The word ping-ponged through my mind for a couple confused moments. I wasn't sure why until I thought about the first time I'd met with Marjorie about the commemoration. "She was all happy about something," I said, remembering Marjorie's weird, secretive grin. "She wouldn't say what it was. She only said it was important and that she was going to put it on display."

"Maybe it was something—"

Before Studebaker could continue, the front door opened and the mail carrier walked in. "I've got that package you've been waiting for, Mr. Studebaker!" she chirped.

Studebaker excused himself and went running.

"Heard what you said!" The ghost with the scar along his jaw crossed his arms over his chest and leaned against the glass-front display case. "What's the story, morning glory? You're asking an awful lot of questions. Seems to me, you ain't getting very far with the answers, neither."

"You got that right." I kept my voice down so Studebaker and the mail carrier couldn't hear me. "There was a break-in, see, and I'm trying to figure out what whoever broke in was looking for."

"And this Nick guy . . . ?" The ghost angled me a look. "He the one who's been calling here?"

"Calling? Here?" I wasn't as dense as I was surprised that a ghost would have been paying attention.

Predictably, the ghost thought dense was the likelier explanation. "Calling. You know, sister, like on the Ameche, the horn, the blower." He held a hand to his ear like he was talking on the phone. "I heard Studebaker jabbin' on the phone just the other day to some fella named Nick. That

Nick, he must have been talkin about sellin', 'cause Stude-baker, he was talkin' about buyin'."

This wasn't news.

Studebaker was walking along with the mail carrier toward the door, and I knew I didn't have much time. "Did he say what he wanted to sell?" I asked.

The ghost grinned. A couple of his front teeth were missing. "That Nick, he must have said as how it was something personal because Studebaker got all excited like. But then he sort of froze. You know, just as he was about to say somethin' else. He listened to the Joe on the other end of the horn say somethin', and I swear, I thought Studebaker was gonna have some sort of apoplexy or somethin'. 'What? What!' he says, and I'll tell you, he's usually such a hotsy-totsy Abercrombie. But I swear . . . I swear, I thought the guy was gonna cry. That's how ex-cited he was."

Studebaker opened the door to let the mail carrier out. "Thanks," I told the ghost.

"Soitenly!" He had already faded away when Stude-baker came back.

"Now . . . you were saying . . . about some of the other things Marjorie may have owned . . ."

But I had already found out all I needed to know.

I thanked Studebaker for his help, promised him that my darling Nick would be in touch with him soon, and headed outside.

The ghost was waiting for me on the sidewalk.

"So you got the lowdown, right, sister?"

There was a couple passing by, so I couldn't answer. I just nodded.

"You wanna share?"

I didn't especially, but I owed him that much. "Nick Klinker's got something personal that once belonged to President Garfield," I told him. "That's what he's been so excited about. It's not just an inaugural invitation, or a newspaper or anything like that. It's got to be something the president actually owned."

"And . . . ?" The ghost waited for more.

"And I think that means it's plenty valuable."

"Now we're talking!" He rubbed his hands together. "You think this Nick is gonna sell it?"

I thought back to the mess that was Marjorie's, and now that I thought about it, I thought back to the night I had visited her at home, too. Just as I was driving away, I saw her tearing through the house as if she'd lost something. "I think Nick would be happy to sell it if he could find it," I said. "And I think—no, I know—that two people know it exists. One of them is Nick, and the other is Studebaker. The only thing I need to figure out now is if either one of them might have wanted it so bad, they were willing to kill for it."

I was sure I was right, and so caught up in what it all meant, I walked away. It wasn't until I heard the ghost behind me that I turned back around.

He was standing outside the antiques shop and he raised one hand. "Abyssinia," he said.

It was a corny joke, but this time, I couldn't help but laugh.

15

Thanks to the talkative ghost, I knew more when I left Chagrin Falls than when I got there. As I drove back home, I made a mental list that went something like this:

1. Both Nick and Ted Studebaker were aware of an item in Marjorie's collection that had once belonged to President Garfield.

2. Whatever that item was, Nick wanted to sell it, and whatever it was, I suspected that it had gone missing. Which brought me to:

3. The logical conclusion, which was that his search for the missing item accounted for why Nick was spending hours over at Marjorie's and why the place had been turned upside down.

But wait (as they say in those awful commercials), there really was more. My incredible deductive powers didn't stop there. I also knew that:

1. Just because she was dead didn't make me think Marjorie was any less crazy, but I had a feeling that whatever that missing item was, it had something to do with the family connection to Garfield that she claimed to have. Because:

2. That would explain why she was so smug about the surprise she was going to reveal at the opening of the commemoration event.

3. It also explained why Nick thought that mystery item would bring in some big bucks. It stood to reason that anything actually owned by a president had to be worth a bundle, especially if it revealed some family secret.

What all this told me, of course, was this:

Both Nick and Ted Studebaker had motives for offing Marjorie. That is, they each wanted to get their hands on this mystery item.

But that didn't mean they were my only suspects.

Even though he didn't fit into any of my numbered lists, I hadn't eliminated Jack when it came to what-was-he-up-to.

Let's face it, he was acting plenty fishy. Sure, he was a great kisser, but there was no way I'd forgotten that turned-around sign.

As luck would have it, just as I arrived at my apartment and was thinking all this, my phone rang. It was Jack, all right, and when he invited me to meet him for dinner that evening at XO, an oh-so-posh steak house in the trendy Warehouse District, I didn't have to pretend to be thrilled.

Yes, I was more than willing to go, and yes (again), I fully intended to enjoy myself. But contrary to popular gossip, I am nowhere near as shallow as all that. I was glad to be seeing Jack again not because I was hot for him (well, I was, but that's neither here nor there). I wanted to see him again because I had every intention of grilling him. And no intention whatsoever of ending up in bed with him. Really. For one thing, I'm not that easy. Ask Quinn. We knew each other for months before that fateful night we finally took the plunge that ended up putting us in over our heads. For another thing . . . well, I have a hard-and-fast rule: no sex with a guy who definitely has something up his sleeve, and just might be a murderer, too.

I told myself not to forget it.

It wasn't easy considering Jack was gorgeous in a gray suit, a white shirt, and a gray tie streaked with blue that wasn't quite as intense as the color of his eyes. He was generous, too; he ordered the most expensive bottle of wine on the menu and insisted I get the twelve-ounce center-cut filet although I told him there was no way I could even eat all of the eight-ounce. He said I'd appreciate having the leftovers for dinner the next day. Fishy or not, I think he must have known something about the salary of a cemetery tour guide.

Oh yeah, Jack was every bit as delicious as our meal, and as charming as hell, too.

But I am strong, remember, not to mention determined. We exchanged small talk over dinner, but when our waitress brought coffee and a vanilla bean crème brûlée for us to share, I knew it was time. I had cut Jack enough slack.

"So how are things at school?" I asked him.

He was as smooth as the crème brûlée. "We don't start until next week. Which is why I decided to stay in Cleveland another couple days. There's so much to see here. Man, I can't believe the whole summer has flown by. Vacation always goes too fast."

"And you must be knee-deep in getting ready for the new school year, what with lesson plans and all. I get so mixed up sometimes!" I made sure I rolled my eyes when I said this, the way I'd seen the truly dim girls do. "I remember you said you were from Hammond, Indiana, but where did you say you teach? Laramie High School?"

"Lafayette High School."

I smiled like I was too dumb to keep track. *Like* being the operative word. "And you teach math, right?"

"History."

I hate a liar who can keep his story straight.

I spooned up some crème brûlée. "A history teacher probably knows a lot about . . . well, history! I mean, presidential history."

"Exactly." Jack took two bites of dessert to my one, and I saw that if I didn't get a move on, he was going to get more than his share. The crème brûlée was that good. "That's how I developed my interest in President Garfield."

"So a history teacher would know about his life."

"Sure." He took another bite of dessert, but his eyes were on me. I do not have an overactive imagination, but I swear, there was a flash of irritation in those incredibly blue eyes of his. I knew what it meant. No matter how innocent my questions, by asking them I was challenging him.

And Jack didn't like to be challenged.

He kept his eyes on mine. A not-so-subtle signal that no matter how innocent or clever I was, he wasn't going to cave. He sat forward and propped his elbows on the table. "Would you like to know what year he was born? It was 1831. Or when he accepted a teaching position at the Western Reserve Eclectic Institute? That was 1856. Just a year later, he was named president of the school. It's called Hiram College now, you know."

"No, no. Nothing like that. That's not what I meant." I didn't know enough yet; I couldn't afford to alienate Jack.

I kept my tone as light as can be. "What I was really wondering about is any family secrets he might have had."

It wasn't my imagination the first time and it wasn't this time, either. That little spark in Jack's eyes tamped back. I hadn't even realized his shoulders were stiff until I saw him relax. He put down his spoon and sat back. Which gave me unspoken permission to finish the dessert. While I did that, I watched him watch me, and damn, but I wished I could read the thoughts going through his head. Did he know I was on to him and his lies about Lafayette High School? Maybe. But there was one thing for sure—he was a cool customer. Too cool to show it.

"You're talking about his affair with Lucia Calhoun," Jack said. He drank his coffee hot and black, just like Quinn did. I sipped. He gulped it down. "That's no secret. Garfield admitted the indiscretion to his wife. She forgave him."

"And there were no children."

"Not as far as anyone knows." Jack sat up. "Wait a minute! Are you telling me you think there were? That there's some kind of proof?" Since I was being coy in the name of detecting, it was just as well that I had a mouth full of crème brûlée and couldn't say a thing. He went right on. "If you did have some kind of proof . . . wow . . . that would create quite a sensation." He smiled at the prospect, but little by little, that smile faded. By the time it was completely gone, there was nothing but worry in Jack's eyes.

A guy who cares enough about me to worry.

It's one of those things that always gets to me. Especially true when Jack reached across the table and covered my hand with his and little sizzles of electricity danced across my skin.

I reminded myself about my "no murderers" rule.

"You told me once that the woman who was murdered

at the memorial . . . you said something about how she thought she was related to the Garfields. Now you're asking about something personal that belonged to the Garfield family. Does this have something to do with the murder, Pepper? Because if it does . . ."

Chalk it up to flashbacks. This sounded a little too much like the horse hockey I'd heard from Quinn, and I knew what was coming next. Jack was going to say exactly what Quinn would have said in this situation: mind your own business.

I pulled my hand out from under his and tucked it in my lap, the better to keep the electricity down to a minimum and keep myself from getting burned.

Maybe I didn't have to because the next second, Jack asked, "Are you looking into the murder? Investigating? Wow! I'm impressed. But I'm worried, too. That sounds dangerous. And I wouldn't want anything to happen to you."

"I'm not exactly investigating," I told him because, since what I was doing, exactly, was investigating, the last thing I wanted was to admit it. "I've just heard some things and talked to some people and it all got me wondering."

The waitress came over to refill our coffee and leave a leather portfolio with the bill in it, and I waited for her to pour, then added sweetener to my coffee. "I guess I just don't understand why people care about old things and history that doesn't matter anymore. I thought maybe you could explain it to me."

Jack chuckled. He didn't even look at the bill; he just took out a credit card and popped it in the portfolio. That was when his cell rang.

He looked at the caller ID and pushed back his chair. "I'm sorry. Really. But I've got to take this."

I gave him a little wave to tell him it was fine by me. Since he already had the phone up to his ear, there didn't seem to be much point in saying anything else. Already deep in his conversation, he walked out toward the lobby and I saw him march out the front door to the street and the place where the poor smokers had to go to indulge their nasty habit.

I sipped my coffee.

And eyed that leather portfolio.

Call me nosey. But then, it is my business, isn't it?

I checked to make sure Jack was still outside and flipped open the portfolio. He'd put a MasterCard inside that looked just like the MasterCard in the bottom drawer of my dresser, the one with Bernard O'Banyon's name on it.

Again, I glanced up. Jack was nowhere in sight and I didn't know how much time I had.

I grabbed the card for a closer look and tipped it to the light so I could see the name embossed on it.

Ryan Kubilik.

I committed the name to memory, but even as I did, I had a feeling I knew what I'd find when I did an Internet search for this Ryan guy.

He'd be dead, just like Bernard O'Banyon.

And I knew what that meant: though I couldn't imagine how or why, there was a connection between Jack and Marjorie. One that involved phony credit cards. And may have resulted in murder.

The thought soured the taste of the crème brûlée in my mouth. Lucky for me, I didn't let it stall me. I tucked the card back into the portfolio and slipped the portfolio back in place next to Jack's coffee cup just as both he and the waitress showed up.

I don't waste time on feeling guilty. But I'm not stupid, either. When Jack slid a look from me to the portfolio and back again, I knew enough to get a little nervous. I also knew not to let it show. In fact, I knew I'd been handed a once-in-a-lifetime opportunity, if not on a silver platter, than at least in a leather portfolio.

Have I mentioned that I looked stunning that night in a little black dress cut up to here and down to there? It was what I'd worn to my former fiancé's most recent engagement party, and I'd pulled it out especially for tonight's dinner to remind myself I was nobody's fool. Not even a teacher from a school that didn't exist.

I leaned forward, and this time, I was the one who made the move. Jack's left hand was on the table and I skimmed a finger lightly over it.

His eyes lit up. "I see you don't want to talk about President Garfield anymore."

I sparkled just enough to look cute without looking too anxious. "All that old stuff, it's all such a silly waste of time," I said, waving away the subject as inconsequential because, let's face it, I now had bigger fish to fry. "But I have been thinking about something we talked about back at the memorial once. You said you hoped Marjorie didn't spend her life scrimping and saving and never buying all the wonderful things she wanted because, in the end, the bills didn't matter as much as how she enjoyed her life."

I felt a thrill shiver over Jack's skin. I skipped my finger up his hand to his wrist and back down again. The smile he sent my way was hotter than the candlelight that flickered on the table between us.

"I was hoping . . ." I didn't do bashful well, but heck, I'd been dating for years, I could blush with the best of them, and I pulled out all the stops. "Marjorie was never one of my favorite people, but I've been thinking . . . and hoping . . . that someday, I could be like her." Even though I was lying through my teeth, I felt obligated to qualify the statement. Not that anyone near us heard or cared, but I couldn't stand the thought that someone might think I was referring to Marjorie's fashion sense, her awful perfume, or those nasty little head scarves of hers.

"Well, when it comes to her spending habits, anyway," I added, just to make things crystal clear. "She didn't let anything stand in the way of getting what she wanted. Somehow, even though she was just a retired librarian living on a fixed income, she managed to build her Garfield collection. I'd like to know how she did that. And I'd like to be able to do it, too. You know, buy the things I want. The things that would make me happy."

If I suspected it was my imagination that caused that spark to flare in Jack's eyes again, I was proved wrong when he moved like greased lightning and snatched my hand in his. His grip was a little too intimate to be just friendly. And too crushing to be taken as anything but a warning.

His smile, though, was as sweet as the crème brûlée, which had turned to a rock inside my stomach. "You're a great kid," he said, his voice as honeyed as the look in his eyes. "You're beautiful. You're sexy. You're smart. But a little advice here from someone a little bit older and wiser: don't be too smart for your own good."

The waitress showed up and Jack quickly dropped my hand. He scrawled a name across the bottom of the charge receipt and added a whopping tip. But then, he could afford to. He wasn't the one paying the bill.

I had added to my *never* list—

Never go to bed with a guy you don't trust.

Never go to bed with a guy who might be a murderer.

And never even think about having sex with a guy who uses a phony credit card to pay for dinner.

Disappointing, sure, but the evening wasn't a total bust. I'd learned something else about Jack: he was up to no good, all right, but something told me it wasn't the no good I thought he was up to.

I smiled when he pulled out my chair. I chatted and laughed when he walked me back to my car and we talked about how he'd come from Hammond, Indiana, some weekend soon so we could see each other again.

When we got to the Mustang, I stopped dead and the bag with my leftover filet in it slipped from my hands and splatted on the pavement.

The light of a nearby streetlamp glared against the message scrawled on my windshield in garish pink lipstick.

Pepper, it said, *you have to love ME.*

"You would be wise to exert an extreme amount of caution. As I have mentioned to you previously, the man who shot me—"

"Was a stalker. Yeah, yeah. I remember." When I got to the memorial the next Monday, I made the mistake of mentioning the Saturday night incident with my car and the cheap lipstick to the president. Now, I waved away his words of warning, and it was no wonder why.

After finding that message on the windshield of my car, I covered for the terror that snaked through me by making up a story to convince Jack it was nothing but a silly joke. That was all well and good until we said our good-byes and my overactive imagination spent the rest of the weekend constructing one frightening scenario after another. Hey, a single woman spends a lot of evenings at home, and a lot of those evenings, I'd spend watching old movies. Oh yeah, I'd seen them all: *Play Misty for Me*, *Misery*, (gulp!) *Fatal Attraction* . . .

My stalker-induced hysteria ranged from kidnapping

to murder—and everything in between. I was on edge. I was twitchy. I was so strung out from not sleeping I'd nearly forgotten to put on my mascara that morning.

Where had it all gotten me? Nowhere but Anxiety City, and I was more than ready for a break. "I'm being careful," I told the president and reminded myself.

"I trust you are locking your doors?"

It was a silly question so I didn't bother to answer. Besides, I was tired of being a marshmallow. With that in mind, I'd gotten to work early that morning and stopped at the administration building first thing. I was armed with a computer printout that listed the addresses and phone numbers of all the Ryan Kubiliks I could find. There were only three of them, but that was OK. That meant I had few phone calls to make.

"You know, that Guiteau fellow, the one who shot me . . ."

The president droned on, but I was so not in the mood for stalker talk. I picked up the phone on the desk in the memorial office and made my calls. As it turned out, the first Ryan I asked for was one-and-a-half and at day care. Not a likely candidate for a MasterCard account. With the second call, I hit pay dirt.

Feeling pretty smug, I thanked the lady on the other end of the line and hung up the phone. "He's dead," I said.

"Guiteau? Most certainly he's dead. He was hanged as a punishment for my murder."

"I'm not talking about Guiteau. I'm talking about the guy whose name was on Jack's credit card." I'd told the president about that when I got to the memorial that morning, too, and never let it be said that it's easy to explain credit cards to a man from the nineteenth century.

His brows dropped low over his eyes. "I once led an investigation of a gold scandal during the Grant Administration," he rumbled. "That was back in '69, and I am well aware that to you, that must seem a very long while ago. Still . . ." His blue eyes sparkled and his shoulders shot back. "When it comes to matters financial, I am sure I am still able to provide some sound advice. Shall we investigate?"

He didn't wait for me to answer. He was already floating up the spiral staircase. I followed in a more conventional way.

It helped that while I was in the administration building that morning, I'd scooped up Ella's extra set of keys, the ones that included the key to the ballroom. I unlocked the door, pulled it open, and stepped inside. It didn't take me long to find what I was looking for, but then, the people who hid it up there in the first place thought they never had to worry about someone discovering their secret.

Not until Marjorie, who had to know everything there was to know about President Garfield, his life, his family, and his memorial did some snooping in places she never should have been.

I was down on my knees, peering into the box I'd found tucked behind a marble column in the farthest, darkest corner of the ballroom, when the president leaned over my shoulder. "Explain this to me again. What are these things? And how do they work? What in the world are they for?"

I reached into the box and ran my hands through the dozens of credit cards in there. The names on every one of them, I was sure, belonged to dead people whose identities had been stolen. It was no wonder why. Phony credit cards were big business, and I didn't mean just for the people who would eventually get their hands on them and use them for shopping sprees they never had to pay for. My theory was that the people who manufactured the cards, then distributed and sold them—the people who were using the memorial as a drop-off and pickup point—were making the really big bucks.

I sat back on my heels and shook my head. "I guess Marjorie was right when she said she was on to a get-rich-quick scheme," I told the president. "Too bad she didn't know it was going to end up costing her life."

16

The first thing I did was tuck those bogus credit cards back where I'd found them. The second thing?

That was a no-brainer.

Murder or no murder, investigation or not, I was out of my league and I knew it. As soon as I got back downstairs, I called law enforcement.

It says something about those magic words *stolen identities and the credit cards to go with them* that the good guys arrived way sooner than should have been humanly possible. But then, I had a feeling some poor schlub flying from Chicago to Cleveland was bumped off the plane that morning.

Just so FBI Special Agent Scott Baskins could have that seat.

Surprised? Come on! I would have sooner shopped for my entire fall wardrobe at the local Goodwill than call Quinn, and Scott was the only other cop type I knew.

He arrived in a dark-colored Crown Victoria and

brought along a team from the local office. They were all clean-cut, grim-faced guys wearing navy blue suits, white shirts, and striped ties. I felt like I'd stepped into an alternative universe adaptation of *The Stepford Wives*.

"Pepper, it's good to see you again." Scott had a hand out to shake mine as soon as he was through the front door of the memorial. The gesture was friendly enough to make it clear that I was the one who'd contacted him and set the investigation in motion, but not so friendly that his fellow G-men would ever have suspected that after I was shot back in Chicago, Scott sent showy bouquets of flowers in all my favorite colors. Though we'd spoken on the phone a couple times since and talked about getting together, his busy schedule always prevented it and I didn't mind so much since I had been busy in my own way with Quinn at the time. I hadn't seen Scott since he was working undercover as a street person while he investigated the goings-on at the Windy City clinic, which snatched the homeless off the streets and used them as guinea pigs in psychic experiments. He made a better impression in his suit and tie than he ever had in his beat-up Army jacket and dirty sneakers.

He wasn't flashy by any means, but Scott wasn't a bad-looking guy. A little older than me, and a hair taller, he had eyes that were as brown and as warm as a teddy bear. Aside from that cordial first *hello*, he was as serious as a heart attack, but then, I suppose that went along with his job description. He walked around the memorial long enough to get the lay of the land and directed the other agents and a couple techie types upstairs to the ballroom so they could begin their work. That taken care of and one hand gently at the small of my back, he ushered me into the memorial office, where Ella and Jim were already waiting.

The office was small, there weren't enough chairs, and it was cramped. Scott didn't let little things like that distract him. He explained what he and the other agents would be doing, carefully outlined the cemetery's role in the process (which in case I need to point it out was pretty much "stay out of the way"), and had me go over everything I'd already told him on the phone. I did, starting from the day Ella asked me to help Marjorie plan the commemoration. Except for mentioning my chats with President Garfield, I didn't leave out a thing. I told him I was suspicious of Marjorie and all the spending she'd been doing. I admitted I was curious about her murder and that I'd talked to a few people concerning it.

In addition to using a digital recorder, Scott took notes as I spoke. He was efficient and very official, and he had an awfully big gun in a holster on his belt. I admit, I was pretty impressed by it all, not to mention just the teeniest bit intimidated; I told him about Jack, too, and about how I knew for a fact he'd turned that sign upstairs around once. I did not, however, elaborate on the circumstances.

"You think this Jack McArthur has something to do with the counterfeiting? Or the murder?" Scott asked.

Since I was being honest, I had to shrug. "I can't say for sure. I only know he lied about a whole bunch of stuff. He said he's from Hammond, Indiana, and that he teaches at Lafayette High School, but there's no school like that in Hammond, Indiana. He turned the sign around that one day, and he had a credit card with a dead man's name on it."

Scott consulted the notes he'd taken when we talked on the phone earlier. "And you saw the credit card with Ryan Kubilik's name on it when this Jackson McArthur took you out to dinner."

I wondered if it was some kind of federal crime to order a twelve-ounce filet and vanilla bean crème brûlée when it's being paid for via a stolen credit card. I gulped and nodded.

When Scott hooked his arm through mine and turned me away so Ella and Jim couldn't hear, I thought he was going to read me my rights. Instead, the smallest of smiles brightened his expression and he leaned close to say, "Which means you go out to dinner with guys who are visiting from out of town, right? Like me?"

Even before I had a chance to answer (and just for the record, I was all set to say *yes*), the office door swung open and Quinn Harrison walked in.

Scott and I were facing the door, standing next to each other with our arms entwined, and Quinn's as-green-and-as-cold-as-emeralds gaze sized up the situation.

Scott's teddy-bear-warm eyes scrutinized right back.

How they both made up their minds about each other so quickly, I don't know. Maybe it was a cop thing, like radar or mind reading or something. All I know is that when Scott disentangled himself from me so he could shake Quinn's hand, the gesture was cold, formal, and just the slightest bit confrontational—on both their parts.

Scott swung around to include Ella and Jim when he explained, "I asked Detective Harrison from the Cleveland Homicide Unit to join us. I thought it would be best if we cooperated with the local police. Just in case there's any connection between their murder case and our counterfeit credit cards."

Even though Scott wasn't holding on to me any longer, it didn't keep Quinn from glancing over at the place where his hand had recently been on my arm. "Connections, sure. They're important." He breezed past us, but the office being as tiny as it is, he could only go as far as the desk.

Jim and Ella were sitting in the only two chairs in the room, and as if they'd choreographed the move, they stood at the same time. They sidled around us and out the door, and Jim mumbled something about how if Agent Baskins needed them, they'd be outside. It was a nice cover. I think that with both a hard-charging federal agent and a big-headed cop in the room, Jim and Ella figured it was going to be tough to get their share of the oxygen.

I wasn't worried. A redhead always gets her share. Of everything. I was also so not in the mood for ego games. Scott and Quinn circled each other like cavemen trying to get the last juiciest bits of the saber-toothed tiger, and only too eager to escape the testosterone overdrive, I strolled behind the desk. "So what are your plans?" I asked.

"We're going to—"

"We've already—"

They answered at the same time, and both shot looks at me like it was somehow my fault.

"We're going to—" Scott said.

"We've already—" Quinn's words overlapped his.

I rolled my eyes. It was the only appropriate response. While I was at it, I sat down. If they were going to keep this up, we might be locked together in the office for who knew how long, and I might as well be comfortable.

Obviously, a dose of common sense was in order, and no one could bring that to a situation like a woman.

I looked at Scott. "Will you take away the phony credit cards?"

It wasn't my imagination. When he realized I'd picked him to speak first, his chin came up just a fraction of an inch and he slid Quinn a quick, sidelong look. "Too soon for that. The other agents are having a quick look around up in the ballroom right now. They're going to leave things exactly the way they found them, and we're going to stake out the memorial and wait to see who shows up for those credit cards. We're going to need your help, Pepper. You said that while you were looking into Ms. Klinker's murder—"

"You were looking into the murder? Oh, great!" Disgusted, Quinn threw his hands in the air, spun around, walked to the door, then rocketed back again. "How many times have I told you—"

"Pepper's given us some useful information." This was from Scott, and when he said it, I sat up and gave Quinn a look that clearly said, *I told you so.* "If it wasn't for her, we wouldn't have known about the identity thefts or the credit cards. It may have nothing to do with your case—"

"Of course it doesn't." Quinn crossed his arms over his chest. His shirt had so much starch in it, I swear I heard it crackle. Or maybe that was just his prickly personality making itself known. "Pepper should know better. Just like she should know to keep her nose out of police business."

"You two obviously know each other." It was the understatement of the year, but I guess I couldn't blame Scott. He was the kind of guy who liked all his ducks in a row. He glanced from Quinn to me and back again to Quinn. "You've worked with Pepper before?"

Quinn's smirk said it all, so he really didn't need to add, "I guess you could call it that."

Three cheers for Scott. Even if he read into the subtext of that one, he pretended like he didn't. Then again, maybe he was just a literal guy. "Then obviously, you know how helpful she can be. She certainly was invaluable back in Chicago when we made the case against that doctor who was defrauding the health insurers and killing his patients."

"Is that what you were doing in Chicago?" Needless to say, Quinn was looking at me when he asked this. "All you bothered to tell me was that you were in the wrong place at the wrong time."

"Because I knew this is exactly how you'd react." I leveled him with a look. Or at least I tried. Quinn is hardly the leveling kind. "I have every right to ask questions—"

"About Marjorie Klinker's murder? That's what you've

been up to, right? Investigating? Have you told Agent Baskins here that sometimes dead people help you out?"

"Of course they do." Scott all but came right out and said, *No duh!* "The way victims live their lives, who they knew, who they talked to, who they associated with . . . you know that's all important to an investigation, Detective Harrison. Pepper knows that, too. I'm sure that's why she finds out as much about the dead person as she can."

The smile Quinn shot my way was brittle. "Not exactly what I meant."

I hopped to my feet and slapped the desk, just for good measure. It wasn't nearly as satisfying as smacking that self-righteous smirk off Quinn's face, but for now, it would have to do. "What difference does any of that make?" I asked no one in particular. "All that matters now is what you're going to do"—I looked at Scott—"about the credit cards. And what you're going to do"—I glanced at Quinn—"about the murder."

"Well, the first thing I'm going to do is—"

They did it again, answered in unison, and this time, they used the same words. I swear, I heard a growl, I just wasn't sure which one of them it came from.

I was only too happy to play favorites. I looked at Scott, giving him the go-ahead to answer first.

"I've got my stuff in the car and I'm going to get it and change. I'm going to play tourist, and so are some of the other guys from the local office. You are going to be our official tour guide, Pepper, and you're going to let us know if anyone comes in who looks familiar. Like that Jack guy."

"Jack?" Quinn had missed that part of the conversation. Now, his eyebrows rose and his eyes narrowed. "Who's Jack?"

"Just some history teacher she went to dinner with." Scott threw off the comment so casually, I had no doubt it was designed to drive Quinn crazy. "We'll start hanging around today, and we're going to stay around until somebody comes to pick up those credit cards." A smile lit his expression. "I'm afraid it's going to be pretty hard to get rid of me, Pepper."

"Well, that's not such a bad thing, is it?" Oh yes, I said this in the perkiest of perky voices. The better to send Quinn up a wall. I knew it worked, too, when a muscle at the side of his jaw twitched. "And what are you going to do while the feds are doing all the real work, Detective Harrison?" I asked him.

There was that twitch again. But never let it be said that Quinn isn't cool under fire. "The first thing I'm going to do," he said, "is talk to you about your investigation." He twisted the last word so that it was as much of a mockery as he thought my detecting skills were. "Maybe you and your dead people can tell me—"

"Oh, I doubt that." I laughed. "It's just like you always say, I waste my time when I investigate. There's no way I've learned anything that could be the least bit useful to you. Now . . ." I went to the door, opened it, and put my hand on Scott's sleeve to escort him out. "I'll show you where you can get changed," I said.

"And this building, it closes at four, right?" He grinned. "Which means you're free for dinner tonight?"

We were already on our way out of the office, but I'm pretty sure Quinn heard me say, "I'd like that very much." I didn't bother to turn around to see what he thought of my response.

B y Thursday of that week, we were still waiting for something to happen, but I wasn't complaining. That meant Scott was still in town, and on Monday, Tuesday, and Wednesday evenings, I went out with him. OK, so he wasn't a ball of fire, at least not when he wasn't on the job. But he was polite and interesting, and occasionally, even funny. He took me to one really nice restaurant in my own Little Italy neighborhood one night, to an Indians game the next, and on Wednesday, to a dive bar I never would have had the nerve to walk into on my own that turned out to be a whole lot of fun, even if the country music on the jukebox was so loud we could barely hear each other talk. Every place we went, Scott paid for everything—and with a credit card that actually had his name on it.

I should know, because one time when he left to use the men's room, I checked.

Other than the fact that I was having a good time, I felt safe with Scott around. I mean, come on, the guy had been trained by the government. I had three glorious days of not worrying about my stalker, at least not until I got home each night, double-checked my windows and my door locks, pulled the miniblinds shut, and closed my curtains.

There were no more messages scrawled on my windshield or anywhere else, no more gifts of flowers or cheap chocolates, and I breathed a sigh of relief and convinced myself that Mr. Doughboy had seen me and Scott together and that he'd gotten a glimpse of that really big gun Scott carried at all times. It had scared him away. Yeah, that's what happened. And I would never see hide nor hair of my stalker again.

Denial is a wonderful thing.

I actually might have enjoyed the euphoria that went along with it, if not for the fact that the longer we waited for something to happen at the memorial, the more on edge everyone got. There were only so many times the dozen or so federal agents who were hanging around the place could go upstairs to the balcony and downstairs to the crypt, only so many questions they could ask, and only so long I could treat them like they were tourists I'd never seen before and I was telling them all about the president and his memorial for the first time.

This undercover stakeout stuff is not for sissies.

Every time I was upstairs, I checked to make sure that sign was turned over, just like it had been the last time Jack was in the memorial. Still, nothing happened.

I guess the feds were used to this sort of waiting game. They took turns, sometimes waiting in the cars parked in various and sundry places around the cemetery where they could see but not be seen, and sometimes playing the role of memorial visitors. A couple days into it, and I already knew how each one took his coffee, what they mostly ordered for lunch (tuna salad on white toast, go figure), and that Scott had somehow made it clear to them that while he was fully prepared to cooperate with the local authorities, Quinn and his detectives—who had also made the memorial their home-away-from-home in the hopes that the two cases were going to tie in and wrap up together—were to be treated pretty much like enemy combatants. If this was what cooperation looked like, I was glad a private investigator worked alone.

Needless to say, with all this going on, the president was grumpier than ever.

I was down in the crypt with no one undercover (or otherwise) around, and he cornered me. "I told you I cannot abide commotion, and this is the way you honor my request? There are more people here than ever disturbing my peace. I have a cabinet meeting this afternoon and—"

I heard the front door open, and since all the agents and the various detectives were in place, I knew it was an actual visitor. I was all set to excuse myself so I could play tour guide for real when Jeremiah Stone popped up out of nowhere.

As always, he tapped the pile of papers he was carrying. "Mr. President . . ."

"Will you sign those things already?" I wailed, and before the president could remind me that I was out of line talking to him like that, I hightailed it out of there.

I got upstairs just in time to see a familiar man head up the winding staircase toward the second floor. I signaled Scott, who was in the rotunda with a sketchbook and a pencil, pretending to be an artist drawing the statue of the president.

"Him." I mouthed the word, pointing up the stairs.

Scott nodded his understanding and ducked into the office, the better to send out a message to all those agents wearing earbuds that made them look like they were listening to their iPods. They were to wait for the signal, then close in.

I guess it was that whole criminal justice mumbo-jumbo thing at work again, because though I didn't think Quinn was anywhere nearby, he caught on that something was up. He'd been in the rotunda, too, looking at a display of historic photographs and he oh so casually positioned himself at the bottom of the staircase, his gun out and behind his back.

"You're not going to get in the way, are you?" he asked me.

I batted my eyelashes in a way that was completely unworthy of me, but necessary in a situation like this. "Scott doesn't think I get in the way."

"Scott . . ." Quinn tossed a look toward the office, where Scott was on the phone, quietly giving instructions to the units outside. "Scott is a jackass."

"He happens to be very nice."

"And you know this how?" Quinn tipped his head, listening for any sounds from upstairs, and when there

weren't any, he gave me that probing look of his, the one
that had brought many a bad guy to his knees.

I was impervious. "We've been out."

"Are you sleeping with him?"

"Is it any of your business?"

"We got the go!" Scott said, racing out of the office and
taking the steps two at a time.

Quinn hurried up after him.

And me?

I stayed right there on the first floor. Not that I was
worried about getting in the way. That would be the day.
And not that I wasn't dying to find out what was going on
up there, either. But I wasn't about to get between Quinn
and Scott in the middle of a bust—not when they both had
guns in their hands. In fact, I ducked into the office, which
meant I had a ringside seat when they came back down,
escorting a man whose hands were handcuffed behind his
back. It was the pudgy Eastern European guy with the
beard, the one who'd been in the memorial the last time
Jack was there.

I didn't see Scott that evening. But then, I think he was
busy grilling the pudgy guy. The next morning while
I was restocking the memorial brochures in the plastic
holder outside the rotunda, he showed up. He was so focused on his case, he didn't even bother with small talk.

"I spent most of last night with your friend, Detective
Harrison," he said.

I was going to say that I'd done the same thing on a
whole bunch of nights, but something told me Scott and
Quinn weren't doing what Quinn and I used to do, so
there didn't seem to be much point.

I sized him up and decided maybe we weren't talking
about the case after all. Until I knew for sure, I put my

game face on. "You don't look all that happy about it," I said, ever observant.

"Harrison . . ." He tossed off the name along with what was almost an eye roll. "Harrison is a jackass."

I nudged the brochures one final time to straighten them, then turned to give Scott my full attention. "Can't argue with you there," I said, but surprise, surprise—no sooner had the words left my mouth than I felt guilty. Let's face it, there was a time I liked Quinn. A whole lot. "He used to be . . ." I couldn't exactly say Quinn was nice, but then, it was hard to say exactly what he was or exactly what we were to each other. It was hard to put my finger on the adjectives that would describe him or our relationship and not include words like *hot*, *sexy*, or *so good in bed, he made my toes curl*. I stuck with the tried and true. "He used to be very nice."

"And you know this how?" Scott crossed his arms over his chest, and the coat of his navy suit rode up and exposed his gun. I don't think he meant the motion to be intimidating, but he had the whole federal agent mojo going on.

I may not have been impervious, but I could pretend with the best of them. My voice was smooth and my expression was blank when I tossed off that most noncommittal of phrases, "We used to date."

"Are you sleeping with him?"

"Is it any of your business?"

He didn't expect me to be so honest. Or so assertive. He caved, but then, I'd seen him in action (no, not when we collared our perp up in the ballroom, on those three dates!). Scott had the whole ubercop personality down pat. That included not wanting to get too personal, and talking about emotions . . . well, that was way too personal.

Since he didn't want to go there, and I wasn't feeling

much like sharing the intimate details of my life with a man I barely knew, I asked the question that had been bugging me all night. "The guy you arrested—"

"Viktor Patankin."

"Patankin. Is he the one who killed Marjorie?"

Obviously more comfortable now that we were talking murder and mayhem, Scott cocked his head, inviting me to go into the office with him. He didn't say another word until we were inside and out of sight and hearing range of anyone who might wander into the memorial. "Patankin claims he's just the middleman."

"For the counterfeited credit cards."

His nod said it all.

"Which doesn't eliminate him as a suspect in the murder. Marjorie had a phony credit card, remember. She was using it to buy her Garfield junk. Even though she wasn't supposed to be up there, she must have found the cards up in the ballroom and scooped one up for her own use. That's why she told Ray she had a get-rich-quick scheme." I had filled Scott in on all these details when he arrived in Cleveland. I'd even turned over the credit card Ray had stolen from Marjorie's and given to me, so he knew exactly what I was talking about.

"She wasn't making it up. She had that card. And she could have gotten her hands on lots more of them. That's why she told Ray she was wrong about the get-rich-quick scheme, right?" Scott didn't contradict me, so I went right on. "But then she saw that she was getting nowhere with Ray and she decided to keep the credit card secret to herself. But if Patankin found out she took the card and that she knew about the cache of them upstairs, he would have been plenty pissed. He could have killed her. That would explain everything."

It really wouldn't. I knew it even as the words left my mouth.

It wouldn't explain the personal Garfield item Nick discussed selling to Ted Studebaker.

It wouldn't explain crazy Gloria Henninger, the neighbor who wanted to see Marjorie dead.

It wouldn't explain Jack and what he was doing hanging around the memorial and how he was connected to Patankin and that sign up in the stairway.

But it would be a start.

Or not.

The *or not* part plonked down on me like a ton of bricks when Scott shook his head. "Unfortunately, it doesn't appear that things are that easy. Patankin told us he was out of the country when Ms. Klinker was killed. Your friend . . ." He tiptoed back into personal territory for a nanosecond, but drawn by the siren song of his case, he shook himself back to reality. "Detective Harrison spent the better part of last night verifying Patankin's alibi for the day of the murder. He said he was in Toronto picking up another shipment of counterfeit cards. We're still checking into that part of the story, but Harrison talked to Customs this morning and they confirm the rest of it. Patankin really was in Canada. He couldn't have killed Ms. Klinker."

"Then who—?"

Scott was carrying a leather portfolio. He flipped it open, pulled out a single sheet of paper, and handed me a sketch of a man.

"It's Jack," I said, looking at Scott in wonder. "How did you—"

"Patankin is a citizen of Uzbekistan and he's not thrilled about the prospect of going back there. He's decided to cooperate and he's singing like a bird. Oh, how I love when that happens!" He allowed himself the smallest of smiles. "He swears he's just the middleman, and this guy . . ." Scott tapped a finger to Jack's nose. "He's the mastermind of the counterfeiting operation."

"Jack?" I studied the drawing again. There was no mistaking the face; Patankin had described Jack to a tee. The hair was right. The eyes were perfect. His mouth was just the way I remembered it. Except that when I remembered it, I remembered him kissing me.

"Nice-looking guy." As if he could read my mind, Scott tossed out, "I can see why you were attracted to him."

"Who says I was?"

"You didn't need to."

"It doesn't really count if he's a bad guy."

"I'm glad to hear that."

I'd suspected that Jack was up to no good, so none of this was much of a surprise. It was kind of shocking, though, to hear he was some kind of Dr. Evil. I did my best to stay focused. "Did this Patankin guy tell you where to find Jack?" I asked.

"Jack . . ." Scott pulled out another paper from the portfolio. This one featured a small color photo of Jack in one corner and an official-looking insignia in the other. I read the printing beneath the symbol. "Interpol?"

Scott's nod was barely perceptible. "One of our agents recognized him from the sketch. That's how we caught on to who he really is. Your friend Jack has quite a reputation." He pointed to the information below Jack's photo. "His real name is Jonathan Bryce-Conway. He's a Brit, and he's wanted in just about every country you can name."

"Jack?" OK, I was repeating myself, and it was annoying, but it wasn't exactly easy to wrap my brain around Scott's information. "I knew he was up to something," I said, "but—"

"When it comes to crime, he's one of the superstars. I can't wait to get my hands on this guy."

"But you've got Patankin. And the credit cards. How are you—"

Scott didn't say a word. He didn't have to. The way his eyes glittered told me everything I needed to know.

"Jack doesn't know you arrested Patankin. And you were careful to make sure the media didn't find out. You're not going to tell anyone now, right?"

He nodded.

"Which means you're hoping Jack shows back up here, either looking for Patankin or those credit cards. And when he does—"

Like I said, Scott is pretty low-key. Except when it comes to his job. Just the prospect of arresting Jack practically made him salivate.

17

I was glad the feds cleared up the phony credit card case. Honest. Of course, Ella and Jim couldn't have agreed more. Seeing as how they're both big-time cemetery geeks, the fact that the memorial was being used by the crooks as a drop-off and pickup point didn't sit well with them. As much of a cemetery fan as I'm not, I can't say I blamed them. Even though I knew better than anyone that they didn't all deserve it, there is a certain amount of respect we owe the dead. The memorial as a stash house . . . that went above and beyond, even in my book.

Needless to say, the president was thrilled to have that part of the "commotion" explained. He was convinced that now that the phony cards were taken care of, things would get back to as normal as they can be when you're dead and running the country as you would have more than a hundred years ago from the inside of a tomb you can't leave without poofing into nothingness.

Have I mentioned how the life of a PI to the dead

can get complicated? In my world, all that made perfect sense.

But none of it helped me much. I mean, not with Marjorie's case. Sure, I could have backed out gracefully. Thanks to Patankin, who was talking up a storm in the hopes of staying in a nice, cushy federal pen like the one my dad was in rather than the nasty place that was waiting for him back home, the feds had plenty of new information to go on; they'd made huge strides in cracking the international counterfeiting ring.

At the risk of sounding too full of myself, let's face it: they couldn't have done it without me. I was something of a heroine and I knew it, and that meant I could throw in the towel without losing face.

But I still didn't know who killed Marjorie, and truth be told, it was driving me nuts. Besides, Quinn was now on to the fact that I was conducting my own investigation into Marjorie's murder, and I knew how his devious little brain worked. He was going to try doubly hard to solve the case, just to beat me to the punch.

And there was no way I was going to let that happen.

With that in mind, I closed up the memorial at four that Friday and went over to the administration building. It's not like I'm a hidebound traditionalist or anything, but on previous cases, I had done some of my best thinking back in my office behind my own desk. It was where I sat now, scribbling the names of my remaining suspects across the top of a legal pad.

Jack. Er . . . excuse me . . . Jonathan Bryce-Conway.

Nick Klinker.

Ted Studebaker.

Gloria Henninger.

As for motives . . .

I added an entry below each of their names.

Jack could have known Marjorie took the credit card,

and I guess if you're a criminal mastermind, that kind of thing pisses you off.

Nick and Ted were in cahoots about something, and if it was something Marjorie didn't agree with, either one of them (or both) could have had a reason to kill her.

Gloria was crazy, and as I'd learned in the course of my PI career, crazy people don't really need a motive. Then again, she did have that statue staring little Sunshine in the face every time the pug went outside for a potty break. In Gloria's book, I bet that was motive enough.

That's as far as I got when there was a knock on my office door and Ella popped in. I turned the legal pad over on my desk.

"I'm so glad you're still here," she said. As is typical of the weather in Cleveland in the fall, it was freezing the day I went out to Chagrin Falls to see Ted Studebaker, and now it was hotter than blazes again. Ella looked a little like a pumpkin in her orange flowing skirt and matching top. She'd been on pins and needles ever since the feds set up the stakeout at the memorial and she hadn't come down from the adrenaline high. Standing just inside my office door, she fidgeted with the string of earth-colored beads she wore around her neck.

"I didn't want to go to Jim with this," she said. "Even though I probably should. And I will. I mean, of course I will. Eventually. But you've been such a help when it comes to things like this, Pepper, I wanted to let you know about it first and see what you think. I'm pretty sure Jim won't mind. After all, he agrees with me that you're just amazing. He said it himself just this afternoon when we were talking. I couldn't be more proud of you if you were one of my own girls. I mean, just look at the way you helped out the FBI! Sometimes I think you're some kind of superhero in disguise."

I wouldn't go that far, but it was nice to be appreciated.

Whatever Ella was going to ask of me, I was more inclined to do it now than I was when she walked into my office. Anybody else, I would have accused of thinking I was shallow and playing to my weakness. Ella? Not so much. Ella didn't have a mean-spirited bone in her body.

"What do you need?" I asked.

She scrunched up her face. "I can't believe it completely slipped my mind, but of course, it did. With everything that's been going on around here lately, it's hard to imagine any of us are keeping anything straight. But there I was, sitting in my office just a little bit ago, finishing up the fall schedule of seminars and tours, and that's when I remembered."

Just in case my blank expression didn't say it all, I asked, "Remembered what?"

Ella threw her hands in the air. Her left arm was loaded with beaded bracelets that matched her necklace and they jangled when they clanked together. "The volunteers' lockers, of course."

I breathed what I hoped didn't look like too big a sigh of relief. This was going to be easy and it involved absolutely no effort on my part except to remind her, "The volunteers don't have lockers anymore."

"Of course." Her smile was shaky. "You were in on the meeting when we decided we would no longer provide lockers to the volunteers. Like Jim said then, it's too much of a liability from a security standpoint, what with having to keep an eye on their personal possessions and then having the volunteers going up and down those steps into the basement. A lot of them aren't as young as they used to be, you know, and I'd hate to think that someone might slip and fall. And it's not like the old days when most of our volunteers lived right in the neighborhood and walked to work. Back then, they needed a place to store umbrellas and coats and things. Now most of our volunteers live outside the area, and they drive here to the cemetery. They leave a lot of their stuff in their cars, and their coats, of course, get hung in the main coatroom off the reception area. You remember how Jim thought that was such a good idea. Jennine can see the coatroom, right from her desk, and we don't have to worry about anything getting misplaced or stolen."

I nodded, and waited for more, but even before Ella said it, a spark ignited inside my brain. Like that idea was the rocket that propelled me, I rose to my feet. "But Marjorie was a volunteer for a long time. That means—"

"She still had her locker."

We finished the thought in unison.

A world of possibilities spun through my head, but before I could get them in any sort of order, Ella continued. "She was told not to use it anymore, but you know how Marjorie could be. She thought she was special and she didn't have to follow the rules like everyone else. I just thought of it a bit ago, the locker I mean, and I went downstairs to check and . . ."

"You found something?" My spirits soared to the ceiling. If the clue I needed to wrap up the case was under my nose all this time, I'd give myself a mental slap—but not until I flaunted my success in front of Quinn. I was moving toward the door even before I realized it and I only stopped when Ella put a hand on my arm.

"I didn't find anything. Not exactly," she said. "I mean, I didn't even look inside the locker. I just came right up here to get you."

"Because . . . ?"

She led the way. "Come on. I'll show you."

I hate basements. They're mostly damp and stinky, and the dark and the quiet along with the moldy smells freak me out. This is especially true at Garden View, where the basement of the administration building is as old as the cemetery itself and had once (back in the olden days) been used to store bodies in the winter when the gravedigger's shovels couldn't penetrate the frozen ground.

Naturally, I wasn't at all sorry when Jim decided to eliminate the locker room down there. It meant I never had a reason to go into the basement.

Except, of course, when Ella had a hold of my arm and was leading the way.

We got to the door outside what used to be the volunteer locker room and she drew in a calming breath. "You ready?" she asked.

"I'm not sure. If there's a body, or—"

"Oh, it's nothing like that," she said. She pushed open the door and flicked on the overhead fluorescent lights.

It took a moment for my eyes to adjust to the dull light. In the recent past, the locker room had been used for storage, and against the wall to my right, there were boxes piled on the tan linoleum floor. At the far, shadowy end of the room was a door that I knew opened up to stone steps that led right into the cemetery. Directly across from the door were two rows of gray metal lockers with a wooden bench between them.

"That's Marjorie's," Ella said, pointing to the left, all the way down at the end of the row and farthest from the door. "It was just like that when I came down here."

"Just like . . ." I closed the distance between the door and locker, taking a closer look. "It was open? It was—?"

Ella nodded.

I stood in front of the locker. Not only was it opened, the lock had been forced, and it didn't take a genius detective to figure that out. The door near the lock was smashed and dented.

The contents of the locker itself looked as if they'd been

put through a blender. "Ransacked," I mumbled. "Just like Marjorie's house."

"What do you suppose they took?"

I'd been so busy examining the locker, I hadn't realized Ella had crossed the room and was standing right in back of me. When she spoke, I jumped.

"Sorry." She patted my arm and leaned forward. "What do you suppose they took?"

I shrugged. "If something's missing, we can't possibly know what it is." I was tall enough to see up on the top shelf of the locker. "Head scarves," I said, making a face as I plucked a pile of the nasty, filmy things out of the locker and handed them to Ella. "Our thief didn't take them, so whoever it was, he had better taste than Marjorie."

"That's mean, Pepper," Ella scolded, but I didn't have to turn around to know she was smiling when she said it.

I poked through the rest of the locker. There was a ratty sweater hanging from the hook on the door, and in the main body of the locker, one of a pair of battered black loafers, an extra bottle of that gag-in-the-mouth gardenia perfume Marjorie always wore, and a pair of black polyester pants. The seam at the crotch was ripped. "There's nothing but junk in here," I said, stepping back to get an overall look and maybe a feel for what somebody could have been after. "There sure isn't anything worth taking. Or is there?"

From where I was standing, the light reflected against something on the top shelf, all the way in the back that had been hidden by the scarves. I reached a hand in, and slid out a pile of credit cards.

"Holy—!" I counted them below my breath. "Six more," I said, and I spread them out like a hand of cards to show Ella. "And all with different names on them. So Marjorie really did have a get-rich-quick scheme. I bet she was planning on using these babies little by little, and thinking that if she did, no one would ever trace them. Whatever our thief was looking for, it wasn't these."

"Which means . . ."

Ella had been in on all the same meetings with the FBI and the local cops that I'd taken part in, but I couldn't blame her for thinking like a civilian. She'd never had to deal with the criminal mind before. "It means that whoever broke into Marjorie's locker, it probably wasn't Jack." I didn't need to fill her in on the details. Because of those meetings, she knew (almost) all about Jack. "If he broke into the locker, he would have taken any cards he found. He'd have to be thorough. Any loose ends might lead right back to him."

"Is that a good thing or a bad thing?"

This, I had to think about. I was relieved to think that maybe Jack wasn't the killer after all. I mean, the thought of kissing a guy who'd just recently tossed a woman over a balcony railing was enough to make anybody shudder.

But I still didn't have all the answers I was looking for, and not having them didn't sit well with me.

"I don't know," I admitted.

"But you're going to find out, right? We need to get things back to normal around here, Pepper. A murder in the cemetery is bad for business. People are afraid to even come visit their loved ones. We need closure." The look in Ella's eyes was so hopeful, how could I possibly let her down?

I n keeping with my promise to Ella, I did something I never, ever do except in the direst emergencies: I went into work on the weekend.

For one thing, there was that whole deal about how the detecting part of my brain worked better when I was in my own office.

For another, I wasn't kidding when I said that the murder and the stakeout had kept us all on our toes. It's not like I'm a cemetery whirlwind, but I do have work to do. And I was way, way behind on it all. Ella was nearly done with that fall schedule of hers, and she'd been bugging me about how many tours I had planned. It was early September. I had to get hopping.

My final reason for going into the office on Saturday should come as no surprise. Now that Scott was knee-deep in his case, we were talking on the phone, but he'd been busy, and we hadn't been able to hang out together. Staying at home—alone—and risking the chance of Mr. Doughboy showing up at my apartment was not my idea of a good time. Even on the weekends, Garden View is fairly busy. After all, it's never a good day to die, and most Saturdays, families come in to buy plots for their recently departed loved ones. Unlike a certain president, I was grateful for the commotion. With people coming and going, I felt safe. Since I didn't have to worry about stalker boy, I could concentrate on my case.

That was what I was doing. Or at least it was what I was trying to do. Too bad my brain was stuck in a loop that went something like this:

Jack, Nick, Ted, Gloria, Ray, Doris.

Then it started all over again.

I was getting nowhere, and it was making me crazy. I'd brought my lunch and I'd just decided to step outside so I could sit at the picnic table behind the administration building. Maybe a little fresh air and sunshine would work wonders on my fact-clogged brain. I was headed out there, just passing the steps that led down to the basement, when I heard a noise.

I knew better than to go down there alone. But I'm not a detective for nothing. (I mean, I am since the whole Gift thing that got me into it in the first place wasn't my choice.

But even on my own and if I didn't have this dumb Gift, I'd still be plenty curious. And have I mentioned plenty anxious to solve the case before Quinn did?)

With that in mind, I looked around for a likely weapon and grabbed the one and only thing I could find, a laser pointer Jim had recently used for a presentation to the Board of Trustees and had left out on the credenza in the reception area. If there was an assailant down there, I was ready. Maybe I couldn't bean him with the pointer, but I could at least blind him long enough to run away.

Since it was Saturday and I wasn't officially on the clock, I hadn't been too worried about what to wear that day. Of course I still looked like a million bucks, but I was a million bucks in skinny jeans, an emerald green T-shirt, and sneakers. Good thing, too. Sneakers don't make noise on steps.

I was at the bottom of those steps, holding my breath and wondering what to do next, when I saw that the door into the old locker room was opened a crack. I knew that wasn't the way Ella and I had left it the night before. I crept closer.

And heard another noise.

It sounded like a muffled gasp, and I wondered if our burglar had caught some other employee by surprise and was holding that person hostage. Or worse. Just in case I needed it, I flicked on the laser and charged into the locker room.

If I had been a little less enthusiastic and a little more careful, I wouldn't have interrupted Ray and Doris doing . . . well, what it was they were doing.

"Ew!" I jumped back and squeezed my eyes shut, the better to let Doris get up from Ray's lap, where she was sitting with her legs sprawled on either side of him and her blouse unbuttoned. I heard shuffling and waited what I thought was an appropriate amount of time before I dared to open my eyes again. By that time, Doris was standing next to Ray. They were holding hands and smiling like lovestruck teenagers.

"What's the matter, kid?" Ray asked. "You've never seen two people canoodling?"

"I've never seen . . . I never want to see . . . You're too old for sex!" I wailed. When I shuddered, the light of the laser pointer did a jitterbug across the wall.

Doris and Ray laughed.

"Never too old," Ray said. He slipped one arm around Doris's shoulders and gave her a hug. "Thanks to that little blue pill you hear so much about, I'm never going to be too old."

"And you two? . . . Together? . . . Here at the cemetery . . ." I am anything but straightlaced when it comes to sex, but I couldn't find my voice.

My embarrassment didn't faze Doris in the least. She smoothed her little old lady black skirt into place and carefully buttoned her blouse. "You're not going to tell Ella, are you? She's such a nice lady, and I love her dearly, but somehow, I don't think she'd approve. Then again, we are volunteers. It's not like we're being paid and we need to be accountable for every minute we're here."

"Not to worry." I congratulated myself for stringing together three coherent words and flopped down on the bench where Ray and Doris had just been—

I stood up again.

"I'm not going to tell Ella. I wouldn't even know where to begin." I glanced around the gloomy locker room. "There's got to be a better place for you two to . . ." I searched for the right words and decided on, "Get together. It's depressing down here. And anybody could walk in on you."

As if he were the teenage boy and I were the angry parent, Ray hung his head. "Well, nobody ever comes into the locker room anymore. That's why we figured we'd be all right. Besides, we've never done it down here before, but we just couldn't wait, you know?"

I did. I didn't want to discuss it. Or think about it. Or think about thinking about it. Murder was a far more acceptable subject than old people sex. I crossed my arms over my chest. The laser pointer made a zigzag pattern against the far wall. "Hey, while you were down here, you didn't see anything unusual, did you?"

Doris giggled. "We weren't looking for anything. We weren't looking at anything. Anything but each other's eyes."

Their sighs overlapped.

I stayed strong. "Somebody has been down here," I told them. "And just recently, I think." It wasn't a warning because, really, what they did and where they did it weren't really any of my business, but I hoped they appreciated the subtle advice. "Ella and I were down here just yesterday, and when we were, we saw that somebody else had been down here, too. We found something interesting."

Ray's expression sobered. He took a step in my direction. "You mean something that relates to Marjorie's murder?"

I reminded myself that, though they weren't on my short list, I had considered both Ray and Doris as my culprits. Maybe I'd need my laser pointer after all. I clutched it tightly in one hand. "You didn't like her," I said, looking at both Ray and Doris because, of course, it applied to both of them. "Ray, you hated Marjorie because she played you for a sucker. And Doris, I'll bet you were jealous."

She made a pish-tush sort of sound. "Marjorie was the one who was jealous of me," she insisted. She looked at Ray, her eyes glistening with mischief. "After all, I've got the hot hunk of a boyfriend she always wanted. That's why she was so mean to me all the time. She knew Ray didn't love her. She knew he was only spending time with her because she was leading him on about the money. Yes, I was angry that she took up so much of Ray's time. But as you can see, Ray and I have worked that out, and I came out the winner."

"But the day Marjorie was killed, you were both in the cemetery, and when I saw you that morning before I headed over to the memorial, you both looked a little guilty and a little flustered. Because . . ." If I wasn't supposed to be a professional detective, I would have slapped my forehead. "I saw the two of you coming out of the copy room. You were doing . . ." I made a funny little waving gesture toward the bench. It was better than actually saying the words. "You were doing up there what you were just doing down here."

"Not exactly," Ray corrected me. "The copy room . . . that's too public. You know, too much of a risk. But we were getting a few smooches in." He grinned at Doris. "Right, honeybun?"

Doris hurried forward to put a hand on my shoulder to console me. "So you see, Pepper, we couldn't have killed Marjorie. I'm sorry to disappoint you." I've got to say, I had to love a woman who apologized for not being a murderer. "I know you'd like to get to the bottom of the mystery, but it couldn't have possibly been either me or Ray. We were busy. You know, together."

Now that we'd cleared all that up, there didn't seem to be anything else to say. Doris was still twinkling like a prom queen, but Ray must have suddenly realized just how awkward the situation was. He shifted from foot to foot. "You think we should all go upstairs together? You know, so we don't look too suspicious?"

"That's probably a good idea. That way, if anybody asks, we can tell them we were down here checking on the envelope supply or something. Only, Ray . . ." Honest, I just couldn't bring myself to say it. I touched the light of the laser pointer ever so briefly to Ray's fly. "You might want to zip your pants first."

18

That was enough excitement for one day. All the rest of that Saturday, I kept my head down and my nose to the grindstone, for once concentrating on cemetery business because when I even did so much as let my brain tippy-toe toward my case . . .

That image burned in my brain, the one of Ray and Doris together? That was just too freakin' creepy for words.

Doing my best to keep the memories to a minimum, I checked and rechecked my fall tour schedule and got all the information typed up and put on Ella's desk so she'd find it first thing Monday morning when she came in. While I was at it, I remembered that she'd been bugging me about writing an article for the Garden View employee newsletter about what it was like to be the one-and-only full-time tour guide in so famous a place. I, predictably, had been stalling. Not to mention dodging and overlooking. Desperate to keep busy, I pulled out all the stops and worked on the article, too, and though it was mostly a lot of hooey about what an honor it was to spend my days among the famous and the dead, I knew it would thrill Ella no end. Not to mention get her off my back.

By the time I had finished everything, locked up my office, and stepped out in the hallway, I realized it was after five and that even Jennine was gone for the day. It was quiet in the administration building. Too quiet. Sure, there were federal agents staked out all around the president's memorial waiting to waylay Jack if he showed, but that didn't do me a whole bunch of good. It was time for me to head home and lock myself in the safety of my apartment.

I would have done it, too, if I hadn't heard another noise from down in the basement.

Believe me, I'd learned my lesson. Even before I started down the steps, I knew I wasn't going to look. All I wanted to do was remind Doris and Ray to lock up when they were done doing what they were doing.

With that in mind, I paused outside the door to the locker room. I heard no grunting. No sighing. No huffing and puffing. Since that was what I was expecting, I dared to take the smallest of peeks. Good thing I had those sneakers on and hadn't made any noise coming down the steps. I saw Jack McArthur looking through Marjorie's locker long before he saw me.

The feds had already come to get the credit cards Ella and I found the day before, but hey, when the moment is right, I'm all about drama. I reached into my purse and pulled out a few of my own credit cards, just so I could wave them in the air when I sauntered into the room and said, "Is this what you're looking for?"

Jack must have had nerves of steel; he never flinched. But then, I guess a criminal mastermind is made of sterner stuff than ordinary people.

His gaze flickered from me to the cards in my hand. "Where did you find those?"

"Oh, come on!" I made sure I smiled. Like it was funny. Like being alone with him didn't scare me and like I hadn't taken the time as I stood there outside the door to call the feds over at the memorial. Hey, I'm not a complete moron!

Just like they asked me to, I did my best to stall Jack. The way to do that, I knew, was to keep him talking. "You know exactly where the cards were. No, wait! You didn't know where they were, did you? That's why you've been looking for them. First in Marjorie's house. Now here in her locker. It was the locker," I said, like it was a nobrainer, and slipped the cards into my pocket before he could get too close a look at them and realize they weren't part of his phony-baloney stash. "Too bad I got to them first."

His blue eyes glittered, even in the miserable locker room lighting. "You're amazing. Have I told you that?"

"So many men have." I tossed off the compliment with a shrug.

He stepped closer. "What else do you know?"

"Everything." Sure it was an out-and-out lie. But as long as I was stalling, I was hoping to egg him on into filling in the blanks of my investigation. "I know you're not a history teacher, but then, I've known that practically from the beginning. Before you say you teach at Lafayette High School in Hammond, Indiana, you really should check to see that there's a school by that name in that city."

He was as smooth as a pint of Ben and Jerry's Karamel Sutra ice cream. "I don't know another woman in the world who would have checked." He gave me a quick bow. "My compliments. You're as smart as you are beautiful."

"And I've got a really good bullshit detector."

Another smile. If the whole criminal genius thing didn't work out, the guy could do toothpaste ads. "Is there anything else I should know you know?"

"You mean about the rest of the phony credit cards? The ones in the president's memorial?"

His eyebrows rose the slightest bit. One corner of his mouth lifted into what was almost a smile. Call me egotistical (and who could?), but I actually think I'd just impressed him.

"That's where Marjorie got the credit cards," I said. He knew it. I knew it. But it didn't hurt to run it all by him, just in case some of my information was off target. "It wasn't this newest batch, either, because this newest batch . . . . well, you'll find out what happened to them soon enough. The ones Marjorie took were from an older cache of cards. She found them and she was using them to feed her Garfield habit. But what, there's some kind of system of checks and balances for phony credit cards? Well, there must be. Because you found out that there were a few cards missing. The trick was, you needed to figure out who took them. At first, you thought it might be me, but let's face it, if I had unlimited access to unlimited spending, I would not still be working here at Garden View, and you saw that right from the start. Marjorie was the only other likely candidate, and she did spend all her time at the memorial. I helped you figure out that part of the puzzle when you asked about Marjorie's spending habits and I told you about her Garfield sprees, right?"

I didn't wait for him to answer. There was plenty more I wanted to know and time was running out. The cemetery isn't all that big, and the feds can drive hard and fast, even when they're trying to be sneaky. "There was no sign of the missing cards anywhere in the memorial so you ransacked Marjorie's house looking for them. No dice. That's why you're looking here now. You've checked everywhere else. How did you find out about the locker in the first place? We just remembered it yesterday."

He shrugged like it was no big deal. "I heard a rumor."

I wondered which of the cemetery employees he'd charmed like he'd tried to charm me. I wondered if that was the same way he'd managed to get a key to the ballroom. While I was at it, I wondered if whoever that employee was, if he'd kissed her, too. Maybe that's what made me testy because, while I was on a roll, I figured I might as well pull out all the stops. "I also know you can drop the phony American accent . . . Jonathan."

This did surprise him. He stepped nearer. "Splendid," he said, in that way that Brits can get away with that would sound corny coming out of an American guy. Just that fast, he lost the phony American accent and sounded like he'd just stepped out of one of those PBS presentations where everybody wears funny, old-fashioned clothes and rides in carriages. "You apparently have me all figured out. Care to share how it happened?"

I didn't. But then, it was a little awkward explaining that the feds were on their way and that they'd better get there fast because I was running out of things to say.

"Care to tell me what all this has to do with murder?" I asked him.

"Murder?" For a moment, he was baffled, as if he really had forgotten that behind the secrets and the scheming and the counterfeiting, there really was a woman whose life had been snuffed out. "You're talking about that silly woman who took those few cards?"

"So you didn't kill her?"

He was either horrified at the thought or he was a mighty good actor. "You know me well enough. Or at least, I wish you did." He looked me over, slowly and carefully. "Ah, Pepper! If only we'd met in another place and at another time. Then you would know I'd never do such a thing."

"But one of your minions would do the dirty work for you."

"Minions?" Jack . . . er . . . Jonathan's laugh was as bright as the lighting was not. "You've been watching too much bad American TV. I don't have any minions."

"Not even Viktor Patankin?"

This time, he narrowed his eyes, and when he looked me over again, I think he was trying to see beyond the surface. "You're a cop."

"I'm a cemetery tour guide."

"Patankin isn't my minion. He's just a silly little man who sometimes performs a few select services for me. Don't tell me he's gotten himself in trouble." He twitched away the thought. "Whatever he says, I'm sure he's got it all wrong. Viktor's English isn't very good. He tends to get things mixed up."

"Except that he's pretty much told them everything, and the feds have the credit cards to back up his story."

He crossed his arms over his chest. "You are a fount of knowledge. I'm impressed. With your good sense and your resourcefulness and your . . ." Again, he gave me a careful once-over. "Your other assets. I don't suppose you've ever considered a life of crime."

"Is that an invitation?"

"Oh, no. This is an invitation." He was standing close enough now to look me in the eyes. "White sand beaches. Palm trees. Crystal blue waters. I've got a place in the Caribbean."

"And my guess is you're not sharing the address."

His smile was his only answer. That, along with, "We'd make a great team." A noise from upstairs distracted him and his smile dissolved in an instant. "Or maybe not. You called the police?"

"Nah, I went right to the top and called the FBI," I said. "Right before I walked in here. I figured it was my best bet."

Footsteps pounded down the hallway, but even that wasn't enough to get Jack flustered. "Don't worry about the credit cards and leaving me in the lurch," he said. "I won't be penniless. There are plenty more credit cards where those came from and plenty of dead people who don't mind in the least when I appropriate their names. I won't suffer. In fact, I'm heading to a place where there's no extradition. You wouldn't—"

"Care to join you? I'll have to pass."

"Just as I thought. Then it's good-bye, Pepper." We were toe-to-toe, and he leaned in close, then paused, asking permission without saying a word.

I gave it the same way.

The kiss was deep, searching, and intense, and when it was over, Jack disappeared into the shadows on the far side of the room just as the federal agents burst in.

They scrambled up the old stone stairway that led out into the cemetery, but they never did find him.

Too bad. It would have looked good on Scott's record to have collared the head of the counterfeiting operation.

Too bad Jack was a crook, too, 'cause he sure was a mighty good kisser.

C all me crazy. Or maybe it was just my hormones talking.

I believed Jack when he said he didn't kill Marjorie.

I was glad. Sure he was a major felon (at least that's one of the things Scott called him when he showed up at the cemetery and read the riot act to the agents who'd let Jack get away), but aside from that teensy character flaw, Jack didn't seem like such a bad guy. Besides, now that I knew he hadn't killed Marjorie, I could relive those couple knee-melting kisses and not feel guilty. Or grossed out.

Of course, the fact that he wasn't willing to cop to Marjorie's murder didn't help out in terms of my investigation. I had eliminated Doris and Ray as suspects, and now Jack was off the list, too. It was time to narrow the field even more.

With that in mind, I called Gloria Henninger and told her to stop down at the memorial the next Monday afternoon and I would take her to lunch.

I know this doesn't exactly sound like an investigative strategy, but believe me, I had a plan. I put it into motion the moment she was through the front door.

"You sure found the memorial with no trouble," I said. Yes, it was a shaky accusation, but desperate times, desperate measures, and all that crap. I pinned Gloria with a look.

She was made of sterner stuff than I'd expected. In honor of our lunch date, she was wearing pink pants and a white T-shirt with a photo of Sunshine on it. Her top lip curled like the dog's. "The memorial is big," she said. "So is the cemetery. It's easy to find."

I wasn't about to let her off the hook so easily. I took a step closer, and since I'm like a foot taller than her, it wasn't hard to look imposing. "You said you'd never been here before."

"Did I?"

If she was going to play hard to get, I had no choice but to get tough. I hoped it would work because it was my one-and-only chance, and if it didn't, I was up that proverbial creek without a paddle. "You lied to me, Gloria," I said, poking a finger in her face and sounding like a detective in one of those corny old movies who reveals the murderer in a big *aha!* moment. "You've been here before, haven't you? That's why you didn't have any trouble finding the place!"

When it came to aplomb, Gloria had exactly none. I was oh so glad. When she realized she'd been found out, she started shaking in her pink Keds.

I couldn't afford to be nice. I pounced. "You told me you'd just heard about the statue here in the memorial. That you'd never seen it. But I found this . . ." I had the brochure I found at Gloria's house in my pocket, and I whipped it out and waved it under her nose. "This was in your living room, Gloria. It's from that rack of brochures right over there." Just in case she'd missed it when she walked in, I pointed. I'm pretty sure all this pointing wasn't necessary, but it sure was dramatic. "You've been here before. I don't suppose that just happened to be the day Marjorie died, was it?"

"Yes! Yes, it was." Gloria collapsed like a cheap lawn chair. Figuratively speaking, of course, because had she really collapsed, I would have helped her. Instead, I watched her snivel for a while and congratulated myself. Getting a confession out of her was going to be far easier than I thought. Gloria pulled a rumpled tissue from her pocket and dabbed her nose. "I was here that morning, all right. I came to . . . I came to . . ."

"Kill Marjorie?"

Her eyes flew open, and this time, I really did think she was going to collapse. Since the floors in the memorial are solid marble, and Gloria is an elderly lady whose bones are probably as brittle as an old bar of soap, I didn't have the heart to let that happen. I took her by the arm, led her into the office, and plunked her down on the desk chair.

"You hated Marjorie. You hated her because she was a pain in the neck who deserved hating. You hated her for the statue in her garden and for the way it upset Sunshine. You came here that morning, and my guess is you had a fight. Maybe you didn't mean to push her over that railing—"

"No! No!" Gloria was crying for real now and I almost felt guilty about it. Almost. She covered her face with her hands. "I wanted her dead, yes. But . . ." She raised her head and looked me in the eyes the way I figured a real perp never would. "I could never do a thing like that. Oh, in my dreams, maybe. But not for real! In fact, I came here that day to bring her brownies."

This sort of bombshell deserved a shake of the head so that's exactly what I did. Maybe when my brain settled again, the news would make sense. It didn't. I had to resort to the old-fashioned way and talk things out. "You hated Marjorie so you brought her brownies because . . ."

Gloria's eyes were rimmed with red. That didn't prevent her from giving me a sly look. All she said was, "Ex-Lax."

I swear, I would have burst out laughing if we weren't talking murder. "You brought Marjorie brownies with laxative in them because—"

"Because I hated that Klinker woman!" Gloria emphasized her point by pounding her fist on the desk. "I was sick of trying to talk some sense into her. Nobody could do that. I wanted my revenge and the brownies were the only way I could think to get it. You know what?" She stood and threw back her scrawny shoulders. "The only reason I'm sorry she's dead is because now I'll never get even."

I was too stunned by all this to say anything so all I did is stand there and watch Gloria march out of the room. Good thing the president popped up right before she walked out of the memorial. He was the one who reminded me that I was passing up a golden opportunity.

"She was here," the president said. "The morning of the murder. Do you suppose she might have—"

"Did you see anything?" I jumped on the opportunity— and on Gloria, figuratively speaking, of course—before she could heft open the heavy front door. "When you came to give the brownies to Marjorie, was she here? Was any-one with her?"

She clicked her tongue. "If I had seen someone here, young lady, don't you think I would have told the police? There was nobody around. Not a soul. Not that Klinker woman, not anybody. I didn't hear anything, either, so don't ask if there was any yelling or screaming or any-thing like that. The place was as quiet as a tomb." Gloria thought about it for a moment before she chuckled. "Tomb, get it?"

I did, I just didn't care. The president and I exchanged looks, and something told me that if he could, he would have asked exactly what I asked. "And the brownies?"

Gloria looked back at the office. "Left them in there. Right on the desk. Figured it was even better that way be-cause then the Klinker woman would never know who brought them. Why? Is it important what happened to the brownies?"

I wondered, and wondering, I said, "Maybe. Because when I got here that morning, there were no brownies on the desk." I did a quick shuffle through the mental notes about my case, sure that no one had mentioned brownies or chocolate or—

Gloria might have been too slow on the uptake to real-ize what was going on, but the president knew exactly when inspiration struck me like a bolt of lightning. An expectant look brightening an expression that was usually somber, he stepped closer.

"What is it?" he asked. "Have you discerned some-thing important?"

Since I wasn't sure what *discerned* even meant, I wasn't

sure about that. I did know one thing, though, and if Gloria thought I was weird talking to the empty air beside me, so be it.

"Brownies laced with Ex-Lax. Get it? That's what we in the business call a big-time clue. It means I know who killed Marjorie."

19

I was pretty sure I knew who the murderer was. But there's this little thing called proof, see, and though I had suspicions aplenty and those brownies helping to point me in the right chocolately direction, what I didn't have was proof.

I did have another thing, though. That was the heart-pounding, blood-thrilling, brain-buzzing certainty that I was one step ahead of Quinn. Oh yeah, I was jazzed, and so eager to wrap up the case before he somehow caught wind of what I was up to and scooped my suspect out from under me, I was ready to go all-out.

Which explains what I was doing in that conference room Ella had reserved for Marjorie and me to sort and store the Garfield memorabilia that would be displayed at the commemoration.

"There's got to be something," I mumbled, thumbing through a pile of old photographs and not caring if Ella knew what I was talking about or not. "We've missed something."

Ella didn't get it, but then, I didn't expect her to. She had a normal life, and normal lives don't include murder. Not routinely, anyway. It was a chilly September afternoon, and she was bundled in a cardigan that wasn't exactly the same shade of green as her ankle-skimming, button-front dress. She poked her hands into the pockets of her sweater. "Something worth putting on display?"

"Something worth killing for."

I knew I wasn't imagining it—her face really did turn the same color as her sweater. She sounded just like I'd heard her sound on the phone when she offered one of her teenaged daughters advice. "If you think you know something that would help solve the case, Pepper, you should leave it up to the professionals. Why not call that nice detective friend of yours."

I stopped just short of throwing her a look that would have caused her to implode. But only because I liked Ella, both as a boss and as a friend. My smile was sweet, but my teeth were gritted when I said, "First of all, Quinn is not my friend. Not anymore. And second of all, he's not nice. Never has been."

"Putting yourself in danger isn't smart."

I was holding a handful of photos of the Garfield family and I waved them in front of her face. "Does this look like danger to you? The only thing I'm in danger of is getting bored to death." I plunked the pictures down on the table and looked around at the mess that was once the neat piles and stacks of memorabilia. "There's nothing here," I wailed. "It's all so ordinary. So dull. I was hoping something that belonged to Marjorie might have gotten mixed up with all this stuff that belongs to the cemetery," I explained. "But whatever I thought I'd find . . ." When I looked around, my sigh shivered through the room—and caught.

"What is it?" Ella was at my side instantly, one hand out as if she thought I was going to take a tumble and she'd actually have a chance of keeping me from hitting the floor. "You look surprised."

"Surprised at how incredibly stupid I am," I told her. I didn't bother to explain. But then, I really couldn't. I was already on my way out the door.

Of course I'd forgotten all about the stuff Marjorie gave me that night I visited her at home and I stowed in the trunk of my car. I mean, who wouldn't? She'd pretty much come right out and told me none of it was all that valuable, so naturally after I dug out that newspaper page I'd shown to Ted Studebaker, I hadn't bothered wasting any brain cells on what any of it was.

What it was, as it turned out, was exactly what Marjorie had promised: not much.

There were a few photographs of James Garfield the soldier and James Garfield the congressman and James Garfield the president. There were a couple postcards that showed the newly opened memorial. There was a poorly done watercolor of the log cabin where the president was born, a half-dozen or so shots of the canopy under which his body had been displayed when it was first brought back to Cleveland, and a couple ancient magazines, their covers promising "new and surprising information" about the president's passing.

It seemed even after she was dead, Marjorie had gotten the last laugh: she said she wouldn't trust me with anything important, and she hadn't.

There was a piece of newspaper at the bottom of what I thought was the now-empty box, and I grabbed it so I could wad it up and throw it away.

Which was when I realized that what I thought was an empty box wasn't empty at all.

I lifted out a sixteen-by-twenty-inch frame and stared at the single piece of paper behind the glass.

Ella was still in that conference room with me, and when I read what was written on the paper and my eyes lit up, she knew something was going on.

"What is it?" she asked. In her excitement, she bounced up on the heels of her flat, chunky shoes. "Is it something valuable?"

"It depends who you ask," I told her, and even though it was late, I headed back to the memorial.

It was time to confront the one and only person who could give me a straight answer.

If Ella knew I was standing up on the marble dais next to the statue of the president, she would have gone into cardiac arrest. National treasure and all that stuff. I was so not in the mood to care. I stood right next to that statue, the framed letter I'd found in one hand and my voice raised so that not even the dead could fail to hear.

"I need to talk to you, Mr. President, and I need to talk to you now!"

It must have been a slow day at the White House. Not two seconds later, he poofed into shape beside me.

"Really!" Honest to gosh, the president's nose was up in the air. "To think you can disturb the chief executive this way!"

"The chief liar, you mean." I held up the frame and its contents. "You know what I've got here? Well, maybe you don't. Because maybe you never thought anybody would find it, that nobody would ever know about it."

He *harrumphed* in a presidential sort of way. "I can't imagine what you're talking about."

"Really?" I gave him a moment to come clean, and when he didn't, I cleared my throat and read:

My dearest Lucia,

You have, no doubt, heard of the misfortune that has brought me to this delicate point in my life. The reports are sadly true. I was shot by a man with murderous intent, and though I did not succumb to the attack immediately, I have been most inconvenienced and in much pain. The doctors tell me there is hope, but I watch them as they turn from my bed, their eyes downcast and their expressions somber. They dare not speak the words. They do not have to. I know that I am dying.

Here I paused and looked up at the president. He was as still as that statue over on my left and as pale as the marble floor at our feet. He didn't say a word so, of course, I had no choice but to keep reading.

I cannot leave this earth, my dear, without conveying to you my last good-byes. Though ours was a fragile and momentary relationship, it has remained as clearly etched upon my heart as if it were the love of a lifetime. I cannot part this world, and from you, my dear Lucia, without imploring of you one last request. Give Rufus . . .

Oh yeah, I admit it . . . I raised my voice here and read slowly and carefully, getting the most I could out of the moment.

Give Rufus Ward Henry my love, and tell him how I do so regret that I was never able to properly acknowledge him . . .

I paused again. After all, this was the big moment.

. . . acknowledge him as being as dearly beloved as are
my other sons.

That was where the letter ended, and besides, I think
I'd pretty much made my point. His eyes glassy, the president swayed on his feet and staggered back, one hand to
his heart.

"I remember now," he said, drawing in a labored breath.
"It was in those steamy days of September. I lay on my
deathbed, weak and delirious, haunted by my past, my
mistakes." He swallowed hard. "My regrets. I was so
much in the throes of emotion and pain, I could hardly
think straight. I called . . ." He passed a hand over his
eyes. "I called to Jeremiah Stone for paper and ink. I
intended . . . I intended . . ." The president stumbled back
toward the center of the rotunda, and when he did, the
scenery around us shivered and shifted. I fully expected
to see that we were back in that White House office, but
instead, I found myself standing in a spacious, neat cot-
tage. There was a window opposite from where I stood,
and through it, I saw a sweep of beach and, beyond that,
the slow rolling waves of the Atlantic Ocean. No way I
was as much of a Garfield fanatic as Marjorie, but at this
point, even I knew enough about the president to know
where I was: at Long Branch Beach along the Jersey
shore, the place where President Garfield died.

I was alone, or at least I thought I was until I saw a
movement underneath the blankets of a nearby bed.

"Stone! Stone!" Even though it was breathless and
thready, I recognized the president's voice. When I stepped
closer to the bed, though, I realized I wouldn't have recognized him as the man under the blankets. Not for all the
world.

His skin was gray. His eyes were sunken. He was at least a hundred pounds lighter than the robust ghost who haunted the memorial.

"Stone!" Even as I watched, the president shifted in bed. A spasm of pain crossed his face. His skin was slick with sweat. His eyes were glassy. "Stone, I must write a letter!"

"Of course, Mr. President."

A door over on my right opened, and as efficient as ever, Jeremiah Stone marched into the room, the ever-present portfolio in his hands. "I am terribly sorry, Mr. President," he said, as oblivious of me now as he'd always been. "I was just discussing a certain matter with Mr. Windom, your secretary of the Treasury."

"All is . . ." Another spasm of pain crossed his face, and the president closed his eyes against it, then opened them again. He wasn't about to let that stop him. Though it obviously hurt, he sat up, and Stone shifted the pillows behind him. "All is well, isn't it? There are no . . . no . . ."

"No problems of national import. No, sir, certainly not." Stone adjusted the glasses pinched to the bridge of his nose. "It was nothing more than a trivial thing we discussed and I regret leaving your side so that I might attend to it. What can I get for you, sir?"

"Paper." The president's voice was so small and shallow, Stone had to lean closer to hear. "Paper and ink. I would . . . I would like to write a letter."

"Certainly." There was a table next to the bed, and Stone set his portfolio down on it. He reached into his breast pocket, pulled out one of those old-fashioned fountain pens, and set that down, too, before he backed toward the door. "I have no blank paper with me, sir, but I will get some for you. I will be back in just a moment. And when I do return, sir . . ." Stone's gaze darted to the portfolio. "There are papers that must be signed, sir. I know it is inappropriate of me to insist so strongly when you are so discommoded, but really, sir, we must get these out of the way before—"

Realizing what he'd almost said, Stone blanched.

The president reassured him with a wheezing chuckle. "I do not hold it against you for nearly saying the words no one else dare speak, Stone. You are an honorable and efficient aide to me, and I cannot fault you for verbalizing the truth. You wish me to sign these papers before I pass into a better place. That is true, is it not?"

Stone nodded.

"We will take care of it when you return," the president assured him. "For now, if you might bring me that writing paper . . ."

Stone disappeared, but honestly, I don't think the president even noticed. For a minute, he was so still and quiet, I thought he might have died. But then he sighed, and like a sleepwalker, he groped toward the bedside table, reached into the portfolio, and drew out a piece of paper. Slowly and carefully, he began to write.

My dearest Lucia . . .

I watched him write out each word, pausing now and then to fight for a breath or reposition himself in bed.

". . . as are my other sons," he mumbled as he wrote, and his strength gave out. The pen dropped out of his hand and onto the blankets. The letter fluttered under the bed.

"I remember desiring to communicate with Lucia on that, the last day I spent among the living." When the president's ghost spoke, I realized we weren't at the seashore anymore. We were back in the memorial. "I remember that Stone went to get pen and paper. But the letter . . . I have no memory of writing it. And yet there it is, framed and in your hand. Are you telling me it was never delivered? Does that mean it never made its way to Lucia? That I never had a chance to say good-bye to my darling?"

"Please!" I turned the word into two emphatic syllables. "All this time, you've held the key to the mystery and all you can think of is your love puppy?"

He had the good sense to look embarrassed—at least for a moment. The next, he was back to his old, blustery self. "It is inappropriate to share such a sensitive piece of information with—"

"Give me a break!" I was pissed, and just to prove it, I stomped one foot on the marble floor. "News flash, nobody cares! Not anymore, anyway. You had a kid with your mistress. Big deal! These days in the world of politics, that's small potatoes."

His chin went rigid. "It should not be. Such a lapse of moral judgment should never be taken lightly. It would surely have destroyed my career if the public knew of my relationship with Lucia. And should they have learned there was a child born from our liaison, that would have resulted in the ruination not only of me, but of my family as well. That is why the boy was raised by a distant relative of Lucia's, why I was unable to acknowledge him as my own. Had word gone out that he was my son, I would have never been elected to office. I would never have been able to hold up my head in public again."

"Yeah, well, that was back in the old days when politicians had consciences. You should have told me about the letter. You should have told me you and Lucia had a son."

"It cannot be of great importance. Not to your investigation."

"It is if your son, Rufus, went on to have a family of his own."

The president glanced away. "He did."

"And if his children had children and their children—"

"Yes. Yes!" I was glad he interrupted me. I wasn't sure about all this genealogy stuff and didn't know how many children's children's children I needed to list.

Rather than even worry about it, I gave him an icy stare. "Yes or no. That's all I want from you. Not an explanation and not a speech. Was Marjorie Klinker really one of your descendants?"

"Rufus was married at an early age. His wife died after giving birth to their first child. He then remarried and fathered a number of children with his second wife. Through that side of the family, there is a convoluted bloodline that—"

"Ah!" I held up a hand to stop him. "Not what I asked. Was Marjorie related to you?"

The president's shoulders never wavered. "Yes."

"Well, damn! Wouldn't that just make her day? Or at least it would if she was alive to hear the news."

Sarcasm—no matter how well placed—apparently doesn't work on ghosts. Or maybe it's just presidents who are immune. Thinking over the possibilities, he rumbled, "You think that unfortunate woman's murder had something to do with . . ." He dismissed the very idea with a lift of his broad shoulders. "No. That is hardly possible."

"It is possible if somebody knew about this letter. And if that somebody wanted Marjorie to part with it. Her nephew, Nick, talked to an antiques dealer about selling a piece of your personal property. Well, it can't get much more personal than this. What if he wanted to sell it and she didn't? She wanted to reveal the news to all the world at the opening of the commemoration. She said she had something to display, something wonderful and valuable. Don't you see? If Nick wanted her to sell the letter and she refused because it was too precious to her . . ."

"Yes, yes." The president nodded. "I understand. Of course I do. They may have quarreled. They may have fought. He might have killed her to get his hands on the letter." He glanced at the frame in my hands. "But he did not get it, it seems. Did he?"

The little piece of presidential one-upsmanship did not sit well with me. Then again, I guess I could forgive Mr. Garfield. He didn't know the whole story.

"Marjorie wanted to pull out this little bombshell at the commemoration," I explained. "And until then, my guess is that she had it at home, where she thought it was nice and safe. But that night I visited her, she was plenty upset by the time Ray dumped her and walked out. So when she gathered the stuff she wanted me to bring over here, she somehow grabbed the letter, too. That explains why I saw her running through the house like a crazy person when I drove away."

Another thought hit and stuck, and I gave myself a mental slap. "It explains that voice mail message she left at my office, too. She said she had to see me the next morning. She said it was important. Of course it was! Marjorie couldn't find the letter anywhere else so she knew I had it. She had to get it back. It was the most important piece of Garfield junk . . . er . . . memorabilia she owned."

The president hung his head, and if I didn't remember he was a politician (which automatically made him a liar in my book), I might have been more inclined to forgive him when he said, "I am terribly sorry. If I had remembered the letter . . . if I thought it had any relevance . . . You believe it does."

It wasn't a question. I nodded, anyway. "If somebody wanted to sell this letter and Marjorie didn't—"

"Then that same person—"

"Killed her. And then when he couldn't find the letter among her things, he ransacked her house and her locker here at the cemetery, looking for it."

The president's brow creased. "It seems to me, that means he might still be looking for this letter of mine. And that if he knew you were in possession of it—"

"He'd be real eager to get his hands on it." I slid the president a look. "Are you thinking what I'm thinking?" I asked.

A smile sparked in his blue eyes. "Only if you're thinking we might still use this letter as bait to catch a killer."

20

Oh yeah, that's exactly what I was thinking, and with the plan in mind, I called in the big guns. Figuratively and literally.

I should have known better. My previous cases had taught me that nothing mucks up an investigation like involving the professionals.

"I still don't think this is a good idea." Scott was so fidgety, I had a feeling he would have paced the office of the memorial if Quinn hadn't positioned himself just to the right of the desk. The way Quinn was standing there—his feet apart and his arms crossed over his chest—it was clear he wasn't about to move and just as clear that Scott wouldn't get past him. Not without a physical confrontation, anyway.

"What if he doesn't show?" Scott asked. "What if he does, and we can't get to you in time? If you're putting yourself in danger, Pepper—"

"Pepper likes to put herself in danger." It was the first

thing Quinn said since he'd shown up in answer to my phone call. "It's one of the things she does best."

I didn't bother to respond to this comment. It was juvenile, for one thing, and for another, it wasn't true. I did a whole lot of things better than I put myself in danger, and Quinn should have remembered that.

"It's too late," I said, responding to Scott because I mean, really, why even try to reason with Quinn? "Ella pulled some strings and got the information out to the media, and the story about it was on the news this evening. They didn't say what it was, but they talked about the fabulous thing we'd found and how it's related to President Garfield and how we're all set to put it on display here at the cemetery. We made a big deal about how, after the commemoration, the item is going to be donated to the National Archives. He's bound to show up looking for the letter. It's his only chance to get his hands on it and sell it before it's out of his reach forever."

Yes, it was brilliant, but I have to admit, the plan wasn't mine alone. Civil War soldier and strategist that he was, the president had actually helped me come up with it. The whole thing made sense to us, and waiting for confirmation from the two guys who would enforce it, I looked back and forth, first to Scott, then to Quinn. When neither one of them said a thing, I gave up trying to be reasonable, flicked off the lights in the office, and headed into the rotunda.

"Hey, what can possibly go wrong?" I asked neither one in particular. "I've got you two superheroes here watching out for me."

Was I trying to convince them, or myself?

Not them. I knew that. Scott was nothing if not good at his job, and he took his responsibilities seriously. Quinn . . . well, he was a royal pain and I was still plenty bitter about the way things had ended between us. But

Quinn was a professional, too. In his deepest, darkest fantasies (and believe me, I knew a thing or two about Quinn's fantasies), I had the feeling he'd like to see me fall flat on my face. But he wouldn't let anything happen to me. Not from a safety standpoint, anyway.

Now all I had to do was convince myself.

Listening to my heart beat out a rumba rhythm in my chest, I stepped into the empty rotunda. It was after hours, and the crowds of tourists were long gone. The chandelier above the president's statue was lit, and it threw a circle of light onto the marble dais. Beyond its glow, the far ends of the rotunda sloped into shadow.

Believe me, I took a good, long look into those shadows before I went to station myself at the table Ella and I had set up to the right of the lighted dais.

The news story we leaked talked about how anxious we were to get our "fabulous" find on display. I'd even appeared on camera to give a quote that went something like, "I can't wait to get started on the commemoration. I'm going to be putting in some extra hours, day and night, to get the display ready."

Anyone who knew me would have seen right through this, of course. Me, extra hours? Day and night? It was ludicrous.

I was counting on Nick Klinker not knowing me that well.

Surprised? Come on! Nick was the logical suspect from the beginning. I'd bet anything Marjorie told him about the letter the moment she found it. After all, the letter proved what Marjorie had been trying to prove all her life—that she was related to the president. Of course, that meant Nick was, too. I could imagine the way her warped mind worked, and in Marjorie's mind, there was nothing more exciting than that news, and nothing that could possibly have made Nick prouder.

I wondered if he shared her excitement, and I realized it didn't matter. Marjorie would have decided the moment she saw it that the letter was the most precious thing in the world. And Nick?

A small noise from the direction of the entryway caught my attention. It might have been Scott or Quinn in the office, but remember what I said about them being professionals. Professionals on a stakeout know better than to make any noise.

My hands stilled over the table where Ella and I had piled much of the Garfield memorabilia the cemetery owned. After all, we needed to make it look like I was knee-deep in commemoration preparations and we'd pulled out all the stops. There were stacks of old magazines and newspapers. There were boxes of photographs of the president and his family. There were framed souvenirs, including the letter we were using as bait to draw Nick to the memorial.

My stomach soured when I realized that, sooner or later, I would actually have to sort through it all. Marjorie or no Marjorie, the commemoration would go on, and without Marjorie, guess who was left holding the bag.

That is, if I lived long enough to have to worry about organizing the commemoration.

The unmistakable sound of stealthy footsteps made my heart bump, and I drew in a deep breath and held it. Scott and Quinn had my back, I reminded myself. Taking care of the rest of the plan was my responsibility.

I told myself to breathe and forced my hands to move, dragging over a stack of magazines and flipping through them like I actually cared at the same time I hoped Nick didn't see through our trap. Could he actually be so dense to think I would be in here alone without locking the door?

If I ignored the next shuffle of footsteps, it would have looked too fishy, so I spun around.

"Is somebody here?" I called into the semidark rotunda, and when no one answered, I mumbled, "You're imagining things, Pepper," to myself, told myself it actually might be true, and got back to what I hoped looked enough like work to fool Nick Klinker.

I guess it worked, because I heard a voice behind me. It was husky and muffled, like he was trying to disguise it, but I'm not a detective for nothing. There was no mistaking that the voice belonged to Nick.

"Don't turn around," he said. "I've got a gun and I'll use it if I have to. Where is it?"

"Your gun? I assume you know where it is."

"Not my gun!" He forgot himself and used his regular voice, and when he realized it, he rumbled and tried to sound all strange and mysterious again. "You know what I'm talking about. The letter. Where is it?"

The framed letter from the president to Lucia was on the table, and I let my right hand drift over to it, the better to tantalize Nick into telling the truth. I rested my fingers on the frame.

"Could it possibly be worth all that much?" I asked him. "It's just an old letter."

"It has historical significance."

"Maybe for loonies like Marjorie, but let's face it, nobody else is really going to care. Not enough to make all this worth your while, anyway."

"I have a buyer."

I paused like I had to actually think about this. "You mean Ted Studebaker. How much is he going to give you?"

"It's none of your business." I still had my back to Nick, and I heard him take another step closer and waited to feel the cold barrel of his gun press into my back. When I didn't, I should have been relieved, but waiting for the touch of the steel only made me more anxious. I sure hoped Scott and Quinn were paying attention.

"Give me the letter," Nick growled.

"You are the rightful owner. I mean, being Marjorie's only living relative and all." I threw out this morsel in an attempt to wheedle a confession out of Nick, just the way Scott and Quinn had instructed me to. "Why not just go home and work on proving you own it. That way you can walk in here, take rightful possession, and do anything you want with the stupid letter."

"I can't take that chance." Another step closer. I held my breath. "What if there's no way to prove it's mine? It's worth too much."

"Was it worth killing Marjorie to get?"

"What?" In his surprise, Nick forgot all about his goofy disguised voice, and hearing him sound genuinely shocked, I spun around. I found him with his mouth hanging open, and yeah, the lights were dim and the shadows edged in on us from every side, but I swear, in that one instant before he stuck his right hand in his pocket, I saw what I saw, and what I saw was that his hand was empty. The second he stuck it in his pocket, though, it looked like he had a gun in there.

Or like he was pointing a finger, pretending it was a gun.

The tension washed out of me and I tossed my head. "Oh, come on, Nick. That's just about as lame as it gets. You don't have a gun."

He made a face. "I figured you'd give me the letter if you thought I did."

"Is that what you told Marjorie that morning you came here to the memorial? That you had a gun? That she had to turn over the letter or else?"

Even with the shadows, I could tell his face went ashen. "I tried to reason with her," he said, his voice squeezed thin. "Aunt Marjorie was not a reasonable woman."

That was neither here nor there. I stuck to my case. "So

when she wouldn't hand over the letter so you could sell it, you tossed her over the balcony."

"No. I didn't. I swear."

He started to shake, and seeing it, I got a fresh dose of courage. I took a step toward Nick. "I know you were here that day, Nick. You took the brownies."

All the gray washed out of his face and left him as white as a sheet. Nick staggered back and swallowed hard. "How . . . how did you know?"

"Because of what Bernadine said. She said you were nervous about the wedding and your tummy was acting up. But it wasn't nerves, was it? It was the brownies. Gloria Henninger put Ex-Lax in them."

All that pale skin was suddenly shot through with a color that reminded me of blood. "I'll sue!" Nick yelled. "That woman is a menace. This certainly proves it. She . . . she tried to kill me."

"But here you are, alive and well." I let this comment settle before I added, "But Marjorie isn't, is she?"

Nick whirled around, then spun back to me. He tugged at his hair, his voice choked and desperate. "Yes, I was here that morning. Yes, when I left, I took the brownies. I love chocolate, you see, and I figured it would serve Aunt Marjorie right to not get any of the brownies. She was . . ." Looking for the right word to describe a woman who was indescribable, he blubbered.

"She was impossible! For once, I wanted to get the best of her, so when I arrived here that morning, I told Aunt Marjorie something she didn't know. A couple weeks earlier, after she showed me the letter for the first time, I smuggled it out of her house and showed it to Ted Studebaker. You know, so that he could value it. I should have sold it to him right then and there, Aunt Marjorie be damned. But no!" He was so overwrought, his voice gained an octave.

"I had to be the good nephew. Just the way I've always been. I had to give in to Aunt Marjorie's whims. Just the way I always have. I returned the letter to her along with the good news about how much it was worth. She said she'd consider selling it and that I should come here to the cemetery and we'd talk about it further."

"And when you did?"

"When I did, she laughed in my face." Nick's eyes were rimmed with red. He swigged his nose. "She told me I was stupid if I ever thought she'd sell that letter, that it was the most wonderful thing in the world and that she'd never part with it. I felt like a little kid all over again, always being corrected by Aunt Marjorie, always being told by her that I wasn't smart enough, that I didn't care enough about family history. She made me so angry . . ." Nick's hands curled into fists. "I wanted to . . . I wanted to—"

"Kill her?"

Nick went motionless and the only sounds in the rotunda were the echoes of his rough breathing. "I . . ." He drew in a breath and it stuttered out of him on the end of a sigh. "I didn't kill her. I swear I didn't kill her. We fought, yes. We yelled. We screamed. But when I left here, Aunt Marjorie was alive."

I wasn't about to believe him, not without proof, anyway. "You were the only one here that morning, Nick," I said.

"Well, obviously not. Someone threw Aunt Marjorie over that balcony. But it wasn't me." He wiped the tears from his cheeks and threw back his shoulders, and suddenly, his voice was as calm as it had been distraught only moments before. "Now you'll need to give me that letter, Pepper. I may not have a gun, but I am a man, and stronger than you. I'm not leaving here without the letter. Even if it means I have to hurt you to get it."

Before I could decide if he was bluffing, Nick darted toward me, and honestly, I think I could have taken him if not for the fact that all the lights came on in the place and Scott and Quinn showed up out in the entryway. I was distracted, watching as they jockeyed for position, each trying to be the first into the rotunda. All they managed to accomplish was to trip over each other.

In the meantime, I lost precious seconds, and in those seconds, Nick closed in on me and I stepped back and bumped into the table. Before I had a chance to figure out which way to run, his hands had already closed around my neck.

"Give me that letter!" he said, his voice deadly serious.

And even though I struggled to breathe at the same time I fought to loosen his hold, I recognized the important word there.

Deadly.

He was stronger than any IT geek had a right to be. He shook me like a ragdoll. "It's mine. Give me the letter. Now."

Never let it be said that Pepper Martin isn't willing to oblige. I was getting nowhere trying to pry Nick's hands away from my neck so I groped for the framed letter. Once I had a hand on it, I swung. Hard.

When the frame and the glass shattered on Nick's head, the noise was as loud as a gunshot.

I guess that got Quinn and Scott's attention. They untangled themselves from the doorway and scrambled over just as Nick's eyes rolled to the back of his head and he crumpled to the floor.

"Nick Klinker, you're under arrest—"

They did it again. Started talking at the same time.

Quinn and Scott exchanged cutting looks. But maybe Scott is the smarter of the two. Or maybe he just knew that the case was officially Quinn's and there was no way he was going to scoop it, anyway. He stepped back and Quinn cuffed Nick and called for the paramedics.

What did I do while all this was going on?

Well, I still had a hold of what was left of the frame, and I looked down at the letter, but I couldn't really see it clearly. That's because my hands were trembling.

"You OK, Pepper?" Scott asked. He put a hand on my arm.

"I'm fine," I lied, but only because Quinn looked up, anxious to see how I was going to answer.

"I'll just . . ." My knees were mushy, and I figured it would be more graceful to sit down in the office than to fall down on the floor, so I headed that way. "I'll wait inside the office."

This, too, was a good plan.

Or at least it would have been, if Nick Klinker hadn't been telling the truth about Marjorie's murder, and the real murderer wasn't lying in wait for me.

I had already slumped down into the chair behind the desk when the office door swung shut, clicked, and locked. Too late, I realized someone had been standing behind it.

"Thank goodness for Nick causing all that commotion. I never could have gotten in here unnoticed if your two cops friends hadn't been so busy trying to one-up each other." Ted Studebaker stepped out from the shadows. Good old Ted, always the showman. He wasn't content using the ol' finger-in-the-pocket-like-a-gun trick. He really did have a gun, a small, silver pistol with a pearl handle. It was aimed right at me.

"Let's get this over with as quickly as we can," he said. He held out his left hand and jiggled his fingers, urging me to hand over the letter. "If I can get out of here fast, we can avoid any messy consequences."

"If you shoot me, Scott and Quinn are going to come running."

This sounded reasonable to me, but it wasn't about to make Studebaker change his mind. "By the time they stop what they're doing and figure out where the shot came from, I'll be out of here. That's the thing about surprise. It's . . ." He grinned. "Surprising!"

"All this for a stupid letter?" What was left of the frame was on the desk and I looked down at the President's fancy, curlicue script. "Come on, it can't be worth that much."

"It isn't." Studebaker stepped closer. "But what's on the back of it . . ."

I hauled in a breath, and if I wasn't so worried about living through the next couple minutes and about how if I didn't, my body would be found with a big, ugly red mark on my forehead, I would have given myself a slap. "Of course, Jeremiah Stone said there wasn't any blank paper in his portfolio. He went to get some, but the president couldn't wait. He grabbed a piece of paper, anyway. And if there was no blank paper, that means something has to be written on the back of this one."

Carefully avoiding both Studebaker's confused "What are you talking about?" and the sharp bits of glass still left inside the frame, I took out the president's letter and flipped it over. Even though the writing on the other side of the paper was stiff and old-fashioned and hard to read, I skimmed over the words and my breath caught.

I looked up at Studebaker in wonder. "This isn't possible. You mean—"

"When word of this gets out . . ." He dangled the word to reflect the possibilities.

OK, so I'm not exactly a whiz when it comes to politics. Or world affairs. Or treaties and such. But even I knew the piece of paper in my hands would blow the lid off international relations.

"That's why you were so anxious to get at this. It wasn't because the letter from the president to Lucia is so valuable. It was for what was on the other side of it. And nobody knew about it but you. When I brought you that newspaper page I wanted to sell, you said you'd have to have an archivist look at it. That's what you did with this. You took it out of the frame, and you saw what was on the back of the letter, and you . . ." There was nothing to be gained from not going for broke. "You killed Marjorie Klinker to get it."

"It would have been easier to kill Nick." Studebaker sniffed. "I was hoping he'd talk his aunt out of the letter and then I could simply eliminate him. I waited for him to leave the memorial with the letter in hand, but then I heard them arguing. She hadn't even brought the letter with her, the stupid woman. After Nick left—"

"You moved in on Marjorie. And when she wouldn't tell you where the letter was—"

"Things got out of hand. Yes. As they are about to get out of hand again." With the barrel of the gun, he motioned me to stand. "I can't say for sure, but my guess is that once a man has killed for the first time, the second time can't possibly be hard. The letter, please. Now."

I got to my feet, and just as I did, I heard the door handle jiggle.

"Pepper?" Scott was outside, and he tried the door again.

"Pepper, are you in there?" This question was from Quinn. "Is everything OK?"

"Tell them it is." Studebaker mouthed the words.

Let's face it, I never have been very good at taking direction. Especially not from a murderer.

I yelled something I vaguely remember as, "Watch out, it's Studebaker and he's the murderer," and dropped to the floor, and just as I did, I heard the crash of the door getting kicked open, the sound of a single gunshot, and a muffled cry from Studebaker. I would like to be able to describe exactly how Scott and Quinn subdued him, but truth be told, I crawled under the desk, and stayed there the whole time.

21

"We've got a mountain of paperwork to fill out." Scott leaned over where I was sitting and looked me in the eye. "I hate to have to leave. You sure you're going to be OK?"

"I'm fine. Honest." I had my arms wrapped around myself to keep him from seeing that I was shaking like a leaf, but I did a pretty good job of sounding cool, calm, and collected. I had to. I'd already given my statement to the cops, but there was one more thing I had to do before I left the memorial that night, and I couldn't do it with the FBI hanging around along with half the Cleveland Police Force and the paramedics who were tending to Studebaker's gunshot wound. (I never did find out if Scott or Quinn was the hero.)

"Somebody's got to lock up when you guys leave," I told Scott, and Quinn, too, since he was standing right behind Scott glaring at me like nobody's business.

"I can call Ella," Quinn said. "She'll come over here and—"

"You don't have to." I guess I wanted to prove to them both (and maybe to myself, too), that I could stand on my own two feet, so I hauled myself out of the chair. "I'm fine. Look." I held my arms out at my sides. Yeah, my neck hurt from where Nick had tried to squeeze the life out of me, but other than that, I really was none the worse for wear. Well, except for my slushy knees and my heartbeat racing a couple miles a minute.

"Go." I shooed them both toward the door. "I'll lock up and be right behind you."

Neither one of them liked being told what to do, but it was a testament to how much paperwork they both had to file after all that had happened that night: both Scott and Quinn walked out. I watched them and all their safety forces buddies troop out the front door, then waited a few minutes for the quiet to settle. When it had, I stepped into the rotunda and onto the dais.

"Mr. President?" I wasn't sure how he was going to take the news I was about to deliver, and my voice was small and tentative.

"Won't do," I told myself, and I raised my chin. "Mr. President," I said, my voice louder this time. "We have a matter of national import to discuss."

He shimmered into shape not three feet in front of me, and now that he thought all the excitement was over, I guess he was feeling a little more relaxed and a lot more jovial. His blue eyes sparkled. "National import? I swear, Miss Martin, you are sounding more like a politician every day. If you were not a woman, I would suggest you might consider running for office."

I had the letter to Lucia in my hand and I held it up so he could see it. "There's something you need to know," I said. "About those last days before you died."

Apparently he got the message. He saw how serious I was, and his brows dropped over his eyes. "You have told me already of the letter I wrote to Lucia. What else can possibly—"

I didn't know how to explain so I didn't even try. I flipped over the letter and held it up for him to read, carefully watching his face as he did. At first he was mildly interested. Then puzzled. Then horrified.

When he was done, he took a step back and blinked, like he was trying to process it all. "If you see fit to pull some sort of antic on me, young lady," he said, "you should know that it is neither amusing nor suitable."

"No, it's not funny at all."

Convinced I was serious and that his eyes weren't playing tricks on him, the president stepped forward, the better to see the paper in my hands. He read it over again, talking it through as he went. "It is a treaty. Between the United States of America and Federal Dominion of Canada, dated September 15, 1881. It sets forth to say that in exchange for the sum of fifteen million dollars in gold . . ." He paused, his head cocked. "That was a great deal of money in those days," he commented before he went back to reading. "It says that in exchange for those fifteen million dollars, the United States would sign over to Canada all the lands of the Montana, Dakota, Idaho, and Wyoming territories. There is room there at the bottom where my signature is meant to go. Thank the good Lord . . ." His eyes bright, he looked up at me. "It is unsigned!"

"You got that right. And this . . ." I waved the paper, but carefully. After all, even I knew a document of historical significance when I saw one. "This is what Studebaker was really after, not your letter to Lucia."

The president's forehead was creased with thought. "But who could have done such a devilish thing?" he asked, and I didn't need to supply the answer. I knew exactly when he figured it out. His eyes flew open. His face flushed. He threw back his shoulders and thundered into the darkness. "Jeremiah Stone! Your president needs you to attend him. Now!"

Oh yeah, Stone showed up, all right, and I don't think I was imagining it: behind his wire-rimmed glasses, his eyes were troubled. But then, I bet he'd never seen anyone as pissed as the president was. James A. Garfield's broad shoulders trembled. His jaw was so tight, I thought it might snap. His eyes flashed as he stood as straight as an arrow and listened to Stone.

"Mr. President." Jeremiah Stone bowed slightly. The overhead light gleamed off the part in the center of his hair. "We are not scheduled for another cabinet meeting until tomorrow, sir. Yet you sound as if you need my help on a matter of some consequence. We shall certainly attend to it, sir. But first . . ." He was carrying his leather portfolio. Of course he was carrying his leather portfolio. This was one ghost on a mission, and he intended to carry it out. Even if it took him more than a hundred years. "There are some papers that require your signature, sir, and—"

"Papers!" President Garfield was a sight to behold! Remember how I once said that if I was casting a Biblical epic, I'd give him the starring role as God? Well, this was an Old Testament God, all right. Furious, and raging like Lake Erie when a sudden storm kicked up. He closed in on Stone, who by this time, was shaking in his boots. The president poked a finger at Stone's chest. "You are the blackguard who engineered this infernal treaty with our Canadian friends to the north." The President poked him again. Stone backed up another step.

"You are the one who sought to profit by it." Another poke. Another step.

"You knew in those last days I was not thinking clearly. You fully intended me to sign the paper without knowing what it was I put my name on and I have no doubt you intended to profit from the perfidy." He poked yet again, and by this time, Stone's heels skirted the edge of the shadows that surrounded the dais. "Even after all these years, your diabolical deed haunts your wretched soul. That is why you still insist I put my signature on the treaty. You have sought, over and again, to make me a partner to your despicable deed. You, sir . . ." The president pulled himself up to his full height, and I swear, in the play of light and shadow, he looked bigger and more imposing than that statue of him nearby.

"You are a vile and pathetic devil, and I want you out of my sight."

With a little yelp, Stone folded in on himself. "But sir, I thought . . . I thought . . ."

"I neither know nor care what you thought then or now, Stone. I know simply that you are a traitor to your president and to your country." The president pointed into the darkness beyond the shadows. "Leave my sight. Now and forever. There is no more cowardly or mean-spirited creature upon the earth than a man who betrays his nation."

"But Mr. President, I—"

"Be gone!" Like a lightning strike, the command shook the foundations of the memorial, and Stone had no choice but to obey it. He slunk off into the darkness, and just as he stepped into the shadows, I saw him pop into nothingness. I knew I'd never see him again.

The president must have known it, too. By the time he turned back to me, he looked like his old self again. He was worn out, but satisfied, too. A small smile played over his lips. "It seems that, after all, I did have unfinished business to attend to. I owe you my thanks, Miss Martin."

"Does this mean you'll go? I mean, over to the Other Side?"

The president looked around the memorial, from the high glittering dome above our heads to those stained glass windows, their colors muted by the nighttime sky outside. "I think I rather enjoy being president," he said. "And without Stone's infernal badgering . . ." His eyes twinkled and he allowed a full-fledged smile to break through his stony expression. "I will no doubt see you now and again," he said. "Good night, Miss Martin."

The light around him was phosphorescent when he shimmered away. I realized that I was smiling, too, when I said, "Good night, Mr. President."

My work was done. One bully of an IT geek taken care of. One murderer caught. One low-down dirty aide to a president finally put in his place after more than a hundred years.

As evenings went, this was a productive one.

With a sigh of contentment and the promise of a nice hot shower, my jammies, and a glass of wine I figured I'd more than earned, I locked up the memorial, started across the wide veranda and toward the steps, and—

Ran right into Ball Cap Guy.

Startled, I jumped back and pressed a hand to my heart. "Oh!" It was hardly up there with clever or even productive things to say, but after all that had already happened that night, I was not thinking clearly. I swallowed my surprise and scrambled to gather the last shreds of a patience that had been long since worn thin by the events of the last few hours.

"Who are you?" I asked the man. "What do you want?"

When I jumped back, I'd left what was still a less-than-comfortable space between us. He shuffled toward me and closed it.

"Pepper." His eyes were on me in a way that made a

cold sweat break out on the back of my neck. I had my keys in my hand and I poked them through my fingers the way those defend-yourself articles in the ladies magazine always advise. I hoped Ball Cap Guy didn't hear the keys clinking together when my hands shook.

"Pepper," he said again, and his voice was soft and reminded me of the sound a too-ripe tomato makes when it gets squished. "Pepper, I want you."

If it wasn't so dark and I wasn't so alone, I might have tried for a smile and tossed off some cute comment like, "That's what all the boys say, but sorry, I'm booked solid."

But it was dark. And I was alone. And I didn't feel much like being cute.

I stepped to my left.

Ball Cap Guy stepped to his right. The security light glimmered against the blade of the knife in his hands.

Honestly, hadn't I had enough excitement for one night? Choked, shot at, now stabbed? It was enough to make me laugh.

Except that it wasn't the least little bit funny.

I swallowed. Or at least I tried. My mouth was dry and sandy. My smile was anemic, but hey, I had to try.

"That's really nice," I said, and I wondered if he could hear me over the noise my heart was making as it slammed against my ribs. "But I—"

"No buts. Not this time." He took another step closer. I gauged the distance to the steps and from the steps to the wide lawn in front of the memorial, and from the lawn to my car. I braced myself and wondered how fast a doughy guy in sneakers could run. "You're coming home with me," he said, and shivers of panic raced up my spine. "I'm going to take care of you, Pepper. I'm going to show you how much I love you."

Oh yeah, this was creepy. I wished my phone wasn't in my purse, but when I made an attempt to fumble for it, he raised the knife. "You have to come with me," he said, and his words were like ice on my skin. "If I can't have you, nobody can."

"You can't." Brave words. Too bad I sounded like a scared little kid. I tried reinforcing the idea with a shake of my head. "You have to go now. Before the cops come back. You saw them here earlier, right? Well, one of them—the guy with the really big gun—he's coming back to pick me up and he'll be here in just a couple minutes. He's kind of cranky. You don't want him to find you here with that knife. If he does—"

"If I can't have you, nobody can!" The words gushed out of him in one breath, and as he said them, he moved at me so fast, all I could do was stumble back against the building. I found myself with my back against the front door and that gleaming knife just inches from my neck.

"When he comes back, he'll find you here," the man purred. "But he's going to find you dead."

Just as I shot to my right and fell to my knees, I saw the flash of the knife. But then I saw another flash, too, one that was brighter and crackled with electricity.

President Garfield popped out of thin air and materialized at my side.

Ball Cap Guy's jaw dropped. His eyes were as round as baseballs and his hands hung loose at his sides. He backed up a step.

"You must leave the premises this very moment," the president thundered. "You must stay far from Miss Martin now and forever. Do you hear me, sir? She does not desire your inappropriate attentions, and she will tolerate them no further. I will tolerate them no further!" The words boomed around us like jet engines, and believe me, Ball Cap Guy got the message.

By this time, he was blubbering. He backed up another step, then another, before he took off running. But it was dark, and he was so busy staring over his shoulder at the president's ghost, he didn't watch where he was going. He hit the top step and tripped, and when he rolled down the wide stairway, I heard a wild cry. Even before he crumpled at the bottom, I saw the dark stain of blood on his T-shirt where he'd fallen on his knife.

I scrambled for my phone, and it might have been easier to get my hands on it if I didn't realize that over on my right, the president was winking in and out, his face pulled tight with agony, his arms thrown out at his sides.

I forgot about the phone and looked around for my keys, and when I couldn't put my hands on either, I spilled my purse on the stone veranda and rooted through it.

"Not . . . to . . . worry . . . about . . . me."

I looked up to find the president with his head thrown back and his eyes bulging. "The living . . ." The words were ripped from him. "More important . . . more important than the dead."

He was right. I looked down the steps and saw that, even though the bloodstain on Ball Cap Guy's shirt was bigger than ever, his chest heaved. I finally managed to find my phone and dialed 911, and yes, I did have to explain that it was the same presidential monument they'd already been to twice that night, and yes, there really was another person there who needed help and needed it bad.

By the time I hung up, I saw that Ball Cap Guy wasn't the only one who needed help. I dragged myself to my feet and hurried to the president's side.

"I'll get the door open," I told him, desperately looking through the dark for my keys. "We'll get you inside and—"

"Too late." Though his face was haggard, the president's eyes were calm. "There's no time, and it hardly matters. Mr. Stone . . ." He grunted in pain. "Mr. Stone was not my unfinished business, your stalker was. I had to . . ." He winked away, and I searched the darkness, praying he'd come back. He did, like the flash of a camera. "I had to face your stalker because I never did deal with mine." The president's expression was calm, angelic. "I do believe I must say good-bye to you now, Miss Martin."

And he disappeared forever.

Nick had an assault charge slapped on his record, and ended up getting a couple years probation. Ted Studebaker went to jail for a whole bunch of years. Ball Cap Guy died in surgery, and I never realized just how tense I was knowing he was around until he wasn't.

My stress levels settled down, and so did my life.

At least my emotional life.

There was still the commemoration to take care of, and Ella and I worked like fiends getting it ready. By opening night, every nook and cranny in the memorial gleamed, and a crowd of interested and enthusiastic visitors couldn't say enough good things about all we'd done. The folks from the National Archives had already come and left with what was being called the Mystery Treaty, the better to make sure it was put on display and preserved with the proper temperature and humidity and all that jazz.

I was glad to have the letter and the treaty gone, but sorry the president wasn't there to watch the way the ad-miring crowds oohed and aahed over the memorabilia of his life. I did my part, talking up his service in the Civil War and all he'd accomplished as a congressman and as president. Even though he was on death's doorstep, he never gave in and signed that treaty, and that made him something of a new national hero.

He was my personal hero, too.

Rather than get all mushy thinking about it, I headed

for the far side of the ballroom that had been opened for one night only in honor of the occasion, where tuxedoed waiters were helping our patrons to fancy-schmancy appetizers and glasses of champagne.

Unfortunately, I guess I hadn't learned to look before I moved. I almost smashed my nose right into an expensive Italian silk tie and the chest of the detective wearing it.

"I couldn't pass up the opportunity to check out your display," Quinn said, and I don't think he was talking about anything presidential since he was giving me and my new off-the-shoulder dress the once-over. I'd bought it to celebrate living through the summer, and I guess I'd made the right choice. When he skimmed a look from my satin pumps to the slim-skirted, blackberry-colored dress, Quinn's eyes lit up. "I thought we could talk. Over drinks. That is, if you're not busy later."

Three cheers for good timing. At that very moment, Scott showed up with a glass of champagne for me. I wrapped one arm through his. "That's so nice of you," I told Quinn, "but I'm going to be busy later." Scott and I turned to walk away, but I wasn't done. I gave Quinn a look over my shoulder. "Besides," I told him, all sweetness and light, "I don't think we have anything left to say."

Scott knew better than to comment. Or maybe he wasn't paying all that much attention. He smiled and pointed to the waiter who was walking around the room, a tray of food in one hand. "That guy over there was telling me about the Rock and Roll Hall of Fame and Museum. I've always wanted to see it. Would you like to go tomorrow? I can't wait to see the exhibits. I'm a huge Beatles fan!"

I agreed because, honestly, I was looking forward to it.

Of course, that didn't explain why even as I sipped my champagne and chatted with our visitors, I kept hearing a song playing from somewhere in the darkest corners of the ballroom. It sounded a whole lot like "A Hard Day's Night."

DON'T MISS MORE PEPPER MARTIN FROM

Casey Daniels

NIGHT OF THE LOVING DEAD

Pepper Martin, heiress-turned-cemetery-tour-guide, has her hands full with work, two hotties, and the ghosts who won't let her rest—or work, or shop—in peace…

The specter of Madeline—a young woman in a lab coat—wants Pepper's help. Before she died, she worked with the sexy, mysterious doctor who claims Pepper is in danger. Little does Pepper know there's more to the story, including a devious doctor—and an obsessive, crazy love.

"[A] charming…blend of romance, mystery, and nostalgia."
—*Publishers Weekly*

penguin.com

"[Features a] spunky heroine and sparkling wit."
—Kerrelyn Sparks,
New York Times bestselling author

FIFTH IN THE PEPPER MARTIN MYSTERIES

DEAD MAN TALKING

CASEY DANIELS
Author of *Tomb with a View*

Heiress-turned-cemetery-tour-guide Pepper Martin is not happy to discover that a local reality TV show, *Cemetery Survivor*, will be filmed at Cleveland's Monroe Street Cemetery—and she has to be a part of it. To make matters worse, the ghost of a wrongly convicted killer needs Pepper's help to clear his name. But digging for the truth could put her in grave danger.

penguin.com